DANGLED CARAT

HILARY GROSSMAN

Booktrope Editions
Seattle WA 2014

Cover Design by Greg Simanson

Previously published as *Dangled Carat*,
Independently Published, 2012

This is a work of creative non-fiction. Some names and details have been changed and creative liberties have been taken.

Print ISBN 978-1-62015-464-9

EPUB ISBN 978-1-62015-474-8

DISCOUNTS OR CUSTOMIZED EDITIONS MAY BE AVAILABLE FOR EDUCATIONAL AND OTHER GROUPS BASED ON BULK PURCHASE.

For further information please contact info@booktrope.com

Library of Congress Control Number: 2014912574

To those I love the most. You know who you are, and this book wouldn't be possible without you. You are truly characters—but in a good way!

CHAPTER 1

December 31, 2003

I NEVER INTENDED FOR IT to happen. The words just came tumbling out without warning...

"It's New Year's Eve, and you know what that means, Marc. Time is up... I told you that you had until New Year's to propose, and, well, here we are. It's New Year's Eve. So, what will it be?"

Despite the deep tan that he was sporting just moments before, suddenly Marc, my long-term boyfriend, turned ghostly pale. He took a deep breath, and it was clear by the expression on his face that he was confused, as well as slightly angry. But could you blame him? Why shouldn't he have been upset? Who wants to be faced with an ultimatum? Especially when the demand is being delivered by someone other than your girlfriend?!

You see, Marc and I weren't alone. We had escaped the frigid New York temperatures and pending snowstorms to spend some time in Fort Lauderdale with our close friends from Utah, Eric and his wife, Jaye. It was Jaye who questioned Marc while Eric and I busied ourselves making grapefruit martinis.

I wasn't surprised by Jaye's question, though how she delivered it did shock me. Jaye, like all of Marc's friends and family, had been pestering him for quite a while about when he was going to marry me. Unlike most long-term relationships with commitment phobic men, I had never pressured Marc about marriage. If our relationship was going to move to the next level, I wanted it to be his choice. I didn't want to live my life wondering if he married me because he really loved me and wanted to spend his life with me, or if he married me because I threatened to leave him if he didn't. But... despite my resolve not to pressure him, I encouraged others to do my dirty work. And no one let me down. Everyone important in his life took on the role with gusto. But of all the people closest to Marc, Jaye had been my staunchest ally.

When Marc didn't reply, Jaye continued, "So, I guess the silence means you are okay with this. I guess you are engaged!"

Eric didn't wait for Marc to regain his senses. He followed his wife's lead. Jumping on the bandwagon, drink in his hand; he patted Marc on the back. "Congratulations, buddy! You are a lucky man!" Then Eric turned and kissed me. "You will be a beautiful bride!" Raising his martini into the air, Eric toasted, "To the happy couple! I hope your marriage is a long and happy one!"

"Woo hoo!" Jaye cheered. "Kiss the bride!"

Marc didn't move a muscle. It was as if Jaye had rendered him catatonic. I jumped up from my seat and pretty much floated over to where he sat, leaned down, and gave him a gigantic kiss.

Marc didn't utter a word, but he did manage to take a humongous gulp of martini. Marc is more of a wine man. He normally grimaces at the first sip of hard liquor, but not tonight. I think he would've been able to down the entire bottle of vodka in one sip.

I took a sip of my drink. This was all great fun to me. Sure, I knew Marc and I weren't really engaged, but we could pretend for the night, couldn't we? Where would the harm be in that? Also, I couldn't help wonder, maybe this pseudo engagement might be the kick that Marc needed to take our relationship to the next level. After all, neither one of us were getting any younger, especially Marc—who at forty-three, was thirteen years older than me.

"So, Marc?" I asked, not wanting to be the only one not joining the fun, "how does it feel to be engaged?"

He grunted in reply. He raised his drink to his mouth, took another sip, and slowly stood up. All eyes were on him as he opened his mouth to speak. "Eric, did you even put vodka in the drink?"

Eric nodded his head.

"I don't believe you. I need more." Marc walked over to the bottle and uncharacteristically topped off his cocktail.

As soon as he sat down, Jaye started up again. With a wink, she said, "So, Hilary, it doesn't seem like Marc answered your question, so I will ask you the same one. How do you feel to be engaged?"

"Wonderful. Fabulous! Unexpected!! Like winning the lottery!!!" I said, my voice getting louder with each adjective I used, as it always does when I am excited.

Eric, Jaye, and I all chuckled. "Did you ever expect to be engaged tonight?" Jaye continued.

Solemnly I replied, "No, never." And then, with a wink, I continued, "But I have to admit I did have some hopes." I turned to Marc and I said, "I guess dreams really do come true. You have made me the happiest girl in the whole wide world."

Eric and Jaye struggled to suppress their laughter.

"You guys are really having fun, huh?" Marc asked.

In unison, we answered yes, and then the three of us burst out in hysterics like a bunch of middle-school kids. Marc was the only one not amused.

I turned around so that I faced him eye to eye. "Oh come on, lighten up. You look so petrified. Don't worry; I know we are not really engaged. Sheesh… You are supposed to be the funny one. Can't you take a joke? Did you leave your sense of humor in New York or something?" I tried to sound nonchalant as I addressed him, but I felt nothing of the sort. After dating Marc for close to four years, I had hoped that eventually he would come around and realize I was the best thing that ever happened to him. There was no legitimate reason for Marc to be so opposed to the idea of a serious commitment and marriage. His parents had been happily married, only separated by the death of his mother. Following in their footsteps, Marc's brother and sister also led happy married lives. Of course, he had a couple of divorced friends, who didn't? But for the most part, like his family, his friends all lived the happy life of matrimony.

The only reason Marc really had for being so against the idea of marriage were the very same reasons you find listed in all the girly magazines under headlines such as "why he will never take a wife". Marc was the poster boy for the fortyish bachelor. He was set in his ways, successful, and extremely self-sufficient. He was a whiz in the kitchen and equally as capable with a washing machine and vacuum. He didn't need anyone. But let's face it: need and desire are two different things. And it had become crystal clear to me, and everyone around us, that he cherished the time we spent together. But was that really enough to change his ways?

Why get my hopes up? Why hadn't I realized by then that I'd end up disappointed or hurt?

"Wow, look at the time," Eric, ever the diplomat, said as he rose to his feet. "We'd better start heading over to my parents' place." Jaye and I scooped up the now-empty martini glasses and rinsed them out in the sink. We locked up the condo and walked over to the house where Eric's parents were staying only a few blocks away, as they tried to escape the cold Canadian winter.

As we strolled, I watched Marc begin to relax ever so slightly. Approaching Eric's parents' front door, Marc let out an audible sigh of relief. I know he felt that the pressure of the night was over.

If only he was right...

Lois, Eric's mom, greeted us excitedly at the front door. She was so happy to have us over for New Year's Eve, as well as her other son, Marno, who was staying with them for the holiday week. "Come in, come in," Lois sang as she hugged and kissed us all.

As soon as we were inside, Jaye announced, "Mom, guess what? Marc and Hilary just got engaged!"

Lois, who had known Marc for about twenty years, and wasn't aware of Eric and Jaye's little joke, brought her hands to her face to try to mask her happiness and shock. She started to screech in joy. Not knowing what the commotion was, her husband, Irvin, and Marno came running into the house from the backyard, fearing something was wrong.

If Irvin noticed us, he didn't show it. He didn't even greet his eldest son, Eric, as he ran to his wife's side. "What's wrong? Are you okay?" he asked, panic present in his voice and demeanor.

"Wrong? Nothing is wrong. Everything is great!" Lois had an ear-to-ear grin. "It's good news! Marc and Hilary just got engaged!"

Irvin and Marno caught the enthusiasm. "What? Really? You?" Marno asked, shocked. "I never thought you would commit. Ever! To anyone! Man, I guess if you live long enough, you see everything."

Eric turned to his brother, and with a smile said, "Shocking, huh?" Before Marno could reply, Irvin exclaimed, "Champagne for everyone!"

Lois floated into the dining room to get the champagne flutes out of the hutch. Irvin popped the top of the champagne bottle that was chilling in the fridge, and Marno started congratulating us. As Eric stood by watching his family, Jaye disappeared from the group and slipped into Lois and Irvin's bedroom. She emerged minutes later with a costume rhinestone ring. "Here." She turned to me. "Give me your left hand." I slowly raised it and she slipped the ring on my left ring finger. "For tonight, this will be your engagement ring!" We both chuckled. Then I hugged her tightly, a goofy smile on my face.

We meandered to the backyard, which was on the inter-coastal, champagne flutes in our hands. Although I knew it was a joke, I couldn't help it. I kept admiring the ring on my finger, pretending it was really my engagement ring. I expected Eric or Jaye to fess up and admit to Eric's family that our engagement was a joke, but they didn't. They just kept letting Eric's family think we were really engaged. Lois kept on beaming, tossing out questions about our engagement. She wanted details. Jaye ended up answering almost all of them for me. After all, if not for Jaye, this "engagement" would not be happening.

"So... when did this happen?" Lois asked.

"Tonight, Mom," Jaye answered quickly. "Would you believe it happened right before we came over?"

"Really? Wow. Were you expecting it, Hilary?"

"No," I honestly replied. "It came out of left field."

"Oh, I love a surprise engagement," Lois beamed.

"Yeah, it was a surprise all right. Hilary wasn't the only one that was caught off guard," Jaye clarified as I tried to keep a straight face.

"How did Marc propose? Did he get down on one knee? Irvin didn't, and I was so disappointed."

"Don't feel bad, Mom, Marc didn't get down on one knee either. But I think he did get weak in the knees." Jaye added, "But you asked how he proposed. Let's just say... I don't think he planned for it."

Lois smiled and took a delicate sip of her drink. I still had a stupid smile plastered on my face. I was having a blast. Well, I was until I glanced over and saw the pained look in Marc's eyes, which was growing more noticeable with every additional comment out of Jaye's mouth.

He was trying so hard to be a good sport. I could see it was getting increasingly difficult for him to let this charade continue. As he got agitated, so did I. In an instant, the joke stopped being funny. It was sad and hurtful. No matter how hard I pretended, Jaye's proposal wasn't real, nor was it going to magically become so. Instead, it started to become crystal clear to me, while looking at Marc's troubled face, that he had no intention of proposing to me now—or, I feared, ever. Would I be okay always just being his girlfriend?

It's amazing how devastating disappointment can be, especially when it's over something that you didn't really expect to occur in the first place, if you are truly honest with yourself...

I removed the rhinestone ring from my finger and thrust it at Jaye. Before bursting into tears, I managed to utter, "I can't do this anymore." Not wanting to cry in front of everyone, as I was humiliated enough, I ran about three houses away and squatted down at the ledge of the inter-coastal. Part of me wanted to just jump in and disappear. Seriously, I was contemplating it. But instead I just stood there, tears streaming down my face, staring into the blue water. This was so not how I'd envisioned this night!

It didn't take more than a moment before Marc was at my side. "Come on," he said, grabbing my hand and leading me back to Lois and Irvin's house. But instead of rejoining everyone, he ushered me around the house to the front porch. "Sit," he commanded.

I did and he quickly sat down next to me. I was sobbing and I didn't care. I tried to cover my face with my hair, but Marc gently swept a long lock away from my face and tucked it behind my ear. He wiped my tears away with his fingers and pulled me towards him, holding me close and tight. Still, he didn't utter a word. I felt safe and protected in his arms, which made me cry harder, until my tears saturated the shoulder of his shirt.

Eventually my sobs started to subside. When they did, Marc slowly pulled away. "Are you okay now?" he asked softly.

I was afraid my voice would crack and bring a fresh set of tears, so I just nodded my head.

"I am really sorry for what happened," he said quietly.

I started to hiccup. "You have nothing to be sorry for."

"Yes, I do."

"No, you didn't do anything wrong. I am the one who's sorry. I could have stopped Jaye and I should have. But did I? No. I'm a fool. I encouraged her to continue. I just wanted it to be true. And now look." Crying again, I didn't want to look at Marc, so I buried my face in his neck, and held onto him tight.

He began to gently stroke my hair, trying to comfort me as I continued to cry. I have no idea how much time passed. It could have been five seconds or five minutes. I was in an emotional fog. Finally, he separated himself and grabbed my face in his hands. "Look at me," he said.

My eyes darted around nervously before I was able to focus on his eyes, bracing myself for what he was going to say.

"It is okay. Stop crying. Please. I want to talk to you."

"I don't really want to talk," I mumbled, as Marc wiped my tears again with his fingers and pushed my hair away from my face. "I'll stop crying. Let's just forget it and go back to everyone." I really didn't want to talk. It would have been easier for me to ignore the disappointment I felt than get hurt more.

"No, we need to talk." I took a deep breath, trying to regain my composure, as he continued. "You know I don't put my feelings into words very often, right?" Marc asked.

"Right," I whispered.

"And you know how hard it is for me to say certain words, right? That is why I try to show you how I feel instead. And I do, right?"

"Yeah, you try." He really did. In my heart, I knew that it was much better to have someone treat you right, rather than make empty declarations about their love and be unkind or unfaithful to you. Normally, I didn't mind the fact that he didn't accurately articulate his feelings. It was a male characteristic I was used to. My father had the same difficulty with words. He hardly ever expressed his feelings. He kept everything bottled up. While he did show both my mom and I his heart and his love for us, he couldn't utter the words. If he did try to say "I love you", it sounded foreign rolling off his tongue. Marc had always reminded me of my father in this way.

But sometimes, actions aren't enough. Sometimes a girl needs to be told what a guy feels, rather than trying to decipher the signs.

As if reading my mind, Marc continued, "So this should mean even more to you, then. I know I don't tell you often enough, but I want you to know just how much I love you. Hilary, I really do. I never thought I would love someone this much."

I honestly knew this already, but when someone has such a difficult time expressing himself, as Marc does, it is natural to wonder and have some doubts. Because of that, I couldn't stop myself from asking, "Really?"

Or maybe I just wanted to hear him say it again. Hearing his words was like grabbing onto a life preserver while drowning.

"Yes, really," he replied, wiping another tear from my face. "And I know that you want to get married. I don't need Jaye or Eric or anyone else to tell me that. But we have to do it when we are both ready, not when everyone else is ready for us to be."

"But what does that mean? You never want to talk about it. And I am afraid to bring it up. I worry that I will freak you out. I don't want to be your girlfriend forever." I was never one of those girls who dreamt about a fairytale wedding. I didn't want to be married for the sake of being married, unlike so many people I've known. I wanted to spend my life with someone I loved, while experiencing both good times and the bad ones with them. I didn't want to be stuck in a perpetual dating situation where we only enjoyed each other's company when it was convenient, fun and easy. I wanted a life partner...

A few months ago, Marc needed minor outpatient surgery. I brought him to the hospital, sat with him while he waited, held his hand when he came to from the anesthesia, and cared for him when he returned home and had difficulty sitting and walking. Although he'd probably disagree, because he was the one that actually had the surgery, it was a wonderful experience. It was so simple and real. We felt like a family. Every step of the way, I'd hoped it would help him realize that he couldn't live without me...

"I know you want more," he answered.

"Is it something you want?" I asked.

"I don't know. I am getting less and less opposed to the idea of marriage. I just can't rush into anything. I have to do it in my time, in my own way. You can understand that, right?" He didn't wait for me to respond; maybe because he sensed my answer would be no. Instead, he just continued. "We have to take our time. We have to wait until we know it is right."

"Know it is right? I already know we are right for each other," I said tenderly. I wanted to add that he did too, but he was just too scared to admit it. But although it was difficult, I managed to hold back those words.

"I know you do. And, honestly, in my heart I do too. But I am not ready yet. We both have to be ready for this to work. Just bear with me. Okay?"

I didn't reply. What was I going to say? No? We wouldn't have even been having this conversation in the first place if not for Jaye.

"I promise you," he continued. "I won't disappoint you, and I will never hurt you. You believe me, right?"

I nodded in agreement, although I wasn't really one hundred percent sure.

Marc grabbed me once again, held me close, and whispered, "I love you, really I do." Then he started to sing one of his favorite Led Zeppelin songs to me, "You will be mine, by taking our time…" I wanted to believe him as we sat on the front porch, snuggled up together. Finally Marc asked, "Are you ready to head back?"

"I guess so."

"Good, dry those tears. Give me a smile, and remember it will be okay." Marc took my hand in his, and together we went back into the house and out onto the back deck.

When we emerged, everyone fell silent. Eric was the first one to come over and apologize. "I am so sorry, guys," he said, hugging both me and Marc simultaneously. As he did, I spotted Lois, with both hands firmly planted on her hips, glaring at him from across the room. Eric may have been a grown man, but it was apparent that he'd been reprimanded by his mother for his actions that evening.

Jaye grabbed me as soon as Eric let go and guided me away from the group. Jaye was ten years older than Marc, and has a son from her first marriage who is only a year younger than me. So while Jaye and I were friends, she often took me under her wing as if I were her daughter. Because of this, we had a special bond. "I'm so sorry for everything. You know that I never intended to hurt you. I know that Marc was originally my friend, but you are my friend now, too. I think of you like a daughter, and I don't want him to take you for granted. He has to understand that you can't be expected to stick around forever."

"I know," I said, tearing up again. I hugged her tight. "Thank you," I said, looking deeply in her eyes. "Tonight was horrible, and I am upset, but I am also thankful for what you did. It had to be done. We had to talk about marriage. We couldn't continue putting it off forever, skirting around it, like we had been doing. Tonight, thanks to you, we were forced to speak. I don't know what will happen next, but whatever does, I think that tonight was very important, and had to happen. And for that I owe you." Despite the reassurance I offered her, I wondered if we would have been better off just letting nature run its course.

"Yeah, I feel the same way too," she smiled. "We can't wait for men to handle anything important. If we did, nothing ever would ever get done!"

Smiling, Jaye and I made our way back to the group. Irvin replaced our champagne flutes with wine glasses and Eric opened a nice bottle of Cabernet. Lois emerged from the kitchen with a tray of cocktail franks and stuffed mushrooms. As we nibbled, we tried our best to put the engagement, or lack thereof, behind us. It was difficult at first, but Eric, always quick with a joke, was able to break the tension and get us all laughing.

Before we knew it, the steak was on the grill and Jaye and I were in the kitchen tossing a salad under Lois's close supervision. Slowly but surely, we began to have the New Year's celebration that we'd expected, although my heart was still heavy.

By the time the third bottle of wine was empty, my tears had been replaced by laughter. However, the emotions of the evening took their toll on all of us. There was no way that we were going to be able to stay at Irvin and Lois's until midnight. I don't think Irvin, Lois, or even Marno could have handled it either. About forty-five minutes before midnight, after Jaye and I had washed and dried all the dinner dishes, we said our goodbyes and walked silently back to the condo.

When we got there, Jaye gave me another quick hug, and then we retired to our separate rooms. Marc tenderly made love to me as fireworks illuminated the sky over the ocean. "Remember, I really love you," he assured me once more, holding me close. He soon drifted off to sleep. Although I was exhausted from the evening, no matter how hard I tried, sleep just wouldn't come. My mind just kept racing. Sure, I knew that he was telling me the truth, but would he ever really be able to fully open himself up to me and embrace a lifetime together?

CHAPTER 2

Friday, July 27, 2001

THE MOMENT I FIRST LAID EYES on Marc, the first thought that popped into my head was "Oh, crap!" The second was, "You've got to be kidding me!" And the third was, "This is going to be uncomfortable. Why didn't just we go for Thai?"

Don't judge. There was a reason for this reaction...

The summer before, I was having dinner with my mother one night at an Italian restaurant several towns away from where we lived. Towards the end of our meal, a large family entered the restaurant. They obviously knew many people who were dining there and were loudly greeting them as they worked their way over to their table, catching our attention in the process. My mom and I quickly went back to our conversation and finished up our meal.

As my mother sipped her coffee and I my cappuccino, one of the ladies from the large group approached us. She was very pretty, with long, straight blond hair that reached the middle of her back, and she was dressed to the nines. "Hi," she said, with a huge smile on her face. She looked directly in my eyes and continued, "I am sorry to interrupt you, but may I ask you a question?"

"Sure." I was very curious. What could this woman possibly need to ask me?

"Are you seeing anyone?" she asked. "Because you would be perfect for my brother-in-law."

Taken by surprise, I quickly answered that I was.

"Okay, then," she replied. "I'm sorry to have interrupted. But I had to ask, as you never know. All right then, have a great night."

"Thanks, you too," I replied.

As quickly as she appeared, she disappeared back to her group.

"How weird was that?" I asked my mom.

"Pretty strange," she agreed. But I could see the wheels turning in her head, wondering who this brother-in-law was. My mom had no doubt in her mind that my boyfriend wasn't the right guy for me.

At twenty-five, I finally let my guard down long enough to have my first real boyfriend, Sam. We started out as friends, but over time, our relationship developed into something more. But there were problems. One day, we would be head over heels in love with each other, and then the next day we'd be ready to stab each other in the eyes, fighting over everything and anything. As quickly as our tempers flared, so did the forgiveness that followed. It was very strange. I am not a confrontational person, but there was something about Sam that brought the worst out in me. We knew how to push each other's buttons and drive each other crazy.

My poor mom never knew what emotional state she would find me in after I dealt with Sam. She spent many a night consoling me as I cried my eyes out over our latest fight. "Love isn't supposed to feel this way," she said. "A relationship should be filled with smiles and laughter, not tears." But did I believe her? Of course not! What daughter listens to her mother?

Okay, maybe I partially listened, sometimes. I would break up with him, but never for long. My resolve would last a few days, or a week tops, before Sam and I would make up.

"What kind of loser must this guy be?" I asked my mom, as I took a sip of cappuccino. "He needs his sister-in-law to scout out dates for him?"

"Maybe you're jumping to conclusions. Maybe he is perfectly normal and she just happens to know his type. Or maybe he is sitting at the table and sent her over to you."

Rolling my eyes, I replied, "Yeah, right, Mom. I'm sure that's the case."

"You know, maybe you should give him a chance. It can't hurt."

I could see the wheels spinning in her mind. But since it happened to be a night that I actually did care for Sam, I didn't even ponder the possibility. "Whatever you say... can we get out of here? I feel weird now." My mom got the waiter's attention, and we paid our check and headed home.

Over the course of the following year, my turbulent relationship continued with Sam, and my mom and I continued to frequent the Italian restaurant. (They had the most amazing chopped salad and baked manicotti.) Initially, after the incident, I was concerned about running into the sister-in-law, but fortunately we never did. Eventually I put the weirdness of that night behind me, although my mom and I still joked about it now and again.

One very warm Friday night in July, my mom and I were debating where to have dinner. I felt like Italian, but she wanted Thai. Since both restaurants were on the same block, we decided to go for Italian, but if we couldn't get a table easily we wouldn't wait. My mom doesn't like to wait for a table. I, on the other hand, never mind sitting at the bar and having a drink before dinner, but to humor her, I agreed that if we couldn't get seated right away, we would head down the street and grab some Thai. As luck would have it, although the restaurant was packed, there was one table left. The maître d' quickly ushered us over to it. As we neared it, I spotted HER, the now infamous (to us) sister-in-law, sitting with three men, next to our table.

My mom immediately recognized her as well. My mother and I have an unusual relationship. Not only do we know exactly what the other person is thinking, we can even have a silent conversation. As we approached the table, that is exactly what we did. She read my facial expression and knew that I was wordlessly saying to her, "Oh crap, it's her! Can we leave?"

She shook her head at me and smiled. Then she whispered, "I'm sure she doesn't even recognize you."

The tables were so close together that in order to get into the booth side, which I did, the maître d' had to move the table out. My mom and I weren't even in our chairs a minute when the sister-in-law turned to us. "Hi," she said. "Isn't it a beautiful night?"

My mom and I said "hi" simultaneously. After I added, "It sure is," we thought that would be the end of the communication, but we were wrong.

As soon as the waiter left our table with our drink order, the woman started to make small talk with us. My initial uneasiness started to drift away. She seemed really nice and friendly. I no longer thought of her as the crazy lady who had to scout out dates for her loser brother-in-law, but instead, a cool lady who had to scout out dates for her loser brother-in-law.

After a few minutes, she announced, "My name is Susan," with a huge smile. Then she pointed to the other men she was dining with, starting with the older one of two men who looked extremely alike. "This is my husband Jay, our friend Bruce, and my brother-in-law, Marc." Brother-in-law, Marc? The brother-in-law? How can that be? I wondered as I checked him out. This guy was cute! He had short wavy brown hair sprinkled with some gray, which made him look distinguished. His eyes were hazel, but the kelly green polo shirt he was wearing made them appear more emerald than brown. And although he appeared to be about forty, his eyes had a boyish twinkle. There was something about his appearance, and the wide toothy grin he flashed me, that made me think that this man would be fun, with a great sense of humor.

The waiter dropped off our beverages and I took a sip of my then-signature vodka martini. It was then that Marc started getting in on the conversation. He and I began kidding around and joking almost immediately. He leaned over, a bottle of wine in his hand, and offered me some. I pointed to my martini and I told him I was covered.

He smiled. I smiled back.

The waiter cleared off Marc's table's salad dishes and brought us over ours. I offered him some of my salad, since he had Caesar and I had chopped. He declined. I smiled. He smiled back.

Their food came. Marc and I were lost in conversation. We continued to laugh, smile, and kid around. My mom sat in silence, just watching us. Jay, Bruce, and Susan's conversation was at a halt too. Or, maybe it just seemed that way to me. Here we sat, in a packed restaurant, and I felt as if we were completely alone.

For whatever reason, this restaurant attracted an elderly crowd. Our two tables were pretty much the only ones in the entire place that weren't occupied by people north of their seventy-fifth birthdays. As soon as the waiter cleared off our dinner plates, my mom headed to the bathroom and Marc sat down in her seat. "I just want to see what it feels like to sit next to you," he said as he smiled at me.

As I arched my eyebrows at him, I asked, "Well, how does it feel?" He pondered for a second, and I noticed the table of two elderly couples sitting to the other side of us. They were watching Marc and me interact as if they were watching a movie. We were clearly their entertainment for the evening.

"I think I can get used to it," Marc replied solemnly.

All too quickly, my mom returned from the bathroom and Marc had to go back to his seat. We continued to chat for a little while as Marc's brother squared away their bill, and the waiter brought over coffee and cappuccino for my mom and me.

As Marc and his family got up to leave, he said, "This was fun. Can we do it again?"

"Sure," I said. "Call me."

"Are you going to give me your number?"

"My number?" I asked, playing coy. "Oh, you want my number, do you?"

"Well, it usually does help," he retorted, "if I am to call you."

"Okay." I rattled off, "766-722" with a twinkle in my eye.

Marc wrote down the digits and stared at the paper. A confused look appeared on his face. "Huh? You only gave me six numbers."

Flippantly, as if I didn't care whether he called — though I desperately wanted him to—I answered, "I know... you need to guess the missing number."

Why I did this, I don't know. It wasn't a plan. It wasn't my signature move (not that I actually had a signature move, mind you)— it just happened.

Marc stared down at his paper, concentrating on the numbers he wrote, and guessed, "Seven?"

I was dumbfounded that he got it right. I didn't think that was going to happen. "Wow!" I exclaimed, "That's right. How did you do that?"

"I'm smart," he answered, his hazel eyes twinkling. And then he was gone.

The elderly foursome to my left was still staring at our table, and I could see their ears perk up as I said to my mom, "Oh my God, I really liked him."

Before my mom could answer, one of the ladies at the adjacent table turned to me. "I am so sorry, honey. I know that we've been staring all night. We couldn't help it. You guys made such a cute couple. I really hope you go out with him."

And then, softly, her friend whispered, "I think he likes you too!"

My mom and I chatted with these people for a bit, not wanting to appear rude, before heading home. In the car my mom said, "He was there that night."

"What night?" Most of the time I am really oblivious!

"When Susan first approached you last year. He was there. I wasn't sure at first, but once you started talking to him, I recognized him. Actually, I wouldn't be surprised if he sent her over to find out if you were available."

"Nah, you're wrong." I said.

"Believe what you want," my mom replied. "You always do."

We drove home the rest of the way in silence. I was beyond lost in thought. I couldn't stop wondering if she was right. Was he there a year ago, and did he really like me then? If so, how strange would that be? It would be almost like fate.

*   *   *

I'll be damned, my mom was right!

I later learned that was exactly what had happened. Marc did see me that first night in the Italian restaurant. He did comment that he thought I was cute when he spotted me from across the room. And when his sister-in-law offered to come over to my table and inquire about my relationship situation, he immediately took her up on it.

I also learned later that this situation was very similar to how Susan had ultimately met her husband. Many years ago, she was in line in a bakery, waiting to pick up pastries to bring to her office, when she started chatting with the older woman behind her. Since the bakery was packed, they had plenty of time to get to know each other. The older woman was delighted that Susan lived in the same town, and made sure to grab her number, because she thought that Susan would be "perfect" for her son, Jay. She was right: Jay and Susan made the perfect couple…

Days passed after that dinner. Although I wished Marc would call, I didn't expect it. In retrospect, I think that is why I was so flippant about giving him my number. I didn't want to let myself be disappointed. Avoidance was one of my best defense mechanisms. He was forty years old, and I was only twenty-seven. I was afraid that he thought I was too young for him, and felt that night was only flirty fun, a distraction from our respective dinner companions.

I was wrong. He called. Marc and I chatted on the phone for over an hour. The light and easy conversation that we had in the restaurant continued on the telephone. When he finally asked me out, I paused. I was thrilled, but I was faced with a dilemma. Sam and I were technically still seeing each other, although that week we were on one of our famous breaks. I was really getting tired of the constant drama that surrounded our relationship, and finally believed my mom: that dating shouldn't be this way. Marc seemed like such a great guy, and I really wanted to go out with him, but could I?

I didn't know what to do. I desperately wanted to get to know him better, but I didn't think it was fair not to tell him about my situation.

"I would love to," I answered, "but I don't know if I should."

"Why not?"

"Well, I am sort of seeing someone," I confessed. "We have an on again, off again relationship, and right now we are technically broken up. But our breakups haven't ever lasted too long in the past, so I feel a little strange going out with you."

"Okay," Marc replied. "But do you feel strange because of this guy, or because of me?"

"The guy, only the guy," I quickly answered. "I want to go out with you, but I just don't know if it is right."

"What can be wrong about it?" Marc asked. "We can call it a friendship dinner. Nothing is wrong with that, is there?"

"Well, if you put it that way. I would love to!" I answered, as I thought: *well played Marc, well played.*

We made plans to go out on Friday, and throughout the week we continued to chat on the telephone and through email. We never ran out of things to say. As for Sam, I didn't speak to him once. Unlike in the past, all his calls went unanswered.

All during the day at work on Friday, I found it hard to concentrate. My mind kept drifting to the evening ahead of me. But by nightfall, as I dressed in my favorite pair of jeans and a fitted black tee shirt, I found myself surprisingly calm, which was unusual for me. I had no first date jitters. I lived at home with my mom. I told her that I didn't expect to be home late. I figured midnight would be tops; after all, we were only going out for a "friendship" dinner.

As it neared the time for Marc to pick me up, my mom, my dog, Hannah Mae, and I left our living room, which was at front of the house, and headed into our den, the farthest room from the front door. I didn't want to seem too eager when Marc pulled up.

We were there for a few moments when the telephone rang. I glanced at the caller ID and saw that it was Marc.

Nice of him to cancel the date two minutes before he was due to arrive, I thought to myself. "Hello," I answered, trying hard to keep any emotion from coming through.

"Hi, it's me. Did you say you lived off of Long Beach Road or Lincoln Avenue?" Both are major roads in the town where I lived, about a mile apart.

"Long Beach Road," I grinned, walking out of the den, towards the living room window.

"Oh. I thought you said you lived off Lincoln Avenue." He sounded mischievous. "I'm on Lincoln Avenue. I guess that explains why I can't find Fonda Road."

I reached the living room window and peered outside. A black Mercedes sports car was sitting in my driveway. "So, where exactly are you now?" I asked.

"Sitting in your driveway, looking at you right now."

And, at that moment, I melted.

I answered the door and ushered Marc in. He sat on the sofa and made small talk with my mom as Hannah Mae, in classic Bichon Frise fashion, feverously barked and jumped around his legs, leaping onto the couch and trying to kiss him. It was apparent that Hannah Mae approved of him. But then again, there wasn't anyone she didn't like, with the exception of the vet and her groomer. We only stayed at my house a short time. Before I knew it, I was kissing my mom goodbye and heading into Marc's car, while he held the door for me.

"Based on where I met you, I already know you like Italian food," Marc said as he drove. I was thinking of bringing you to a small Italian restaurant near my house. Sound good?"

"Sounds wonderful," I replied.

"Good," he said with a smile. "Let's stop off at my house first for a drink, and then we'll go for dinner. I noticed when we met you were drinking a martini, but did you ever have a chocolate martini? I make a killer one."

"Nope, I never have. But it sounds delicious." I was impressed that he remembered what I drank.

Marc and I lived about ten miles apart from each other, but we might as well have lived on different planets. I lived inland; he lived on the beach. Although his town was only twenty minutes away, I never went there. I thought of it only as a place where people belonged to beach clubs. I didn't know people actually lived there.

As we drove, there was a major traffic jam from an accident of some kind, so Marc took a detour. Even so, traffic was at a standstill. As we approached a red light, Marc reached into his glove compartment and removed a box of tic-tacs. Then he reached into his back seat and grabbed a bottle of water. Turning to me, he held them both out. "Well, I know I promised you dinner and a drink, but it doesn't look like we're getting anywhere anytime soon. So here is some warm water, if you want. And the tic-tacs can be dinner. So, if we are stuck here all night, at least I didn't lie... I've got dinner and a drink for you!"

This may have been a little corny, but it is totally my sense of humor. I cracked up. If I'd any doubts before, I knew right then and there that I was going to have a great night.

As we continued to joke around, traffic began to ease up. Before I knew it, we arrived at his home on the beach. As soon as we left the car, I was overwhelmed by the fragrant scents of the ocean. Marc ushered me through his garage into what appeared from the outside to be a tiny, attached town home. But looks can be deceiving, and what I found inside was anything but small.

The garage door opened up into his dining room. As we stepped in, I was amazed at the open floor plan. Since there were practically no walls, but lots of mirrors and windows, it appeared that the dining room, den, and kitchen were one gigantic room. His kitchen was filled with gleaming stainless steel Viking appliances. The den had an enormous fireplace, and more electronic contraptions than I had ever seen in my life. "What is all that stuff?" I asked Marc as I pointed to what looked like the cockpit of a spaceship.

"Oh, that's just my stereo equipment," he said casually.

"You mean all that stuff does is play music? It doesn't transport you to Mars or make a cup of cappuccino?" I asked.

Marc chuckled. Spotting two objects that were bigger than me on both sides of the electronic substation. I said, "Don't tell me those things are speakers?"

"Okay, I won't," he said with a smile.

"But they are, right?" What kind of place was I in anyway?

"Yeah, they are. What do you want to see next?" he asked. "Up or down?"

"Tough one," I replied. "Let's do down first."

He led me to the basement. The first thing I spotted was hundreds of bottles of wine in wooden shelves. "Wow, I've never seen a real wine cellar," I remarked. "Those shelves are really cool. They look handmade."

"They are. I made them."

"What?"

"Yeah, I made them."

"You?"

"Yeah, me. Don't look so shocked," he gently scolded. "Look over there." He pointed to the back of the basement, where there was more power tools lined up than you would find on an aisle in Home Depot, all of which were in pristine condition. "Those are my tools."

"Hmm," was all I could muster. He was handy? Really? What Jewish guy do you know that can change a light bulb, yet alone work these contraptions? I certainly had yet to meet one. Growing up, my dad paid electricians enough money to have easily covered a year of my college tuition, just to point out to him that appliances weren't broken but rather simply unplugged. And here this guy had power tools that he uses? I started to fear that he was either a liar or an exaggerator.

"Enough about my tools, let's continue the tour. Okay? Here is my little gym." He pointed his finger in the opposite direction from the wine. His workout area—complete with a treadmill and stationary bicycle, as well as a full standing weight center—didn't seem so little to me.

"Wow, you call that little? I guess you don't belong to a gym, huh?"

"No. No need." He walked further in his basement and pointed. "And here is my drum set."

"You drum?" I asked.

"Yeah, you can say that. I was in a few bands in my day."

"Wow, that is cool. Can you play something for me?" I asked.

"Nah. Maybe later."

"Oh come on. Please? For me?" I gave him a flirtatious smile.

"Well, if you twist my arm, I guess I can play something. Here, put this in your ears," he said as he handed me some cotton. I did as instructed and watched as he tentatively tapped his sticks on the drums.

Rap. Tap. Tap. Rap. Tap. Tap...

Okay. He said he was in a band? And all he is able to do is tap on these drums? Are they just for decoration? I probably could do better. This wasn't looking good.

My reverie was broken when out of nowhere, his arms and legs flared at a speed I didn't think humanly possible. He was making love to the drums. Never before had a drumbeat sound like music to my ears. But this did.

When he finally put his sticks back in the case, winded but smiling, I let out a huge cheer. "Wow, when you said you played drums, I didn't realize you really played drums."

"Yep! What, did you think I lied or exaggerated?" he asked, as if reading my earlier thoughts. "Oh, you will find out I am just full of surprises." He grabbed my hand and led me away from the drums. "Let me show you the rest of the house, so I can make us that drink I promised. I'm getting thirsty."

We walked up from the basement into the dining room, and up a few stairs into a huge room overlooking the ocean with the largest TV I had ever seen. "This is the living room," he announced. We walked up a few more stairs and he led me into a bedroom, complete with a king-sized bed.

It was beautiful. "Is this your room?" I asked.

"No, it is a guest room."

"Wow."

Then he walked me into another bedroom, as big as the first, with a full bathroom, and a balcony that overlooked the ocean. "This must be your bedroom?" I asked.

"Afraid not, it is another guest bedroom. My room is upstairs."

We walked up another flight of stairs, and he announced as he paused in the doorway, "This is my suite."

"Suite?" I asked, trying to keep my eyeballs in my head.

The bedroom was huge, with an amazing view of the ocean, complete with an enormous balcony. Then he walked me into his spacious bathroom, with a tremendous Jacuzzi tub and a steam shower.

All I could mutter was, "Wow."

"You like this, you'll love my closet." With that, he walked me up another few steps and into a closet that ran the entire length of the house. It was wide open and spacious, scattered sparingly with a few pairs of jeans and some polo shirts.

They say that the way to a man's heart is through his stomach. But I swear, the way to a girl's heart is through her closet. And this closet was the kind of closet that dreams were made of.

"You like?" he asked.

"Like?" I asked. "'Like' isn't the word for it. This closet is bigger than my bedroom!"

"Yeah, it's pretty nice. I thought you'd like it." He turned around. As I followed him out of the closet, all I could think of was how I wished I could have stayed in that closet forever. That's how nice it was.

Who was I kidding? All I could picture was how amazing it would be if I could live there...

Marc didn't lead me downstairs. Instead, he walked over to the sliding glass door, which opened onto the balcony. He grabbed my hand and guided me outside. The smell of the sea was so strong. "I love this smell," I remarked as I inhaled deeply. "And look at the white caps from the crashing waves," I said as I pointed. "They're beautiful."

"I think someone else is more beautiful," he said as he moved a little closer to me. I offered him a sly smile in return. After a few moments of gazing at the ocean in silence, he placed his right hand on the small of my back and his fingers slid under my tee-shirt and slowly across. His gentle caress stopped when he reached my side. He squeezed gently. A small electric current jolted through my body. I am sure I wasn't the only one who felt it, but unfortunately he remembered about that drink, and loosened his grip all too quickly.

I followed Marc downstairs and into the kitchen where, as promised, he prepared a chocolate martini. Just as I anticipated, it was delicious. We settled down in his den and began an easy conversation. Out of nowhere, his cat appeared.

"Alex, say hi to Hilary," Marc told his cat.

Cat? I didn't know he had a cat!

I have always been a dog lover. I wanted a dog for as long as I could remember. But growing up, I had very bad allergies and my allergist warned my parents not to get a dog. It wasn't until I was about twenty that my mom and I got Hannah Mae—and, of course, I ended up being allergic to her, but I loved her too much to let my respiratory issues get me down.

But as much as I loved dogs, I despised cats. As a kid, I had nothing but bad experiences with felines. My friend's cat scratched me from head to toe when I was about nine. Then, when I was about thirteen, I babysat for a family whose cat hissed at me and jumped at me the entire time I was at their house. I think that all the cats I had contact with sensed my fear, causing our dislike to become mutual. I expected the same thing with Alex.

But unlike the others, this cat came up to me and started circling my legs. Being in a brave mood, I told Marc about my fear. He showed me the proper way to handle Alex. I followed his instructions, and my heart melted as Alex let me pet him while he softly purred.

Marc was amazed. "Alex never does this with anyone. Usually he runs away and hides when someone is over. I have to tell my neighbors about this. They will never believe it. He really must like you. I always knew he had good taste." I smiled at Marc and figured that this was just a line. Little did I know, Marc was telling the truth about Alex not liking anyone!

Alex stayed by my side the entire time we were drinking our martinis. When we were finished, we headed over to the restaurant, which was only a few blocks from his house. It was clear that Marc was a regular, because as soon as we walked in, the owner came out from the kitchen in his chef uniform and greeted him. Marc introduced me to him, and I could see him sizing me up. I must have passed muster because he promised to send over some appetizers on the house.

The waiter handed Marc a wine menu, which he studied with great intensity. After a few questions he selected a bottle. The waiter promptly returned with it and poured a teeny bit in Marc's glass. He swirled it, sniffed it, and then tasted it. "It is good," he told the waiter, who then filled my glass, and then Marc's.

As soon as the waiter left the table, Marc raised his glass and toasted "to a great evening". I clinked glasses with him and repeated his sentiment, already feeling that it had been a great night, though it was only the beginning. We looked over the menus and Marc asked me what I wanted. I told him pasta and shrimp fra diavolo. When the waiter approached our table for our dinner orders, Marc ordered for me. There was something special and romantic about this. I felt like a princess.

As we drank and ate, Marc and I really started to get to know each other. "So, what made you start playing drums?" I asked.

"It's the only instrument that's also physical. I was a very hyper kid."

Interesting... he seemed very calm and collected now. Controlled, even.

"How old were you when you started playing?"

"Thirteen."

"Your mom must have loved your choice of an instrument." I couldn't help but chuckle as a mental image formed in my head.

"Yeah, she was less than thrilled when I'd practice. But she was a good sport about it though. My dad, on the other hand, had less patience. I drove him crazy. The last thing he wanted to listen to after working all day was me banging on my drums. But they got over it."

I took a bite of my salad. "How?"

"I was playing for about a year and a half and we had a battle of the bands at school. We were up last. When we took the stage we played Emerson, Lake and Palmer's 'Welcome Back My Friends'. The crowd went wild. The other bands started packing up their equipment. They knew instantly we won! My parents were in shock, but they loved every second. They were so proud." Marc took a sip of his wine and rolled his eyes. "Of course, my dad told anyone who would listen that he taught me how to play. What about you... any musical talents?"

"No! I don't have a musical bone in my body. I've got others, though. I can crochet, draw, and I like to write. But there is nothing musical in me, and it's not for a lack of trying... I've attempted everything... cello, piano, recorder, flute—I can go on, but I was awful at everything. Oh, and I can't sing either. When I was in fifth grade, I was one of three kids who weren't allowed in chorus. And I don't mean as an after school activity. I mean the chorus class that was part of the curriculum. I had to take music history instead and write reports. If that isn't bad enough, when I waited tables I would be tipped extra to not sing happy birthday!"

"Well, you never tried the drums, did you? Maybe there is hope for you yet. I guess I'll just have to teach you."

I liked the idea of the lesson, but had no false illusions that anything musical would ever come out of my body.

The waiter cleared away our salad plates and refilled our wine glasses. "So, you're an only child?" Marc asked. "What was that like? Were you spoiled?"

I thought for a moment before answering. "In some ways, yeah, how could I not be? But for the most part I'd say no. I didn't have the typical childhood. When I was really young, my grandmother lived with us. She had her leg amputated and my mom had to care for her. Basically her needs came before my desires. So, in a lot of ways, I wasn't really an only. Then, when I was fourteen, my dad had a massive stroke and passed away."

"Wow, that couldn't have been easy."

"No. It wasn't. I was actually alone with him when he had his stroke."

"Really?"

I took a sip of wine before continuing. "Yeah, my friend Kathleen and I were shopping in town together. When it started to rain, we called my dad to pick us up. Kathleen lived on my block, so he dropped her off first. As soon as we walked in our front door, he started acting strange and talking funny. He was trying to tell me he bought chocolate covered donuts, but he kept slurring his words. At first I thought he was joking around, because that was what he did. He was a jokester. But then I realized that he couldn't figure out how to remove his sneakers. That's when I knew something really was wrong. First I called 911 for help, and then I called my mom, who was at work. As soon as I hung up with her, he collapsed on the floor. Somehow I managed to pull him away from the door so the paramedics could get in.

"He was paralyzed on his left side, but was able to speak for about a week. Then he had to go on a respirator. He only lived for three weeks and three days after his stroke. It is so hard to lose a parent, but when you are that young… your life just changes, instantly. Childhood is gone."

I didn't really want to elaborate further exactly how my life changed after my father passed away. I completely withdrew into myself. I stopped hanging out with all my girlfriends. When I needed their support the most, I was unable to relate to them. Their typical teenage problems seemed minor and trivial to me, just as my grief was foreign to them. I suffered from severe anxiety. I was petrified of something terrible happening to my mother. Except for when I was in school and she was at work, I never left her side. I even slept with her. Although I always dreamt of going away to college, when the time came, I was unable to do so. I was too afraid to leave her. And while I was interested in boys before my father died, afterwards I cut myself off. The wall surrounding my heart was just too high. I wasn't able to let anyone in for fear that something would happen to them, or that I would get hurt. Sam was actually the first guy I let into my heart—which was probably why, despite our problems, I had such a difficult time ending the relationship in the past.

"I know. I lost my mom a few years ago," Marc softly said, and fell quiet just as the waiter approached our table with our dinner.

I wanted to get back to the topic of his mother, but I got the feeling he didn't want to talk about his mom, which I could easily understand. It took me many years to be able to easily talk about my father's death.

"I know you have a brother because I met him, but do you have any other siblings?" I asked.

"Yes, a sister, Ilene. She's also older than me."

"Cool. So you were the baby! My turn..." I smirked, "Were you spoiled?"

"Of course!"

Why didn't that shock me? Marc definitely struck me as a guy who liked to get his way.

"How's your dinner?" Marc asked.

"Delicious! And your chicken?"

"Excellent. Do you like to cook?"

"Don't know if I would say I like to, but I wouldn't say I didn't like to either. Honestly, I don't cook much, living at home and all, but I do make a killer chili and a mean tomato sauce."

"I love to cook," Marc announced as I remembered his state of the art kitchen, which I actually expected to have been more for show than use. "My mom and sister taught me. I find cooking very relaxing. I'll have to cook for you one of these days."

"I'd love that," I answered as I took another sip of wine.

Nice! I was excited. Dinner wasn't yet done and he was already talking about another date...

I felt a connection was definitely forming. The meal was a blur, and ended way too quickly. But fortunately the night wasn't over. We headed back to his house to continue chatting.

Earlier in the evening, I spotted two electric scooters in Marc's garage. He explained he had them for his nieces and nephews when they visited. When we arrived back at his house, I asked him if we could ride them. I figured he would think it was juvenile and refuse, but instead he eagerly obliged and we proceeded to ride them, laughing like teenagers for about a half hour.

When we put the scooters away in the garage, Marc opened the door to his house and walked inside. I followed him. He stopped at the rear sliding glass doors, which opened onto his deck. "Take off your shoes," he instructed. I did as I was told. He opened the door and gently took my hand.

"Let's go to the beach," he announced.

Hand in hand, we walked on the grass behind his neighbors' houses until we reached the fence which opened onto the beach. It was such an unusual sight to see lawn meet sand. The beach was very long, and slowly we made our way to the shoreline, where we stood side by side as the cool water lightly swept over our toes.

After a while Marc led me to the lifeguard chair. He ascended first and then helped me up. We sat there in silence for quite a while, just gazing out to the sea.

It was the most beautiful sight ever. There is something so magical and romantic about a beach at night, and this night was picture perfect! There was a soft, gentle breeze. The moon was full and its glow illuminated the entire ocean. The tide was low, making the waves so tranquil and small. Yet the sound of them quietly crashing onto the shore and the rock jetties was musical. It was all so peaceful and calm. Somehow it felt like the ocean was transformed into a glass lake. I was mesmerized.

Eventually Marc wrapped his arms around me and pulled me close to him. He placed his hand under my chin and gently turned my head to him. "I know that this is a friendship dinner," he said with a wink and a smile, "so would it be okay if I gave you a friendship kiss?" I smiled and nodded. I'd been waiting for this moment all night. And I loved that he asked about the kiss. He leaned over. Slowly and gently he ran his fingers down my check until they reached my chin, which he cupped as he angled my face closer to his. Our lips touched and instantly parted. As our tongues entwined, desire surged through my body. I felt everything but friendship at that moment. I also knew that no matter what happened with Marc, I would never see Sam again. And I didn't.

One kiss led to another, and then yet another. We snuggled up together on that lifeguard chair, talking and kissing. All too quickly, Marc broke away from our embrace. "Come on, let's go," he announced as he took my hand and started to descend.

"Already?" I asked, disappointed.

"Don't worry," he said. "I'm not through with you yet." Still holding my hand, he led me away from the shore back to his house, where he had a large hammock. "I think we'll be more comfortable here, don't you?"

"I don't know about this. I'm a klutz! Every time I go on a hammock, I fall off!"

"Not this time," he whispered as he swept me up in his arms and gently placed me in the center of the hammock. He then got on and lay down beside me, wrapping his arms tightly around me and pulling me close. "I'll keep you safe," he said. "You're not going anywhere."

That was perfect, because at that moment, there was no place in the world I'd rather have been. I made myself comfortable in the crook of his arm and nuzzled his neck. He smelled so good, a mixture of masculine and beach.

Holding me in place, he rolled onto his side to face me. He gently stroked my cheek. In return, I wrapped my arm around his neck, pulling him closer. Our lips locked, but this time the kisses were longer and more passionate. Hungry, even.

He shifted once again so he was lying on his back. But unlike before, this time he maneuvered me as well, placing me on top of him, so that my back was against his stomach. He slipped his hand under my clothes. As his fingers explored my body, shivers of desire soared though my veins. I felt his erection hard against my back. It didn't take long for my fingers to reach him and playfully tease.

Tangled in each other's embrace, we snuggled on the hammock for what seemed like minutes, but really were hours. When we finally entered the house, I was shocked to see it was four o'clock in the morning.

Marc drove me home, and I was astonished to see my mom awake in the living room with Hannah Mae barking like a maniac by her side. "Oh my God," I sung as I walked into the house. "I had the most amazing night of my life."

My mom gave me the stink eye. "Oh really? I'm so glad you had an amazing night," she sarcastically replied. "Personally, I had the most awful night of my life. You leave here and tell me you won't be out late, and then you never come home and you never even call? So what do I do? I try your cell phone and of course it's off! I was so worried." Pointing at my dog, she said, "And the more I worried, the more she barked. She was driving me crazy. All I could think was that you were murdered!"

"Sorry," I said sheepishly. "I didn't realize it got so late. I lost track of the time."

Still angry, she pointed at the Movado watch that I bought myself a few months earlier as a holiday present after years of wanting one.

"Oh, I'm so glad that you bought yourself that thousand dollar watch. It is really useful, if you don't bother to look at it."

"I said I was sorry. I am sorry. I know. You are right. I should have called."

"Yeah, you should have," she spat out.

"Okay. Enough with this, I got it that I am a terrible daughter. Can we please move on? Tonight was amazing. Let me tell you, first..."

"No." She cut me off. "You can do whatever you want, but I am going to bed. You may have had the time of your life tonight, and I am very happy for you. But I, on the other hand, had an awful night. I was worried sick. My stomach hurts, I have a headache, and I am exhausted. We will talk in the morning." And with that she headed upstairs to her bedroom, without as much as a backwards glance. I was dying.

With a loud sigh, I floated upstairs. Fortunately my mom's anger didn't last long, because as soon as I finished brushing my teeth, she was in my room. "Okay, I tried playing hard ball, but I can't do it. I can't handle the suspense. I need details. Tell me everything!" she said as she crawled into bed with me and shut off my light.

As I started to tell my mom every detail of the evening, from the very first moment, I noticed that the bedroom light next door flicked off. What I didn't know as I relived the very best first date ever with my mom was that our next-door neighbor, Judy, a recent widow, couldn't sleep that evening either. When she noticed that my house was ablaze with lights and spotted my mom pacing around, she began to worry about us, keeping an eye on our house. She was only able to fall back to sleep when she realized that both my mom and I were home safe and sound. The next morning she called to find out what happened, and my mom told her that I had an amazing first date. Judy wanted to hear more, so we made plans to have dinner with her that night.

I repeated the story I told my mom the night before to Judy over Chinese food, and watched the delight on both ladies' faces. I felt as if both these widows were reliving their own dating experiences through my story. It was wonderful. I felt their joy and their excitement, especially when I shared that Marc called me earlier in the day to make plans for Sunday.

CHAPTER 3

Wednesday, August 15, 2001

"HE WANTS ME TO SLEEP OVER on Friday," I blabbered into the phone as soon as my friend, Cassie, answered.

"Hello to you too," she snickered. I could just see her eyes roll. I knew each and every one of her facial expressions by heart, which was no easy feat since she had so many of them. Cassie could never be a poker player. Her face always showed her every thought and emotion. I have known her since my freshman year of college, when we met waiting tables together. Although she is only two years older than me, sometimes it feels like she could be my grandmother, especially when she stands on ceremony or is a stickler for formalities, like she was doing right then. It drives me crazy every time!

"Sorry. Hello, Cassandra. How are you this fine evening?" I asked, sarcasm dripping out of my voice.

"That's more like it." I could just see her smile spread over her face. Little things made her so happy. "I am very well, thanks for asking. And you?"

"Enough with this crap, okay? Did you hear what I said? He wants to cook me dinner and then have me to sleep over on Friday."

"Yeah… So what? I know you want to."

"Yes, but…"

"Are you afraid he can't cook?"

"Yeah, that's what I'm afraid of… Have you lost your mind?"

"No. Actually, I don't think I am the crazy one. Seems to me someone else is blowing things a little bit out of proportion. You have known this guy for what? Two weeks? And have hung out with him a bunch of times already. You two have done pretty much everything else, so what's the big deal?"

She had a point.

"This is different… it's so planned. It feels awkward."

"Please! Personally, I think it is a good idea. It gives you plenty of time to spend with him, and if a little something- something happens, all the better! I know you want it…"

"Yeah…"

Before I could say anything further, she interjected. "I hear a 'but' coming. Don't be an ass! You're just nervous. Get over it!"

She was right. I was worried. Sam was the only guy I'd ever slept with. While he was six years older than me, and a father, he had a very immature side—which was one of the reasons we constantly fought. I always thought of him as a boy. Marc, on the other hand, was a man…

"But—"

"But nothing," she scolded. "Put on your big girl panties, and… No! Wait. Put on some sexy undies and enjoy yourself…" With that, she hung up the phone.

Friday quickly approached. I made sure to leave my office exactly at five, which was no easy task. I raced home, took a shower, grabbed my pre-packed black knapsack, and headed over to Marc's house by the beach. I would be lying if I said I wasn't still nervous, but the butterflies that were floating around my stomach were more of the excited variety than the worried kind.

His front door was open, so I walked right in. I found Marc in the kitchen, opening a bottle of red wine. "Hi," I said as I leaned in for a kiss. As usual, I melted a little.

"Dinner is all set." He pointed to the pots on top of the stove. "Why don't we go into the den and relax a little bit first," he said as he grabbed the bottle. I followed him and found that he'd put some time into setting this evening's stage. Although it was a gloomy and rainy night, you wouldn't know it from the glow in the room. Candles were ablaze all throughout the room, including ones in sconces on the wall.

"Wow, someone was busy," I remarked.

"Just trying to make it special," he replied as he filled up the wine glasses that were already strategically placed on the coffee table.

"Should we toast?" I asked.

"Sure… How 'bout to a wonderful evening…"

We clinked glasses and took a sip. He flicked on the stereo and the room filled with the soft, sweet sounds of classical music. It was just enough to add ambiance, but not too much to take away from us being able to have a conversation.

"So, do you like mussels?" Marc asked about forty-five minutes later.

Pretending I didn't understand, I reached for his arm and grabbed his bicep, giving it a gentle squeeze. "Yep, I like muscles a lot."

He chuckled. "Excellent! I am doubly covered then, because that's what I made for dinner. Wait here. I'll be right back."

With that, he went into the kitchen and emerged carrying two bowls of Caesar salad which tasted like restaurant quality. "Where did you get this dressing?" I couldn't help but ask.

"Get it? I didn't get it. I made it."

I arched my eyebrows, showing my disbelief.

"Okay, fine. I sort of made it. I can't lie to you. I confess, I cheated. I use a really good jarred dressing and then I doctor it up with some freshly grated parmesan cheese, lemon juice, and some anchovies. I grind it all together with a mortar. So I guess it is semi-homemade."

"So, you really can cook? Impressive…"

"Oh, you ain't seen nothing yet…" he replied, sounding cocky.

I washed our salad dishes and loaded them into the dishwasher while Marc finished the dinner prep. We each carried our bowls of linguine and mussels with a spicy red sauce down into the den. He was right, dinner was amazing.

When we finished our feast, together we cleaned up the kitchen. We were very much in sync. It was easy, comfortable, and felt so homey. But the best part—the cleanup was fast.

We returned to the den and Marc changed the CD. There is nothing like the Bee Gees, or any seventies music for that matter, to get you on your feet dancing, which was exactly what we did. Although as the music picked up, our movements slowed down. The space between us decreased and we meshed into each other's arms. Tenderly we embraced as our mouths met. As we kissed, Marc moved his right hand away from the small of my back and placed it on my left cheek. Slowly he continued his caress down my neck, over my shoulder, across my breast, down my side, and returning it to the small of my back. Once he reached my behind, he tenderly squeezed it. His fingers slid up under my skirt and he began to fondle my ass and lower thigh. He moved his palm agonizingly slowly down my leg. When his fingers reached right behind my knees, he lifted me up, cradling me.

I tightly wrapped my arms around his neck as our kiss deepened. He carried me up the two flights of stairs to his bedroom and gently placed me on the center of his bed. "Don't move," he commanded, and proceeded to light the several candles which were on the night tables next to his bed. The rain must have stopped, because he also opened the sliding glass balcony door, letting in a cool, ocean-scented breeze.

Marc leaned back down on the bed and kissed me with passion and desire. His hands started out on both sides of my face, but tantalizingly slowly made their way down my neck, over my breasts, before finally reaching my waist and removing my shirt. I reached over and grabbed the bottom of his polo. I gently slid it up and off his body. I ran my fingers through his chest hair. As I leaned in to kiss his muscular chest, his fingers deftly unhooked my bra, freeing me. He gently pushed me back down onto the bed. Leaning down slowly, he removed my skirt and panties, caressing my behind and legs as he did.

He tossed my clothes onto the floor and eased himself onto the side of the bed, away from my reach. "I just want to look at you first," he said as his eyes darkened, while he studied my body. It was sweet torture.

Finally, he reached out to me, captured me in his embrace, and announced, "Enough looking, touching time!"

CHAPTER 4

September 2001

MY RELATIONSHIP WITH MARC seemed to be moving at a fast and furious pace. I would come into work every day, where I was the assistant controller for a beverage alcohol importer and distributor, to find a sweet email waiting for me from him. These notes always made me smile. I couldn't think of a better way to start off my day. We were spending an enormous amount of time with one another, and when we weren't physically together we would talk on the phone for hours. Our relationship was easy, fun, and stress-free. I didn't worry about anything when I was with him. I was able to be myself, and I loved it. I was sure Marc felt the same way.

But without any warning, about a month after our first date, the pace and extent of our communication totally changed. The morning emails were no longer waiting for me when I logged onto my computer. My cell phone didn't ring at night, and Marc stopped making plans to see me. At first, I chalked it up to the fact that he must have been busy at work; after all, he did own his own technology company. I convinced myself that he was dealing with a situation that demanded his full attention. But as the days stretched on, and exceeded a week, I started to get concerned and curious. I didn't have any idea what had happened to cause him to stop calling me.

I stayed up at night, wondering how I could have judged his feelings so wrongly. Every action before now pointed to the fact that he cared as much about me as I cared about him. But obviously that couldn't have been the case. I vowed not to reach out to him. I wanted to stay strong. If he had something to say, he could reach out to me. I felt my protective walls coming up once again.

Stubbornly, I stayed true to my resolve and didn't call, although I would be lying if I said I didn't come close. My curiosity about what happened peppered my every thought. I found it difficult to focus on anything but the demise of our relationship.

One bright, sunny morning I got into work and turned on my radio to the funny morning show I always listened to. I logged onto my computer and opened my emails. Just as I did the day before, I sent a silent prayer up to Cupid that there would be an email from Marc. It had been almost two weeks since I heard from him last. But of course, there wasn't. My disappointment was profound. So much so that I really didn't catch what was just on the radio.

I heard something about a plane and a building, but nothing really registered; I was too focused on my dating disaster. This morning show was famous for pranks and practical jokes, and I figured this was another one of their stunts, and I was not in the mood to be amused. But I slowly became aware that the hosts weren't laughing. Instead I heard cries, screams, and panic.

I listened in disbelief about how a plane had just hit the World Trade Center. Details were sketchy at first, but more and more information began coming through the radio at a fast and furious pace. As it became clear that this wasn't an accident, shock and terror overcame me. My office was a mere twenty miles from the attack. We were all crying and clinging to each other, scared for ourselves, scared for our country, and scared for our friends and relatives who, like us, simply went to work that morning.

In an office shared by four girls, one had a portable television set by her desk. She whipped it out, and turned it to the local news station. The five of us gathered around it. One girl suggested we take each other's hands and pray. And as we did, in shock and disbelief, we watched the second tower fall to the ground.

It was surreal. We were standing there, but none of us were really there. Our heads and hearts were with our loved ones and the innocent people we never had the chance to meet. Being so close to lower Manhattan, there wasn't one person in my entire office who didn't lose or come close to losing someone they knew that day.

Phones started ringing as we all checked in on those we loved the most. Some people immediately fled the office, while others like me, who had a long commute, decided to stick around. I felt safer at work than I would on the road, where I would have to spend an hour in my car driving from the north shore of Long Island to the south shore where I lived. Those of us who remained tried to comfort each other as best as we could, answering telephone calls from clients all over the world who were worried about our safety.

Eventually we all went home. There were hardly any cars on the road by that time, and most traffic lights were not properly functioning. Everywhere I turned felt abandoned, desolate, and empty, just as so many of our hearts did.

When I finally arrived home, my mom and I clung to each other, thankful that we were both safe and sound. Our phone didn't stop ringing for a second as concerned family and friends checked in. There was one call that was notably missing: Marc's.

I was fuzzy on the details of Marc's job. I knew that he owned his own business in the technology field, and that he frequently visited customers. Where these customers were located, I hadn't a clue. Could he have been in the city today? Was it possible that he was in the World Trade Center? Oh my God, I started to panic, could he be... gone?

As my mom hung up the phone for what felt like the millionth time in the past hour, I turned to her and said, "I'm worried. Do you think Marc could have been there today?"

"Oh God, I don't know," she answered, worry apparent on her face.

"He never called me," I said. "Do you think that could mean..."

She interrupted. "It could mean anything. I am sure he is okay. Let's not forget that he hasn't called you in over a week."

"Yeah, I know, but..." I paused and rubbed my face. "It's different now. Now I am worried."

"I can understand that. Why don't you call him, then? Make sure he is alright, and maybe while you're at it, find out what is exactly going on with him, anyway."

"I want to, I really do." I took a deep breath and vocalized my fear. "But if he is fine, why didn't he care if I am?" A tear slowly ran down my face. "Everyone and their uncle called today. Sam even called me."

"Well, don't seem so surprised about that. Did you think he wouldn't call you? He'll find any excuse he can think of to call you. He wants you back. I know it and you know it. He never thought you were serious when you ended it with him. He expected you to come back, like you always did. But since you didn't, now his pride is hurt."

I knew my mom was right, but Sam was the furthest person from my mind. I didn't even respond to her statement as I began my rant. "Clients even called me from Australia to check in on us. I could have been there today. He doesn't know I wasn't. Why doesn't he care if I am alive or dead?"

"Hilary, calm down. Stop jumping to conclusions. First, obviously there is an issue somewhere between you and him, and I suggest you find out what's going on, or you'll keep driving yourself, and me, crazy. Second, I think you are being a bit melodramatic about him not caring if you are alive or dead. You don't work in the city, nor do you visit clients there. He wouldn't expect you to be there. And besides, you have no idea what he could be dealing with today, and who he could have lost. So, if you are worried, just call him. It's the right thing to do anyway. And if this is the last time you speak to him, at least you will know that you did the right thing and checked on him in the midst of a catastrophe."

I knew my mom was right. I really did want to call him. But I must have paced around the house for about an hour before I was able to successfully finish dialing his number. When the call finally went through, and he answered, he greeted me as enthusiastically and happily as he possibly could have, given the situation. This confused me even more.

"Hi, I just was worried about you," I softly said. "I didn't know your schedule or anything, and I was afraid you could have been there today. I just wanted to make sure you are okay."

"I am fine, thanks. I was thinking about you today too."

I bit hard down on my tongue. I wanted to ask "really" but I didn't want him to see my insecurities. Instead I simply said, "I am okay. Did you lose anyone?"

"No, not that I know of yet, anyway. I have been on the phone all day and night. What about you?"

"I just found out that one of my cousin's friends was there and that he is missing. I was just with this guy," I said as a tear streamed down my face. "My cousin had a barbeque on Labor Day; he was there with his wife and daughter. She is only six."

"I'm sorry."

We chatted for a little while about where we were when we learned about the tragedy. Marc also shared that when he was a little boy he was fascinated by architecture and building. Dreaming of growing up and becoming an architect, he watched the World Trade Center being built from square one, as he studied the buildings' design. Also, he shared that one year, when asked what he wanted to do for his birthday, he told his parents that he wanted to take his friends to the construction site, and even though they didn't understand his fascination with the building, they of course obliged. Both of our voices cracked many times during the conversation.

But as we continued to talk, eventually the conversation grew lighter. Before I knew it we started falling back into our old normal banter, as if nothing had changed between us. It was bizarre. I knew what I had to do, so I worked up the nerve to ask, "So what's going on?"

"Going on? What do you mean?"

Nervously, I blurted out, "With us. Are we done?"

"What?" He sounded confused.

"Done, as in no longer seeing each other?"

"No, why would you think that?"

"Um, I don't know. Maybe it has something to do with the fact that all of a sudden you stopped emailing and calling me and have made no attempts to get together with me in almost two weeks." I took a deep breath and continued, trying to make myself sound more confident and secure than I felt. "It's okay if that is what you want. I understand. I get it. But what I don't understand is why you wouldn't have said something to me about it. I would've hoped you'd have at least told me you didn't want to be with me anymore."

There was silence on the other end. Hannah Mae must have sensed my nervousness, because she came up to where I was sitting and nestled in my lap. I kissed the top of her head as Marc cleared his throat and began to speak. "You're right. I should have said something to you. But it's not what you think."

I rolled my eyes at Hannah Mae, and she licked my nose in return. "What do you mean it's not what I think?"

"I don't want to break up with you. I really like you, and I want to continue to see you. But things were moving too fast. We were spending too much time together. I'm not ready for that. I am just not ready for a relationship."

"What does that mean? Are you seeing someone else?" I asked.

"No."

"Do you want to see someone else?" I asked, trying to clarify for him. Again, without a pause, he replied, "No. Not at all."

"Then I don't understand. What's the problem? What do you want?" Why are men so difficult, I wondered?

"It's hard to explain," he said tentatively.

"Try to." I said, stroking Hannah Mae's head.

"Okay," he said with a deep breath. "I want to continue to see you. I really do like spending time with you, but I don't really want a relationship right now. And that is what I feel we were starting to have."

"A relationship?" I felt a major headache coming on.

"I am not really explaining this too well, am I?"

"Um, no, you're not."

"Okay, I guess I just want to take things slow. I want us to get together when we want to get together. I don't want to feel like we have to. I don't want an 'every weekend' kind of commitment. I need space. I need my own time, and I need to take things slow. Does this make any sense to you?"

Strangely, when he finally spit it out, it sort of did. Although I didn't like how he came about sharing his feelings with me, I could actually understand where he was coming from. I honestly wasn't ready for a heavy relationship either, especially after putting to bed, finally, all the drama I had with Sam. But more than that, after two years of having my CPA license, about a year earlier I'd started a new position. I finally felt I had a career, as opposed to just a job. I wanted work to be my focus rather than a man, even though I really did like Marc a lot. But rather than express any of this to him, I simply replied, "Yeah. I think I can understand that."

Marc let out an audible sigh of relief. "Good. Now that we got that squared away, want to have dinner on Friday?"

As I hung up the phone and started to think about Friday night, another thought popped into my head. Was Marc telling me the whole truth? After all, it is so difficult to navigate through a man's brain. There is so much empty space there, sort of like the hollow drums that

Marc played so expertly. Did he really not want a relationship, or was he just afraid to have one?

When I saw Marc on Friday, it was as if no time had passed. We picked up exactly where we left off. We went to a local restaurant for dinner and had a wonderful time. Over the next few months, we continued to see each other, although there was no rhyme or reason as to when we would get together. Some weeks we would spend several nights together, but other weeks, I wouldn't see him at all. I let Marc take the lead, and I only saw him when he initiated it. I never tried to make plans with him on my own. I didn't want to appear needy, nor did I want to experience rejection. I made sure to have plans with my friends and family instead. I didn't want to him to think I had nothing going on in my life and I was just sitting by the phone waiting for it to ring. Which of course, let's face it, technically, I was.

Something about our relationship always troubled me. Even though I stayed over at his house, I tended to see Marc during the week, but hardly ever on the weekends. The weekends, he explained, were when he spent time with his family. From what he told me, I knew that he was close to his brother and sister and their children. I could understand him wanting to spend time with them, especially the kids, but I just never could understand why he never included me.

Why couldn't I accompany him to his niece's dance recital? I wondered. I could sit in the audience and clap when appropriate. Why wasn't I able to go bowling with him and his nephews? This bothered me, but I didn't push it. In fact, although difficult, I never uttered a word about it to him. I felt if he wanted me there, he would ask me to join. I couldn't help but wonder if he was hiding something? Could one of his nieces or nephews be his child?

*   *   *

In mid-November, uncharacteristically, following a Wednesday date, Marc invited me over Saturday night. He had candles aglow, and the fireplace blazing. He cooked up a delicious filet of sole with sautéed broccoli, and his now famous Caesar salad. We had two bottles of pinot grigio, which was more wine than I'd ever drunk in my life. I was having a blast.

After dinner, we went upstairs to his room. I got ready for bed first. In the bathroom, after brushing my teeth, I threw something into the garbage, and when I did, I felt my stomach drop to the ground. There were condom wrappers on the top of the pail. I knew they weren't from me, because although I had been there only a few days earlier, when I left for work Thursday morning, I threw out a pair of pantyhose—and there were no pantyhose in the pail.

I was in a panic and a little drunk. I didn't know what to do, but I knew I couldn't stay in the bathroom forever. So I returned to the bedroom and wordlessly hopped into bed. Marc didn't realize I was upset: he just went into the bathroom.

As he cleaned up, my mind raced and my stomach sank more. I finally had the answers that I didn't want. No wonder he hardly ever wanted to see me during the weekends. He was obviously seeing someone else, and sleeping with them as well! Was I only here tonight because she was busy?

I felt like someone had kicked me in the gut. Part of me had figured it could have been a possibility, but I'd really never allowed myself to believe it. And now, thanks to the evidence, I had my proof. But what should I do?

The way I saw it, I had two options. I could say nothing, ignoring what I saw, or I could confront him about it now. I knew I couldn't wait and confront him later. If I was going to say something, I had to do it now, when it was fresh in my mind, and when the evidence still was in the trash. No matter how much I may have wanted to, I couldn't pretend I didn't realize what was really happening, nor could I be with someone I knew was sleeping with someone else. So as Marc lay down in bed next to me, I made my decision.

Thankful for the liquid courage the wine provided, I blurted out, "You are seeing someone else." I meant it as a question, but it came out more of a statement.

"I am what?" Marc sat up in bed and faced me.

I repeated my original words. "You are seeing someone else." Then, to clarify, "I saw the condoms in the garbage."

"You saw the what in the where?" he asked, anger flashing across his face.

"I saw the condoms in the garbage. Why didn't you tell me you're seeing someone else? I thought I was the only one."

"Why would you think I'm sleeping with someone else? Do I strike you as a liar or a cheater? I've told you that I'm not seeing anyone else, haven't I? So you think I am just lying to you. After all this time, don't you know me at all?"

I was so upset. Why do people, when they are wrong, twist the conversation around and place the blame on someone else? Why was he getting mad at me and making this my fault? After all, I was the innocent and hurt one! "I believed every word you ever said to me," I replied, anger and wine getting the best of me as I sat up and stared him in the eyes. "I never questioned you when you didn't want to hang out, nor if you went days without communication, did I? No, I gave you all the space you needed. And I did so because I could understand where you were coming from, and I thought I was the only one you were involved with. But I guess I was wrong."

"Oh, you are wrong alright," he said, still sounding very angry. "You are wrong to think I've been with anyone else. First of all, do you think I'm an idiot?" He didn't wait for me to respond, he just continued. "I am not an idiot. If I was cheating on you, believe me, I would be smart enough not leave evidence in clear sight for you to find. But I am not a liar or a cheater. If I want to be with someone else, I have news for you, I will be with them. But I won't be with you. I am not the type to mess around behind someone's back. I wouldn't want that done to me, so I certainly wouldn't do that to someone else."

I hated myself, but I believed him. Was I a moron or a fool? "But what about the condoms?" I couldn't help but ask.

"Oh, the condoms… Did you even bother to look at them?"

"Um, no. Why would I?"

"Yeah, why would you? They were expired," he stated matter-of-factly.

"I didn't know that condoms expired," I replied.

"Yeah, they do. So, I was looking out for you, actually, and I went through them and threw out any that were expired. So if you'd have bothered to look at them, instead of just jumping to conclusions and thinking the worst of me, you would have seen that the condoms were never used. They were all sealed."

With that, he lay down on the bed. I absorbed everything he said, as a tear rolled down my face. I wanted to believe him and instantly regretted thinking the worst of him, but at the same time I knew that I'd made the right decision to ask him about it. If I ignored it, I would always have worried and wondered. I lay back down and softly whispered, "Sorry."

"Yeah, me too," he replied. I couldn't tell if he was being sincere or sarcastic.

We lay there, both on our backs, in silence for what was probably a minute or two but felt like an eternity. I tried to gauge his state of mind, but since his eyes were closed, I couldn't. I'd been walking on eggshells for months trying not to push him emotionally and scare him away. Did I just blow all that effort?

Willing to risk sounding naïve, "Do you hate me?" I asked.

He turned and faced me, and softly said, "No. I am not thrilled with you, but I far from hate you." His eyes were kind, compassionate, and sad. He extended his arm to me, and said tenderly, "Come here."

I rolled into his embrace, and for a second it felt wonderful, until a wave of nausea hit me. I didn't know if it was the stress of the evening, or all the white wine that I drunk, or both, but I did know that I was going to be sick. I ran toward the bathroom as fast as I could, holding my mouth, praying desperately that I would reach the toilet in time. But I didn't. Why would I? Just when I thought the night couldn't have gotten any worse, I threw up all over Marc's beige bedroom carpet.

The next morning, still beyond mortified and barely able to face Marc, I couldn't wait to get out of his house and head home. Before I left, compulsion got the better of me. I couldn't stop myself from digging into the garbage pail, through the paper towels which I used the night before to clean up my mess, to inspect the condoms and make sure they were indeed sealed. Which, of course, they were... oh, and yes, they were expired too! How I hated myself.

As I drove home, I couldn't stop replaying the disaster of a night in my head. I was sure that I would never hear from Marc again. But this time I didn't blame him. In fact, although I was disappointed and ashamed at how it had to end, I totally understood.

To my shock and disbelief, he called me later that night, and made plans to see me on Monday evening. When I hung up the phone, I realized something. He may have convinced himself that he didn't want a relationship and would never commit to anyone. But in all his thoughts and plans, he didn't account for one thing.

Me!

And in that moment, while I had doubts about what our future would be, and wondered why he reacted so extremely to my accusation the night before, I didn't have any doubts that somehow, I'd managed to get under his skin.

CHAPTER 5

January 1, 2004

I GLANCED AT THE CLOCK next to my side of the bed in our rented condo in Fort Lauderdale, and saw that it was only 3:15. How could that be? It felt as if I had been in this bed for a month instead of just a few hours. No matter how hard I tried, I was unable to rest my racing mind. I rolled over to face Marc, who continued to sleep peacefully, snoring loudly. It amazed me that the evening's events and our fake engagement fiasco didn't interfere with his beauty rest. If only I was so lucky...

It occurred to me that it was ironic that this engagement debacle fell on New Year's Eve, because this holiday had been a turning point in our relationship earlier on. The first year Marc and I were dating, I got my hopes up that we would spend New Year's Eve together. I was so optimistic and confident that I actually broke my self-imposed rule and broached the subject with him a week or so before the holiday.

When I did, I wasn't prepared for his answer. "Oh, New Year's is a difficult holiday for me," he explained. "My mom passed away in December, and ever since I don't really like to celebrate the holiday."

I was able to relate to this; after all, I also lost a parent. I understood your outlook on life, including holidays, changes after a parent dies. Marc's mom died about six years before we met, of a brain aneurism. What I wasn't able to understand or relate to was what he told me next. "I am going to go New Jersey to spend the day and night with my friend Louis."

"Louis?" I asked. "Why?"

"Well, his father died around the same time as my mother. Ever since that happened, we usually hang out on New Year's Eve together and reminisce about our parents," he explained.

"But Louis is married, and has two kids, right? You are going to hang out with all of them?"

Marc answered yes and changed the subject. I ended the conversation and hung up the phone. I didn't believe his story for one second. Two grown men celebrating New Year's Eve together alone was hard enough to imagine, especially if one or both of them had a girl available to spend the holiday with. But a grown man traveling to another state to hang out with his friend and his friend's family to mourn the passing of their parents who died six years earlier was ludicrous!

I was flipping mad. I didn't care as much about not spending New Year's with him as I cared that his story was so ridiculous. Did he think I was a fool? Why was he lying to me and who was he spending the holiday with?

I became pretty cool after this conversation. When he asked me out for dinner that week, I told him that I already had plans; as a result, I didn't see him the entire week leading up to New Year's. I wasn't sure what I really wanted to do, or how I felt. I was confused. As soon as I made one step forward with him, before I knew what happened, I would find our relationship back at square one. Did I really want to continue walking on this emotional tightrope?

Bright and early on New Year's Day, 7:30 AM, to be exact, my house phone rang. It was Marc. He sounded upset and nervous when I answered. "Happy New Year," he said softly.

"Um, thanks, you too," I replied with a chill in my voice.

"Did you have a good night?"

"Yeah, I had a wonderful night! I went out with a bunch of friends," I answered, although in actuality Cassie came over my house and we ordered a pizza, watched a movie, and dissected Marc and my relationship the entire night. Cassie thought I was crazy to want to continue seeing him. I really couldn't disagree with her.

I didn't question him about his night. I wasn't interested in hearing any lies. Since he called me so early in the morning, I really wondered what, if anything, he did the night before.

"Nice," he said. "What are you doing today?"

"I am going to my aunt's house for an early dinner with my mom," I replied, which was also a lie.

"Oh, I was hoping you could hang out with me."

"I would love to," I answered honestly, because I really did want to spend time with him, but I didn't want to be too available. "But I have to be at my aunt's at four o'clock."

"Well, it's not even eight. How about you come over for an early lunch? We can hang out a while before you have to see your aunt."

I thought for a moment, and decided to go for it. After all, what harm could it do? Besides, I missed him.

When I got to his house, he seemed extra happy to see me. I think he realized that he hadn't done the right thing the night before and felt bad about it. I didn't mention it once. Based on the time he called me, I figured that his plans didn't include a romantic evening with another woman.

When he opened his refrigerator to prepare lunch, I saw there was a bunch of cut up pieces of cheese and veggies. I assumed he had company over the night before, but I didn't know who was there. It was troubling. I knew from what Marc told me that he was very close to his family, but he never included me in any of their plans. The same went for friends.

I wanted to question him about the food. But I knew if I did, I would then have to address the fact that he lied to me. I didn't really want to go there. So I ignored what I saw and vowed not to tell anyone about it. It is easier to lie to yourself than hear others tell you that you are a fool.

It was an awkward afternoon. My guard was up and I think he knew it. We ate lunch, we chatted, and he taught me how to play chess. Hours passed before he attempted any physical contact with me.

When he finally leaned over and kissed me, it was deep and passionate. I welcomed it and wanted it. It became clear that he wanted more. So did I, but I refused to let anything happen. The night before he didn't give me what I wanted, what I needed, so I didn't want to be so available for his desires.

"I can't," I muttered as I broke away from his embrace.

"What?" Clearly, he wasn't expecting that reaction from me.

"I don't want to start anything we can't finish," I replied, trying to sound playful.

"And why can't we finish?"

"It's getting late. I have to be at my aunt's soon."

"Come on," he replied and kissed me once again, as his hands reached under my sweater. "You can be a little late, can't you?" he asked, followed by yet another gentle kiss.

"No, I really can't. Sorry." I stood up and adjusted my clothes. "In fact, I really should get going now so I can make it there on time." He followed me to his front door, held me tightly, and kissed me one more time goodbye. I don't think he expected such a hasty exit. To be honest neither did I, but I was proud of myself.

Marc called me later that night, and we spoke on the phone for an hour. I decided to try putting New Year's Eve out of my mind. I hoped in time I would learn what he really did with whom, but I knew if I wanted to continue our relationship, I would have to stop worrying about it.

Marc prepared a beautiful and romantic dinner for me that Friday night. He set the stage perfectly—an amazing bottle of wine, music on the stereo, candles illuminating every room including the bathroom, a blazing fire, and filet mignon and shrimp grilled to perfection.

When we first started dating, Marc asked me what music I liked and I didn't have a real answer. Sure, I liked music, and listened to the radio, but I was never crazy about any particular band or singer. Music was in the background for me. It never was a focal point. Marc, on the other hand, was passionate about music. He hated the fact that I didn't know his favorite bands and had missed out on what were, in his view, the great musical events of history. So he made it his personal mission to teach me everything he knew.

We would spend evenings in his den, sitting beside a blazing fire with a glass of wine while he would play CD after CD, explaining who the bands were and giving me history on them. He also shared stories about how the music touched his life. He told me how his brother, Jay, heard Led Zeppelin for the first time in Central Park when they played as a warm up band at a concert. I was able to feel the excitement Marc must have felt when he saw Pink Floyd's "The Wall" at Nassau Coliseum as a teenager with his best friend, Evan. He described the emotion he felt getting a new tape of The Who and bringing it to the boardwalk, down the block from his childhood home, and listening to it surrounded by all of his friends.

I was a quick study. Fascinated by his stories, I started to hear music in a different way. As I became more knowledgeable, his approach changed. We continued to have leisurely evenings by the fire listening to the stereo, but instead of him lecturing me on the bands and the songs, he would play "name that tune" with me. In the beginning I always got it wrong, but I had a blast guessing, and he enjoyed watching me trying to figure out who I was listening to. Over time, I started getting more and more songs right. He would love to stump me, and I loved shocking him with my newfound knowledge.

As we ate our filet, we were playing "name that tune". I was doing extremely poorly, but having a great time. Finally Marc selected a song I knew, *Bridge over Troubled Waters*. I didn't rush announcing the band. Instead, I enjoyed the music a little and waited for a full verse to play.

"Taking pity on me and finally choosing an easy one! Simon and Garfunkel," I exclaimed as I turned to face him. I expected Marc to break into a smile as he always did when I managed to guess correctly. But he didn't. Instead I saw he was crying.

I was shocked. I sprung to my feet and went to the chair where he was sitting. "What's wrong?"

He looked embarrassed as he brushed his tears away. "I'm okay," he tried to assure me. "This song just reminds me of my mom. She loved it."

I hugged him tightly. I understood the pain of losing a parent. "Tell me about her," I softly asked after I released him from my embrace. I was so eager to for him to open up to me. He always kept his thoughts and feelings so bottled up. Finally was he going to let his guard down?

"No. I don't want to," he said as he shattered my hope. "It is too difficult for me to talk about. I'm not good talking about feelings." And as quickly as he opened the window to his soul, he closed it. But it did mean a lot to me that he allowed me a small glimmer into his heart, and he felt comfortable enough to let himself go, if only for a few moments.

The next morning, I was getting ready to head home, but Marc asked me to go shopping with him instead. He wanted to get new chairs for his dining room, and wanted me to help him pick them out. His chairs were upholstered in black fabric, which didn't mix well with the shedding of his white cat, Alex.

I enthusiastically agreed and we drove around, visiting numerous furniture stores in the area. I was relieved to find that we had very similar tastes. We had a blast looking and measuring everything. He totally valued my opinions. Eventually, four stores later, we selected the perfect chairs. They were high backed and made of oak, which matched his decor perfectly. We were having such a great time shopping we also went looking for an area rug, which we found. I loved that regardless of what happened between us, whenever he looked at the chairs he would remember me.

We arrived back at his house around six. After we were there for just a few minutes I said, "I guess I should be going."

"Why? Do you have plans tonight?"

"No, but I just figured you had enough of me," I joked. "Two days is usually your limit, isn't it."

"Yeah, it is," he replied, his eyes twinkling, accompanying his boyish grin. "I usually get a little nervous," he said as he waved his right hand by his heart, "but today feels different. I'm not nervous. I want you to stay."

So I did. We went out to dinner, to the very same place where we had our first date. I wouldn't say that Marc had a one-eighty after that day, but I do think that it was a slight turning point in our relationship. We started spending more time together, and it seemed that slowly his jitters began to take a back burner more times than not.

Chapter 6

March 2002

"THIS WEEKEND IS going to be very crazy for me," Marc announced as we ate dinner in an Italian restaurant near his house about a month later.

"Really? What's going on?" I asked as my mind jumped to conclusions. Just when I started regularly seeing him on the weekends, was he getting nervous again? Was he trying to prepare me for not spending time with him?

"My friend Boya is coming over. We're gonna take down the half wall between the dining room and the living room. Right by the staircase," he clarified. "We're going to put up an oak railing instead. It will make the house much more open and airy."

Although I couldn't quite picture what he was explaining, it did seem exciting. Finally I would get to see his handy side. "That sounds like a lot of work. You're going to be pooped when you are finished. Why don't I come over at night and cook you dinner."

Surprise crossed his face. "You'd want to do that?"

"Yeah, I'd love to."

It is funny; Marc always seemed surprised when I offered to do something nice for him. We were only dating for about two months or so when I offered to take him out to dinner the first time. I wasn't being pushy about it, nor was I trying to force a date with him. I just wanted to pay for dinner for a change. I thought it was the right thing to do. He was shocked as he explained, "No one ever buys me dinner."

I decided it would be easier to cook at my house and just bring the food over since I didn't know what shape his house would be in with the construction. I prepared chili and a salad, since it was easy to transport, while being hearty and light at the same time.

As I seasoned the dish, my mom entered the kitchen. Panic stricken, she cried out, "Watch the cayenne pepper! You don't want to kill the poor guy, do you?"

"I know what I'm doing, Mom," I said, rolling my eyes. "He likes spicy food."

"Hilary, there's human spicy and your kind of spicy. Make sure you make it human spicy." My mom was right—I'm a little insane when it comes to spices—I swear I must have asbestos for a tongue. But I ignored my mom's advice and continued cooking the chili how I saw fit, which included lots of liberal dashes of cayenne pepper.

I drove a large Tupperware container of chili over to Marc's house a few hours later. He just finished work and was having a celebratory drink with his friend.

I was shocked at what he had accomplished. The workmanship was amazing, and he was right—the room was transformed. His friend only stayed a few more minutes, and as soon as he left, Marc went upstairs to clean up. I busied myself in the kitchen heating up our dinner.

I was so excited that I'd finally met one of Marc's friends. I couldn't wrap my head around why Marc never included me when he had plans with other people, especially his family. Most times, I didn't let it bother me; I just took it in stride, figuring it had to do with his commitment-phobic ways. But other instances weren't so easy to shake. Like about a month before, when Marc was planning to fly to Utah to attend a conference hosted by Eric and Jaye. We had plans to have dinner the night before he was due to leave New York, but those plans never materialized. The morning of our dinner date, he called me and told me that he had to cancel. When I asked why, he told me he had to have dinner with his brother before he left town.

Now seriously, what was that all about? I could understand wanting to see your brother before going on a long trip, but he was only going to be out of town a few days. Where was the urgency?

I tried to reason to myself that there was nothing wrong with him hanging with his family. But the part I couldn't get my head around was why I couldn't go with him. After all, he was canceling our date to spend time with them. And to make matters worse, it wasn't like I never met his brother or his wife. If not for Susan, I never would have dated Marc in the first place.

As usual, I didn't let on how upset I was. I didn't want to give him the satisfaction, or make him feel pressured into seeing me. It was his life, and if he wanted to be with his brother more than me, so be it. "I hope you have a very good time," I simply said, keeping all emotion out of my voice.

Although I should have known better, a part of me expected him to change his mind at some point during the day. Of course, that didn't happen. I also figured that he would reach out to me at some point during the day or the night, but again, that didn't happen. By the time I went to sleep, I was fuming.

I didn't feel any better when I woke up the next day. I was hurt, to say the least. Like so many other times in the past, I was convinced that our relationship was over. I don't know why, but I always figured when it was time for him to move on, he would just stop calling me, rather than leveling with me. Communication had never been a strong suit of his, and he made it clear from day one that we didn't have a relationship anyway.

I spent the morning moping around the house and the afternoon at the hair salon with my mom. I vented to my hairdresser, Thelma, as she cut my hair. She tried to be encouraging, but I sensed she thought the relationship was headed nowhere fast.

When my mom took my spot in Thelma's chair for her cut and blow my cell phone rang. It was Marc. Cautiously, I answered, "Hello."

"Hi," he replied. "I just wanted to tell you I got to Utah." I was glad he called, but confused with the mixed messages. He had no reason to feel the need to check in, especially after last night.

"Oh great," I answered, trying to sound upbeat, but not too excited. "Did you have a good flight?"

"Yeah, everything was perfect, but I really can't talk long," he said, "I know I messed up last night. I shouldn't have canceled on you. I'm really sorry."

I pulled the phone away from my ear for a second and stared at it, as if asking, "Is this really happening?" Trying to sound confident and unfazed, I answered, "You did what you felt was right. There is no need to apologize."

"But I have to. I was wrong. So can I make it up to you?"

"I don't know," I replied. "What do you have in mind?"

"I'll be back on Tuesday. Do you want to have dinner on Tuesday with a handsome guy?"

"Dinner on Tuesday with a handsome guy, huh? That sounds nice. Who is the guy?" I couldn't help but tease.

"Yum, that smells good," Marc remarked, breaking my reverie. He kissed me gently as he took the spoon I was using to stir the pot with and placed it on the counter. "Why don't we relax a while before dinner?"

He grabbed the bottle of wine from the counter and two glasses and walked into the den. I shut off the stove and followed him. He flicked on the stereo and I sat beside him. "I can't believe the job you guys did! It's amazing. Tell me about it."

"Nah, I have some other ideas," he replied as he slipped his hands under my shirt and kissed me with longing and urgency.

Eventually I had to feed him...

After we finished the salad, I scooped the chili into two large bowls and garnished them with shredded cheddar cheese and corn chips.

"Wow, this looks great," Marc said with a smile, dipping his spoon in the chili. He took one bite and the smile disappeared. He started sputtering and coughing. Tears ran down his eyes. I ran into the kitchen and got him a bottle of water. He took a long, deep gulp, as sweat oozed from every pore. All I could think was: great, I almost killed him. One day, I really have to start listening to my mother.

Once he regained his composure, I apologized.

"Don't worry about it," he replied as he dipped his spoon back into the bowl. "I like it. I just didn't realize it was that spicy. But now that I know, I will go slower."

"You don't have to eat this. I can make tuna, grilled cheese, or something."

"Don't be silly," he answered after swallowing a spoonful. "I just have to get used to spicier food if you are going to keep cooking for me."

CHAPTER 7

FROM: MARC@WORK
TO: HILARY@WORK
Sent: Wednesday May 22, 2002 2:54PM
Subject: Dinner
Tonight???

In less than a minute, I fired back a reply.

From: Hilary@work
To: Marc@work
Sent: Wednesday May 22, 2002 2:54PM
Subject: Re: Dinner
Wow. A man of many words. :) I would love to.

I smiled to myself as I hit "send" and returned my focus to the
spreadsheet I was working on when my computer beeped, alerting me
to another email.

From: Marc@work
To: Hilary@work
Sent: Wednesday May 22, 2002 2:56PM
Subject: Re: Dinner
Good… because Alex misses you….

Typical, I thought, as my fingers struck the keys…

From: Hilary@work
To: Marc@work

Sent: Wednesday May 22, 2002 2:57PM
Subject: Re: Dinner
But, more importantly, does his dad????

Even though I compulsively clicked on the send and receive button,
I waited almost ten minutes for a reply.

From: Marc@work
To: Hilary@work
Sent: Wednesday May 22, 2002 3:06 PM
Subject: Re: Dinner
What do you think?

Even though we'd been seeing each other for about nine months,
and I had a key to his house, this exchange was characteristic of our
communication. Sure it was cute and fun, but it was also extremely
frustrating. Marc would never come out and express his feelings. He
kept all of his emotions bottled up. When he finally felt the need to
share, rather than addressing it straight on, he would just transfer his
feelings onto the cat!

I never used the key that he gave me. I was reluctant to let myself
in unannounced. I guess it came with the territory of him being so closed
off emotionally.

"Why don't you ever come over and surprise me?" Marc asked as
we ate dinner that night. "You do have a key, you know."

"Yeah, I know. It feels strange to just let myself in."

"Don't be silly. That is why I gave it to you, so you can use it any
time you want, not just hold onto it. In fact, use it on Friday," he instructed.
"I have to work late. I won't be home until about ten, and I want you
to be here when I arrive."

It felt very peculiar being alone in his house on Friday night. Of
course I conducted a little snooping mission, but I didn't find anything
of interest (although I didn't try too hard). Flashbacks of the expired
condom night came flooding back to me. So I decided it was best that I
try to stay out of trouble.

I grabbed a bottle of water from the refrigerator and settled in on
the couch and turned on the T.V. Within moments, Alex, the cat, was
by my side purring. I reached over and began to gently scratch his head.
His purrs became louder. Before I knew it, Alex was sitting on my lap.

Although Alex seemed to have liked me, his affection was mostly shown from a distance. Sure he would let me give him a little pet here or there, but in all this time I had been at Marc's house, never did he sit on my lap this way. It was shocking.

He stayed with me for an hour or so until Marc opened the garage door. As soon as the cat heard the sound, he abandoned me. It was almost like he didn't want Marc to get jealous!

I met Marc at the garage door and his face lit up. He clearly was as happy to find me there as I was to be there.

The next morning as I was getting ready to shower, I picked up the towel I used the night before, which I left on the side of the tub. It was wet and heavy, and the smell assaulted me. "Yuck!" I screamed.

"What is it?"

Pinching the towel and holding it as far away from me as possible, I replied, "I think Alex did something." It didn't take more than a whiff for Marc to confirm my suspicion.

"That is so strange, he has never peed on a towel like that before," Marc replied.

A few days later I slept over Marc's house again. I packed my favorite jumpsuit to wear to work the next day, which I hung in his closet. My outfit was very long, and the bottom of the pants draped on the bottom on the closet floor. When I went to get dressed the next morning, I saw that the bottom of my pants was saturated, and the now-familiar smell was unmistakable. I showed my outfit to Marc, and again he was shocked. "I don't understand what he is doing," Marc told me. "He has never done anything like this before."

"Maybe he's sick," I suggested.

"I doubt it. But I will call my cousin, Ira. He's a vet."

Later that day, Marc called me. "So I spoke to Ira about Alex peeing on all your stuff."

"And?"

"He said that Alex is testing you out. Alex isn't used to sharing me with anyone, and you have been spending a lot of time here lately. He wants to make sure you are worthy of his affection."

I rolled my eyes. Great! It wasn't bad enough I was dating a commitment phobic man, but he had to have a commitment phobic cat too!

CHAPTER 8

BY THE TIME SUMMER rolled around, my newfound appreciation of music wasn't the only change that was a result of my relationship with Marc. Little by little, my life changed for the better.

For example, when I first met Marc, I never exercised. I didn't see the need. I figured I was already thin, so why bother? I never considered that there were other benefits besides looking good in a pair of designer jeans or a bikini.

It was easy for me not to work out. I spent many years having to be fairly stationary. When I was eleven years old, I had a major growth spurt, growing seven inches in less than a year. Soon after, I was diagnosed with a severe case of scoliosis. My doctor kept a close watch on it, and the summer before my thirteenth birthday, I was put in a back brace.

If the transition to becoming a teenager wasn't difficult enough, I had to wear my brace for twenty hours every day. It was a huge plastic contraption that went from my hips up to my shoulder blades in the back, and under my breast bone in the front. Not only was I no longer able to play any type of sports, or be a camp counselor as I'd planned for that summer, I couldn't even wear normal clothes. Nothing would fit over the thick plastic. I was petrified about what I would wear when school started. Fortunately, I got lucky. Leggings and oversized shirts were that fall's fashion.

My parents worried how I would emotionally handle wearing my brace. I reassured them that I would be fine. I even remember telling my mom that I didn't care if anyone made fun of me, because if they did, I wouldn't want them as a friend. She thought this was so mature. It would have been, if I was telling the truth. But I wasn't. I lied to them.

I did care. Children, especially teenagers, are cruel and hurtful. It crushed my spirit to walk through the halls of my junior high school to taunts of my classmates, who never seemed to tire of their jokes.

Initially I was supposed to wear my brace for eighteen months, but I ended up having to wear it for close to three years. Eventually my classmates found other outlets for their hostilities and stopped their teasing. While they may have forgotten "Back Brace Girl", I never forgot how I was treated. My circle of friends greatly diminished, and I became very quiet and withdrawn at school.

When I finally got out of my brace, all those years of inactivity really took a toll. I couldn't run a hundred feet and not get winded, so I didn't. And I had no plans to, until Marc showed me the light, or more appropriately, showed me the gym. He made sure that I realized that it was just as important for my body to look good on the inside as it did on the outside. Exploring the world of physical fitness made a huge change in my life. I started feeling physically better than ever, and working out proved to be an amazing stress reliever. This was a good thing, because trying to figure out what was going on in Marc's brain all the time was very stressful.

He also made me more conscious about what I put into my body. Usually, in a couple, the girl is the health freak, eating only salads while the guys are busy slamming down cheeseburgers, but Marc was different. I think it had to do with the fact that his sister, Ilene, was a dietician, and enlightened him about the dangers of additives and chemicals in our food.

I was skeptical at first. I honestly thought Marc was a wee bit crazy and compulsive, until he did something to prove me wrong.

One summer night, after we had dinner, Marc opened up his freezer and removed a container of ice cream. He was about to throw it into the garbage when I grabbed his arm.

"What are you doing?"

"Getting rid of it. My neighbor brought it over last night and I am not eating it!"

"But why?" I asked, perplexed. "Ice cream is your favorite food. You can eat a gallon yourself in one sitting."

"You are right, I love ice cream, but this isn't ice cream, it's chemical cream! Look at the ingredients."

I scanned the back. Sure, I couldn't make out most of the words on the label, but so what? "I don't know what half that stuff is, but what does it matter? It looks like ice cream and tastes like ice cream, it has to be ice cream," I declared.

"Ya think so, huh?" Marc asked, flashing me a smile. "Let's just leave this container here." He placed it in the center of the stainless steel sink. "You tell me in the morning if you still feel the same way."

I crooked my pinky and extended my hand as I said, "You're on."

The next morning, I woke up with no thoughts of ice cream in my head. Marc has a bad back and neck, and needs to do a stretching routine first thing every morning. If he doesn't, he's in pain for the rest of the day. As he did his exercises, I went down to the kitchen, fed the cat, and started to prepare a pot of coffee for us. Looking into the sink, I found the container of ice cream and lifted it up carefully, expecting to find a melted mess. Instead, to my amazement, I found the container of "ice cream" warm, but fully solid. It never melted!

"Oh my God! Marc!" I yelled, repulsed. "Come down here! Look at this! I can't believe it!"

Coming into the kitchen, Marc took the container from my hands. "Yep, told you. It's full of chemicals. There is nothing natural about it. If it doesn't melt in the sink, what happens to it in your body? Ponder that one for a moment." He went to the utensil drawer and took out a spoon. Handing it to me, he asked, "Still think that's ice cream? Want some?"

Food and exercise aside, I was impressed with Marc's compassion towards others. The development where he lives has twenty-four-hour security. There are four guards that walk the grounds on a rotating schedule, keeping an eye on the forty-eight homes, as well as the residents of the beach community. Rain, sun, sleet, or snow, they patrol. If anyone needs assistance, they are just a phone call away to offer help.

These men do not make a lot of money. In fact, most of them, sadly, are just getting by. Whenever Marc cooks dinner, he usually makes extra. The majority of these leftovers do not go into the fridge for a future lunch. Instead, he calls the security guards and gives the food to whichever man is on duty that evening. It doesn't matter what Marc prepares, these guys are thrilled to get the call.

Beyond the surface of this small gesture of kindness, I saw the bigger picture. I believed that if he was so compassionate, and took such good care of strangers, he would take amazing care of me if I needed help one day. My theory was tested and proven to be right.

I left Marc's house early one weekday morning to head to work. I had only driven a short ways when suddenly I heard a loud pop. I almost lost control of my black Jeep Liberty, wrestling with it to avoid swerving off the road. I stopped and tried to pull over, but there wasn't a shoulder. Not sure what to do, I grabbed my cell phone out of my pocketbook and dialed Marc.

In retrospect, I probably should have just called triple A for help. But calling them never even dawned on me. I felt safer reaching out to Marc.

Bordering on hysterics, I screamed into the phone, "Something happened!"

"Oh my God, what's wrong? Are you okay?"

"Yeah, I'm fine, but my car isn't. I don't even know what happened. One minute I was driving, and the next it sounded like a gun shot. I probably have a blowout. I don't think I can drive it. Something's really wrong with my tire."

"Where are you?"

"I just turned onto Brookville," I said, slightly panicked. The street was a one lane, extremely curvy road, which intersects a swamp. It was not in the best of areas. It started off in a very desolate area, which was where I was. It was about a two mile ride before you entered a residential area where you could safely pull over.

"You can't stay there," he commanded.

"What do you mean? I can't drive this car!"

"You have to try. You are not safe where you are. Someone will hit you."

"I know, but…"

"But nothing… You have no choice. You have to get somewhere safe. Take a deep breath, calm down, and start driving that damn car! I am on my way. Don't stop until you reach the first side street, and when you get there, stay in the car and keep the doors locked. I will be right there."

He hung up the phone and I knew that he was right. I wasn't safe where I was. I really didn't think I could drive my car, but I knew I had to. I took a deep breath, as instructed, and sent a prayer up to my dad that I would be able to maneuver that hunk of junk out of there. I pressed my foot down on the accelerator. I hoped my Jeep would spring into action, but it wasn't so cooperative. No matter how hard I pressed down on my gas pedal, the truck barely moved. It crept down the winding road, making what sounded like scratching noises as I drove.

I anticipated getting honked at by drivers behind me, or at least a finger or two... after all, this was New York... but no one did anything. All the cars behind me were extremely patient, which freaked me out even more. I finally reached the side street where Marc told me to wait. I pulled over to the curb, shocked that I'd made it, and shut off my engine. I looked up and found my car was surrounded by men with worried looks on their faces. I slowly rolled down my window, afraid from my ordeal, and more than slightly scared of all these men.

"We saw you driving down the road; we never thought you would make it. Are you okay? Do you need help?" one of the men asked me.

"No, I am okay, thanks. My boyfriend is on the way. I guess I am worse off than I thought." My joke was met with grim expressions.

Another man chimed in, "Don't get out of the car. Wait for your boyfriend to come. But if he doesn't, we will be at the corner, installing a traffic light. If you need help, let us know." I looked where he pointed and saw lots of equipment and several trucks parked. It was amazing; I had never noticed anything when I drove by. I couldn't decide if his concern about me staying inside my car had to do with the fact I wasn't in the best area of town, or if he was afraid I would freak when I saw what my SUV looked like.

Either way, I didn't want to think about it, so I just thanked them and waited. Who says there aren't nice people in the world?

Marc arrived moments later. As soon as I saw him, I jumped out of my Jeep and ran into his embrace. My adrenaline drained away, and I realized I was totally shaken up. "Are you sure you're okay?" he asked as he held me and gently stroked my hair.

"Yeah, I'm fine." I told him about the construction men. "I don't know why everyone is freaking out. It's only a flat tire, right?"

"You didn't look at your car, did you?"

"No, you told me to stay inside it, and shockingly, I listened."

"Come here." He grabbed my hand and walked me around to the rear passenger side of my car. My tire wasn't blown out; it was underneath the chassis of my truck. My wheel had cracked off. He and I were both shocked at how I managed to drive with only three wheels.

He took over the situation from there. He called a tow truck to cart away my vehicle, and then he went over and thanked the guys who ran to my aid. He gave them money to use for lunch as a sign of appreciation.

And he cancelled all of his day's meetings so that he could accompany me as I arranged a loaner vehicle from the dealership and look for a new car, because I never wanted to drive that truck again!

Finally, I felt that Marc and I really had a real relationship. There was only one problem; he still kept me isolated from everyone he was close to. I thought it was bizarre and it drove me crazy! But it was equally strange when he decided that it was time for me to meet his friends and family. He didn't start out slow and introduce me to a person or two. No, in one weekend's time, he managed to introduce me to all the key people in his life—his sister Ilene, her husband Stephen, their children, his brother Jay's sons, his cousins and their children, his neighbors, even his friends from Utah, Jaye and Eric, and his best friend from childhood, Evan, and his wife Tania. It was like a bizarre coming out party.

It was overwhelming to be introduced to so many people in such a short period of time, especially for a formerly shy girl like me. I struggled to keep names and relationships straight as I turned on my charm. I was really working it hard. I hit it off with everyone almost immediately. And as I did, I realized why Marc kept me away from everyone for so long. While I feared that he felt his family and friends wouldn't like me, he knew they would. He didn't want to have them tell him how much they liked me, and how good a girl I seemed to be for him, and how he should marry me, which of course, was exactly what happened!

When I think about Marc's friendships, I am in awe. He managed to stay extremely close with all of his childhood friends. Sadly, this is totally unlike me. I have developed many friendships over the years, but I never put in enough time or effort into them to maintain them through thick and thin. If life changes made the relationship difficult to maintain, or if a mutual interest was lost, I would just let my friendships wither and die. But not Marc. He made sure to never let this happen. His loyalty to others always amazed me, and was one of the many things I admired most about him. I thought, it may take a lot to get into Marc's heart, but once you were there, it was hard, if not impossible, for you to be removed… or so I hoped.

Evan was one of these long-term friends. They met when they were four years old. Evan's family moved next door to Marc's in Belle Harbor, Queens. The boys started to play that very first day, and when they discovered that Evan's first name was Marc's middle name, the friendship was solidified.

Regardless of whatever life changes occurred, Marc and Evan remained the best of friends. Unlike most of Marc's friend's, who married girls close in age to them, Tania was also thirteen years younger than her husband, which made us exactly the same age. Needless to say, she and I hit it off immediately.

Evan's a doctor. While he specializes in cardiology, he is also an internist. Almost a year after I met Evan for the first time, I mentioned to Marc that I needed to find a doctor, as it had been years since I'd had a physical. When Marc suggested I see Evan, I was taken aback. "How can I see him as a doctor? He is your best friend, and we have dinner with him! That is too weird!"

"Hey, I am able to do it; you should be able to do it too. And it is stranger for me. Look how long I know him?" Marc quickly added.

"Yeah, but that is different."

"How?"

"I don't know. It just seems different."

"Do what you want, but wouldn't you rather see someone who knows you and cares about you rather than some stranger?"

I pondered it for a couple of minutes and realized that as always, Marc had a point, even if I didn't like it. So, I reluctantly agreed to schedule an exam with him. Marc came with me for moral support because he knew that I would be nervous. It was very strange. Somehow, in that exam room, Marc's best friend Evan turned into Doctor Evan. I no longer felt uncomfortable around him, even though we'd just had dinner together a couple of weeks prior. I felt very at ease, just as I would have with any other physician. At the end of the exam, he told me that normally he does a breast exam on his patients, but would skip it on me if I felt uncomfortable. I didn't even give it a thought. I told him to just do what he normally would, I was fine.

When I got into Marc's car, following the exam, he eagerly asked me how I did, and if I lost my nervousness. I proudly told him I did, and how halfway through the exam, I started seeing Evan in a different light. "I didn't even feel funny when he gave me a breast exam," I announced.

"Oh, great," Marc replied, his eyes twinkling as usual. "Now my best friend is feeling up my girlfriend!"

I laughed. It wasn't what I told Marc that I thought was so funny. I was laughing at what I didn't share with him.

As Evan was finishing up the exam, he questioned, "So how are things really going with you and my friend?"

"Really good."

"Does that mean he's going to come to his senses and marry you one of these days?"

"I don't know. You are his best friend. Shouldn't you two be talking about this stuff?"

"Yeah, well, you of all people should know how he is when it comes to talking. But if he doesn't smarten up soon, let me know. I'll prescribe something that will help him come to his senses!"

CHAPTER 9

January 1, 2004

I MUST HAVE FINALLY fallen asleep at some point during the night. When the sun started to stream through the blinds of our rented condo in Fort Lauderdale and awaken me, I blissfully and momentarily forgot where I was and what day it was. But as soon as I rolled over and caught a glimpse of Marc still deep in sleep, and snoring, the memories of last night's faux engagement debacle came flooding back to me.

I continued to lie there facing him, listening to the ocean loudly cascading in the background. Eventually he broke out of his slumber and smiled at me. By the grin on his face, I thought he might have temporarily forgotten about the previous night too.

He yawned deeply, and stated, as a matter of fact, "You were up all night."

"I know." I replied as I leaned over and kissed him. "Sorry," I said, and smiled. "Did I keep you up?" Based on his loud snoring all during the night, I knew I didn't.

"No. I did wake up a bunch of times, and saw that you were up. But you know me. I fell right back to sleep. Did you sleep at all?"

"I think I might have dozed a little bit, but I'm not sure. I just kept replaying last night over and over in my head."

"I'm sorry," he answered, sounding very sincere.

"It's okay," I said as I sat up. "It wasn't all bad. Eventually I started remembering all the good times too. Hey, do you remember the time when we first started dating and I was walking down the den steps carrying the wine glass and I fell?"

"How can I forget that?" he asked as he chuckled. "I thought that was a one-time accident, I didn't realize I'd found myself a super klutz!"

I was laughing too. "Did I ever tell you what was running through my brain as I started to slip?"

He scrunched his forehead as if he was trying to recall. "I don't think so."

"There was no doubt in my mind that I was going down, and I was fine with it. Not like it was my first time falling down a flight of stairs, nor my last," I joked as I smiled. "But was I worried about me? No, not at all! I was mortified that I was going to break your wine glass. As I was tumbling, all I kept saying to myself was, 'please don't break the glass, please don't break the glass'."

"And you didn't," he remarked.

"I still don't know how I managed that one. But you know what sticks in my head about that night?" I asked.

"Besides you being a lucky klutz?"

"Yeah, besides that." I rolled my eyes. "What sticks in my mind is how you didn't even care about the glass at all. You were so worried I'd hurt myself."

"I remember. The glass wasn't important, you were."

"You were so sweet and thoughtful," I said. "It reminds me of how you were always so honest with me about your feelings. You never once pretended to want something you didn't. You made it clear to me from the beginning that you didn't want a commitment. I know your feelings, and I should have known better last night. I never should have allowed myself to get so swept up in the fake engagement. But I couldn't help it. Things have changed from when we first got together. Our relationship has changed. And I wanted your feelings about marriage, and me, to have changed too. I don't want to be just your girlfriend forever. Seriously, I just wanted Jaye's proposal to be real. And it wasn't. And it hurt. A lot..." My voice trailed off and a tear rolled down my face.

Marc sat up. I could see he was starting to get a little upset, but I didn't care. "I told you. I am trying. But we need to take our time and wait until we are both ready. Can you do that?"

I just nodded my head. I had so much I wanted to say but I was frightened to say any of it. In a lot of ways, I walked on eggshells around Marc. I was always so worried about scaring him off.

"Do you think you'll be able to snap out of this, or will you be moping around for the rest of the trip? We can always go back to New York earlier."

I wiped my face, knowing he was right. My being upset and sulking wasn't going to make him go down on one knee and pop the question. The only thing I was going to accomplish was make myself, Marc, and our friends miserable. I sure didn't want that. "Oh, I can snap, Sir!" I replied as I saluted him.

Marc patted me on the head like a puppy dog. "That's a good girl. Come here." He opened his arms and engulfed me in a huge hug followed up with a tender kiss. "Let's get out of bed and get some coffee. And yeah, I love you."

The "L" word said two days in a row? It was a new record for Marc.

Unlike him, I have no issues saying the word. In fact, I am the opposite. I say it often. I never hang up the phone or leave the house without saying it to my mom. I easily say it to my close friends and family. And if I wasn't so afraid of freaking him out, I'd say it every day to Marc. I never wanted anyone that I love to doubt my feelings again.

When I was a little girl, I was not overly affectionate with my father. He always would beg me to kiss him. Out of spite, I refused. I looked at it like a game, especially when he would pretend to get calls from a little girl named Barbara, who didn't have a daddy, and wanted one to kiss.

When my dad suffered his stroke, he was in the hospital for three weeks and three days. He was paralyzed on his left side but was able to speak, initially. Two weeks after he was admitted, he had a blood clot which settled in his lungs; he was transferred to the intensive care unit and was put on a respirator. Seeing my father in that hospital bed with so many tubes, I hated myself for being such a brat, refusing to kiss him in the past. I vowed to God if my dad was able to make it, I would kiss him all the time and make sure he knew how much I loved him.

As I prayed, my dad got worse. He developed an infection and his temperature soared to a hundred and six degrees. For two days, as the doctors tried to find the source of the infection, my dad hung on, laying naked under an ice blanket. The last time I saw my father, I was with my aunt. She told me to make sure my dad knew I loved him. I took her advice. I held his hand and gently stroked it. With a cracking voice I said, "You know I love you, right, Daddy?" Somehow, despite the fever, despite everything, my dad managed to nod his head yes. I kissed him one final time. Moments later, he was gone.

I always ponder what I would have felt later if my aunt hadn't prompted me. Would I have spent the rest of my life wondering if my dad died not knowing how much I loved him?

*   *   *

By the time we entered the kitchen, Eric and Jaye already had a pot of coffee brewed. Eric also must have picked up some newspapers, as he was surrounded by them. The first moment or so was a little awkward, because Jaye, who could read me like a book, was able to see I was still upset, although I was trying with all my might not to show it.

Marc poured coffee and handed me a cup with a sweet and affectionate smile. As we all sipped coffee, we fell into our normal comfortable routine, with Marc and Eric cracking jokes and bantering back and forth. Jaye and I couldn't help but laugh hysterically.

After about an hour of lounging around over coffee and the news, Jaye and I ditched the boys and went for a walk on the beach together, as we often did. Jaye is a runner, and for years she has tried to get me to run with her, to no avail. No matter how much I try to force myself to enjoy the sport, I hate it. It isn't like I don't like to exercise. I love to bike, swim, and rollerblade, but I simply cannot stand to run. Now, when we are together, she forgoes her run and walks with me instead.

At first we were silent as we strolled along the deserted beach. But after a few moments, she stopped in her tracks and faced me. "Look at me," she commanded. "Are you sure you're okay?"

"Yeah, I'm fine."

Jaye raised an eyebrow at me, clearly not believing it.

"Really, Jaye, I am," I tried to assure her—and myself too.

"You're not mad at me, are you?" she asked, sounding nervous.

"Mad at you? Are you nuts?" I exclaimed. "Hell no! I am not mad at you at all. In fact, I love what you did last night. Actually, I am thankful that you did it."

"Okay, good. I was worried," she said as she let out a deep breath. "I felt really bad; I didn't expect it to snowball like that. I kept Eric up all night. I kept telling him that I shouldn't have pushed Marc so hard. You, of all people, know how Marc is. He likes to take everything super slow, over-analyze, and do everything his way. That's fine, but sometimes he needs a nudge or two."

"Well, you sure gave him a good nudge last night," I said as we resumed our stroll. "And you are right, he needed it!"

Jaye was laughing too. "I know! I did good, didn't I? But don't worry. I wasn't the only one, right?"

"Oh, yeah, I know," I said, smirking. "But I also know you are the best!"

It seemed to me that everyone in Marc's life was trying to convince him that if he would just abandon his fears and marry me, he would find happiness. His family and friends would joke about it in front of me, making it almost a game. However, Jaye approached the situation differently. Except for last night, she would never mention marriage or commitment to Marc in my presence. She would wait until she was alone with Marc and seriously question him about his feelings for me and for our future. She would confide to me later that she told him that he was being selfish, explaining to him that if he saw no long-term future for us, he should be honest with me and let me go, before I got really hurt. I think that Jaye understood my real fear—that I would keep falling more in love with Marc, only for him to abruptly end our relationship one day.

"Of course I am. But seriously, Eric and I, and Marc's family, are not giving up until he comes to his senses and marries you. We are all on your side because we know you are exactly what he needs."

I smiled, as I wondered if Marc would ever realize it too…

Then my smile faded as I said, "Jaye, level with me. Please. I know that everyone is rooting for me to become Marc's wife, but honestly, you've known him forever. Do you really think that is going to happen? Or do you think I'm just hanging onto false hope?"

"What do you think?" Jaye asked.

"I don't really know," I answered honestly. "I have very mixed feelings. Sometimes I really think that he has changed, and has come around to opening his heart and sharing his life with me. But then, just when I think I made some headway, he goes and pulls one of his stunts."

"What do you mean? He's not still playing games, is he? I thought we made more progress than that." I love the way she said 'we'. It was like my relationship with Marc was a group project, and all of Marc's friends and family had a hand in it—which of course, let's face facts, they did.

A couple of summers before, Jaye and Eric were visiting Marc, along with another couple who had two small children. I spent a couple of days with them and assumed that I would spend Saturday night with them as well. What I didn't know was that Marc had purchased tickets to see a concert with his nephew, Adam.

When his friends learned about his plans they decided that they would try a hot new restaurant in Manhattan which they'd all heard a lot about. I was clearly a fifth wheel. When care for the children came up, without meaning to, I offered to babysit, although I had no desire to watch them. I was hurt and upset, but felt I needed to offer, as clearly I was the only one in the group who didn't have anything else better to do.

Jaye and Eric, as well as the kids' parents, seemed hesitant at first. Marc, on the other hand, jumped at the opportunity. He was excited that I offered to help out. His enthusiasm really pissed me off. Did he really think that is what I wanted to do on a Saturday night?

I didn't know how to get out of my babysitting duties, so I headed out of the room to think and kick myself in private. As soon as she thought I was out of earshot, Jaye called out to Marc and with a stern whisper asked, "Can I speak to you for a moment, alone?"

She took him outside. I have no idea what she said to him, but moments after they came back inside the house, I brought him right back outside and confronted him myself. "You need to get me out of babysitting, because I'm not doing it. And speaking of stuff I am not doing, I am not sticking around now either. I'm going home."

He looked confused. "Why are you upset? You just offered to babysit. Why are you are you changing your mind?"

"Did you really think I want to babysit while you guys all go out and have fun? If you haven't noticed, I am not in high school anymore! My babysitting days are done, thank you very much. I only offered because I felt I had to. After all, suddenly I found myself free and available, just standing here watching everyone else make plans. What else was I supposed to do? I couldn't very well have said I was busy, now could I?"

"You didn't have to offer."

He totally missed my point. Now I wanted to kick him.

"You're not joking, are you?" Shaking my head and rolling my eyes, I continued my questioning. "You really don't get it? Do you seriously have no idea why I am upset? God! I think that makes it even worse."

I'm not sure if it was the fire in my eyes, or whatever Jaye said to him had sunk in, but slowly I watched as realization and understanding registered on his face. He apologized. He gave his concert ticket to his other nephew, Gabriel. He called his nieces and arranged for them to come and watch the children so he and I could join his friends at dinner.

Looking back, I don't think he intended to hurt me. I just don't think he gave any thought to his actions or how they would make me feel. I think he was just used to living his life alone, not worrying about how his actions affected others.

I sort of regretted mentioning Marc's recent stunt to Jaye, but since I brought it up, I guess I had to share the story with her. Besides, I did want her opinion and insight. "I am probably making it sound worse than it is," I answered, trying to downplay it.

"I'll be the judge of that. What happened?"

"About a month or two ago, I was at his house all weekend. I got there Friday night after work and we spent all day Saturday together. I figured we were going to spend the full weekend together, because that is what we have been doing lately. In fact, honestly, before this day, I don't remember the last weekend we were apart."

"Which is exactly how it should be after all this time," she said sternly.

I didn't let her tone deter me. "So Sunday morning comes, and he tells me that he made plans to have dinner with a friend of his from high school and his friend's sister, both of whom he hasn't seen in a really long time."

"Okay."

"He never mentioned these people to me before, and I didn't think much of it. But I did figure that I would be going with him. Is that crazy? Wouldn't you have?"

"Of course," she answered, looking at me like I had fifteen heads.

"Wrong! Around five o'clock he reminded me about the dinner, and then asked me if I was going to have dinner with my mom."

"He what?" she said, sounding outraged.

"Yeah, you heard me. I was flabbergasted."

"So what did you say?"

"I told him no, that I wasn't having dinner with my mom. I fought the urge to call him an idiot for asking."

"That couldn't have been easy," Jaye said with a smile.

"You know it! I told him that my mom wasn't going to be home and that she had plans. And I didn't lie, she did. She had a wedding to go to. So then I played dumb and said something like, 'Oh, I guess you don't want me to join you, huh?', thinking that he would say, 'don't be silly' or something. But he didn't."

"First of all, why would he assume that you would be having dinner with your mom after you've been spending the weekends with him? And why in God's name would he not want you to join him?"

"You got me, Jaye. I have no idea."

"What happened next?"

"He told me since they are such old friends, it was probably best that he just went out with them alone."

"Oh, no he didn't," Jaye stammered, working herself into a state.

"Oh, yes he did… but it gets better," I replied sarcastically. "I told him that I probably should get going so he had time to get ready for his important dinner—because let's face it, at that moment, all I wanted to do was get the hell out of his house. I wasn't about to sit there and keep him company until he was ready to go out and enjoy his evening. I was so hurt and flipping mad. So I went and grabbed my bag, and gave him a casual goodbye. And do you know what he said?"

"I'm afraid to ask."

"He told me to call him tomorrow. Like, what the fuck?" I took a deep breath. "All I kept wondering was: did he lose his mind? Did he really think that after all this time we've been together, he was going to just send me home so he could have dinner with old friends, who he hasn't seen in, like, forever, and I was gonna call him the next day as if nothing happened?"

"Well, I should certainly hope not," Jaye answered.

"Oh, don't worry. I had no intention of ever calling him again. And I think he knew it. If my mumbling 'yeah right' when he told me to call him didn't give him a clue, then it was my demeanor when I left the house. I was cold as ice, and hurt as hell. There is no doubt in my mind that as I pulled out of the driveway he realized he really blew it. But I did well, I didn't cry until I was safely alone in my car."

"Well, that's good. I'm glad he didn't see you cry."

"I had no desire to go home and sit by myself. Nor did I have any desire to reach to a friend and try to make spur-of-the-minute plans. I didn't want to tell anyone what happened, nor did I want anyone's advice. I am tired of everyone telling me I am crazy for dealing with his shit. So I drove to a shoe store halfway between my house and his, and wandered around. I was there for about a minute, when I called my mother, hysterical. The poor lady, she was at a wedding, and she was trying to console me!

"Your poor mom," Jaye answered. I knew she could relate—her son is my age, and she has shared in his dating dramas.

"She didn't know what to do or what to tell me. She kept reminding me she was at a wedding, which didn't really help my emotional state, if you know what I mean."

"Yeah, I can understand," Jaye grinned.

"So I got mad at her and hung up. I wandered around the store for a few minutes, barely able to see past my rage. Now, you know I am really upset when a new pair of shoes can't lift my spirits."

"Oh, yes. Usually retail therapy solves your problems," Jaye said. "But enough about shoes, what happened next?"

"I cried all the way home, and when I got there I collapsed in a heap on the couch. My dog tried to comfort me. I was about to confide my woes to her since I knew that all she could do was listen to me rant, but I didn't have the chance. The phone rang, it was Marc. He apologized for being an ass. His words, not mine," I clarified. "He told me that he canceled his plans because he wanted to spend the night with me. He asked me to come back over so we could have dinner together."

"And?"

"I didn't want to rush back over there. I didn't want him to think I was desperate for him to call me back…"

Jaye interrupted, "Like you were."

"That's beside the point. I told him I started a laundry and I had some stuff to take care of, and I would be back over in a few hours. I sat in the den playing Snood on the computer for two and a half hours until I felt I'd made him wait long enough. So… what do you make of this? Shouldn't we be past this stuff already?"

"Okay," Jaye said and sighed. "I don't really know what to make of this situation. I have no idea why he didn't want to include you. But at least it ended well. He knew that he did wrong, and he knew he hurt you, and he cared enough to fix it right away. You know as well as I do that the Marc of the past wouldn't even realize he did anything wrong or care. Don't get me wrong, he isn't mean; he's just oblivious. But that is changing. Don't you see it?"

"Sure I do. But Jaye, come on, this isn't normal, especially after all this time."

"Hilary, you're right. It isn't, but he has commitment issues, and major ones at that. I don't know why, but he does. I don't even know if he knows why he does. I have known him for almost twenty years. I've told you this before, and I am going to tell you again. In all that time, I never met any of his girlfriends. Ever!"

"Not even Allison?" Allison was the girl Marc was dating when his mother suffered her fatal aneurysm. She accompanied him to the hospital during the four weeks his mother was in critical condition, and comforted Marc after she passed away. Knowing how upset he was, she surprised Marc with a cat on his birthday a month later.

At first, Marc didn't want any part of having a pet. I guess his commitment issues carried over to four-legged creatures as well as the two-legged kind. But as Marc tells the story, Allison didn't let his protest bother her. She assured Marc that she could return the cat the following day when the shelter reopened. She did, however, request that he kept the cat overnight. Reluctantly, he agreed.

The entire evening while Allison was at Marc's apartment, the cat remained in his carrier case, petrified to venture out. Allison didn't stay the night; she wanted to give Marc a chance to bond with the feline. Marc was sure that it was pointless, as he'd already made up his mind about having a pet, but he humored her.

Marc went to sleep as the cat remained in its case. However, something happened in the wee hours of the morning. The cat must have felt safe, because he left the security of his case and ventured into Marc's bedroom. He jumped up on the bed and made himself comfortable on Marc's chest. Marc awoke to the cat's gentle purring, and his cold heart melted. He knew instantly that the cat wasn't going anywhere. He named the cat Alex after Allison, which I always felt was an intimate reminder of past love.

Marc and Allison broke up about six months later. It is strange, but after Marc moved to the beach, he learned that Allison married his new next-door neighbors' best friend's son. Since she sometimes visits with her in-laws, I actually met her myself a few times and played with her children. It really is a small world.

"No, not even Allison," Jaye assured me, although I wasn't sure I should believe her... "I heard about her, sure, but I never met her. You are the only one I have ever known, yet alone become friends with. You are different. Very different," she stressed.

"I knew that the first time he had you come over when we were in town. I told Eric if anyone was going to capture his heart, it would be you. And that was years ago, and I still believe it. So do I know where this relationship is going to end? No, I have no idea. All I do know is if anyone is going to become that man's wife, it will be you. But you have to decide if you are willing to stick around to try and make it happen. You have to do what you feel is right for you." She sighed. "I love Marc, really I do, but I love you also. You have to follow your heart. If you don't want to stick it out, no one will blame you for giving up. And if you love him, and are able to accept the relationship for what it is and what it may become, or what it may remain, that is wonderful too. But whatever you do decide to do, make sure that you consider your feelings. You tend to put other people's needs and wants in front of your own, which is a wonderful characteristic, but not when it comes to something like this. Make sure you're getting what you want and need. After all, it is not all about Marc."

CHAPTER 10

MY CONVERSATION WITH JAYE helped me immensely. She didn't tell me anything I didn't already know. My mom and my friend Cassandra had been telling me the same thing for months, but having the words come from someone in Marc's camp made all the difference.

She also made me think. When I boarded the plane for our Florida getaway, I never expected to return home sporting an engagement ring. I never expected Marc to propose during our trip. I was only disappointed because Jaye proposed to me. If she hadn't mentioned marriage on New Year's Eve, all of these feelings and doubts would have remained on the back burner. So why did I need to stir the pot when I was happy? I'd have plenty of time to worry about the future and our relationship not going anywhere when the proper time came. For now, I was still content, so I thought I might as well enjoy myself.

And enjoy I did. The rest of time in Florida flew by, and the "M" word was not mentioned again. Instead, the four of us lounged on the beach, joked and laughed while enjoying delicious wines and beautiful dinners. In what felt like the blink of an eye, it was time for us to fly home and return to real life.

As soon as the plane took off, Marc fell asleep, which was typical, and my mind raced. When I was about ten years old, my parents had a wedding to attend. Since I wasn't invited, my mom arranged for me to spend the day with my cousin, Robin, and her husband. When we got to their house, Robin told my mom that she was going to take me to a large, outdoor flea market. My mom handed Robin money and said, "If Hilary says she likes something, buy it for her. She will never ask for anything."

Remembering this story, I realized that now, twenty years later, not much had changed. I still didn't ask for much. I had always feared disappointment and rejection. If you don't ask, you can't be told no. At my core, even though I may have pretended otherwise, I was still an insecure girl. And if I was honest with myself, I think that was the reason why I had been willing to accept my relationship with Marc completely on his terms. I didn't feel like I deserved a guy like him, and I was afraid if I pushed my wants and needs too hard, he would end the relationship. I felt settling was better than losing him.

The ironic thing was, while my insecurities may have been responsible for my relationship lasting as long as it had with Marc, my relationship with Marc had helped me lose the majority of my insecurities. I had changed so much since I'd met him, and I continued to see personal growth.

While Marc may not have been great at expressing his feelings, he was an amazing listener. So many times throughout our relationship, I would share problems I was having, mostly related to work. As a new manager, I didn't know how to handle a lot of situations. He would always listen to me and guide me. He would say, "Don't be afraid to stand up for what you believe is right. If you disagree with something, say it." But my favorite was when he would tell me, "You are smart, you are talented, and you are beautiful. You just need to believe in yourself, because when you do, anything is possible."

He made me believe in me.

*   *   *

We were home from Florida for a week when my cell phone rang at work. "Hey Cassandra, is everything okay?"

"Everything is fine, why would you ask?"

"Because you never call me at work," I replied.

"Well, I know you just got home from Florida with Marc, and I know that you have been spending more time at his house than yours, so I figured if I wanted to talk to you, it'd be best if I called you at work."

I took a deep breath, knowing it was going to be one of "those conversations".

Cassandra didn't disappoint. "So, I've got to ask you, how often do you sleep there, anyway?"

"I don't exactly have a schedule," I said as I rolled my eyes. "But lately about four or five nights a week."

"Do you think that is a good idea?"

"Cassie, seriously, you are worse than my mother."

"Do what you want. It is your life, after all. Who am I to say that you are making it too easy on him. But that isn't why I called. Guess who I just bumped into?"

"I don't know who?"

"Ms. Pancakes."

Cassandra and I waitressed together all through college. Of course we knew some of the regulars real names, but for the most part we gave them nicknames based upon their orders. Ms. Pancakes, also known to us as Jen, was about ten years older than we were. The entire time that Cassie and I worked in the restaurant, she would come in every weekend morning with her boyfriend. That was at least eight years ago.

"Really? I loved Jen and Danny."

"I know. Me too. Guess who just got married?"

"Really, it is about time! Jen must be so happy."

"No, she is not. She is crushed. Danny got married alright, but not to her. She told me the whole story. They dated for thirteen years, and she lived with him for five of them. She wanted to marry him and he kept telling her that he wasn't ready yet. He just needed a little more time, he'd say. She didn't push it, like you. Then one day he comes home from work and told her he met someone else and is moving out. If that wasn't bad enough, he also told her that he realized that he never loved her, and that is why he couldn't commit to her. Six months later, he was married."

I was speechless. Jen's story was my biggest fear...

"I will take silence to mean I hit a nerve," Cassandra said simply. "Good. Think about it for a while and don't be foolish. I've got to go to a meeting now."

*   *   *

A week later, I saw Jaye and Eric again. Along with Marc, they are involved in point of sale software, so they participate at the National Retail Federation's trade show every January in New York. Since Eric and Jaye live out of town, they always stay at Marc's house for a few days before heading into Manhattan to be closer to the venue. This year would be no different. Eric and Jaye arrived on a Thursday night, and Marc made sure I was there when they came. As soon as they walked in the door, I saw that Jaye was sporting Lois's chunky rhinestone ring. She made sure to wave the symbolic honorary engagement ring in Marc's face every chance she had. It was apparent to all of us that he read her loud and clear, although we avoided the subject like the plague during their stay.

A month later was Valentine's Day. Marc had never been big on celebrating special occasions. He was more of a believer that you should try to make every day a special occasion, rather than waiting for a holiday, birthday, or anniversary. His favorite quote was, "You should live every day like it's your last. One day it will be, and then you'll be prepared!"

We planned on cooking dinner at his house and enjoying it besides a fire over a bottle or two of wine. While romantic, it was typical of our normal weekend nights (his motto does come in handy). Our plans were delayed a bit as his next-door neighbors, Ann and Warren, were bringing home a new kitten. Earlier in the year, they'd had to put their beloved cat, Elmo, to sleep, and they were devastated.

Ann and Warren had lived at the development for about a year before Marc moved in. They had a son and daughter who were both older than Marc, and obviously me. From the moment he settled in, they took him under their wing and treated him like another son. In turn, Marc looked out for them and would help them around the house. When I entered Marc's life, they were just as warm and inviting to me. Warren was in the garment industry. He represented numerous designers and was responsible for introducing the lines to the retail trade. Since I was the sample size, whenever he took on a new line of clothing, he made sure to give me samples. Sometimes he would invite me over and hand me a bag of apparel. It was a fashionista's dream come true. Thanks to Warren, I was always dressed in the latest trends. It was wonderful.

So when they wanted us to meet the cat for the first time, Marc and I jumped at the opportunity, especially since they were still deciding on a name for her.

They couldn't decide between Valentine, Cupid, or Sweetheart, and needed us to be the tie breakers. As soon as they let the cat out of the carrier, Marc and I sat down on the floor. Shockingly again, the cat sat in my lap first. I gently petted her golden fur, as we admired how cute she was. We decided her name should be Valentine.

I could have sat there all night stroking the little princess. In retrospect, I should have, because it was the first and last time that she would ever let me get close to her. When Warren and Ann went on vacation the first time after they adopted her, I took care of her. She was none too pleased by their abandonment, and I think that she blamed me for their departure.

But Marc had other ideas besides playing with the kitten. "She is gorgeous," he told Ann and Warren, "and I am sure Hilary could sit here and play with her all night, but we've got to head out." He extended his hand to help me off the ground. Before I took it, I kissed the kitten's head one last time. Then we kissed our neighbors good bye and headed next-door to his house.

He sensed my disappointment about having to leave the kitten so soon. "I know you wanted to still play, but I wanted to get out of there. I want to be able to enjoy the night with you." Who can argue with such a good reason? Besides, although little Valentine was a cutie, Marc was more my style.

As soon as we got in, he turned on the stereo and lit the fire. I cut up some cheese and brought two wine glasses into his den. Marc opened a bottle of Barolo and poured us each a glass. I raised my glass and toasted, "To us!" as I always did. We clinked our glasses and took a sip.

When Marc and I first started dating, he always got me long stemmed roses for Valentine's Day. I think he felt that it was something that a girl would expect, more than something he believed in. The first year or two, I gladly accepted them, because I was looking for a sign of feelings. But as our relationship deepened, and I knew that I occupied a special, if maybe not permanent, place in his heart, I asked Marc to stop getting me roses. I know it sounds strange, but I actually hate flowers, especially roses.

Though typically roses conjure up images of love and romance, they remind me of a crazy man. I used to wait tables at a Friendly's by my house and I had a steady customer who came in every Sunday for breakfast. From his first serving of pancakes and bacon, he took a liking to me, and always requested to be seated at one of my tables. At first he seemed like a nice, friendly man, almost thirty years my senior. He would always order a four dollar breakfast and leave me a ten dollar tip. I had no complaints; I figured he was just generous. But my feelings changed when he started showing up every Sunday carrying a dozen roses for me. Then I realized that he had ideas where our relationship was heading, ones that extended beyond the boundaries of patron and server. It became uncomfortable, but I took it in stride. I accepted the roses each and every week, but would leave the flowers at the restaurant after my shift was over. If the roses weren't bad enough, one morning he overheard me telling another customer that my birthday was the following week. He arrived for his Sunday breakfast the next weekend with his usual dozen roses for me and a small jewelry box. He insisted I open it at the table, and when I did, I found that the box contained diamond earrings.

I was able to rationalize flowers, but diamonds was going too far. There was no way I was going to accept them, and I told him as much. He didn't seem to understand why I was so upset. But he ended up putting them back into his breast pocket when I refused to take them. I thought I made my feelings crystal clear and I never expected to see him again. However, he showed up again the following Sunday, carrying roses as usual, but this time in the middle of the bouquet was the jewelry box containing the earrings.

Once again, I had to explain to him that I couldn't accept it. Once again, he made it clear that he didn't understand why. This game was repeated for weeks, until I got sick one Sunday and missed my shift. When he learned I wasn't working, he had a conniption fit in the middle of the restaurant, which ended with him throwing the roses onto the floor. I quit waiting tables soon after that, and never told him I was leaving.

Marc got up from the couch and placed another log into the fireplace. He adjusted the volume on the stereo before once again sitting down. We sipped our wine in comfortable silence, staring into captivating flames that were dancing to the music. I didn't know what it was, I couldn't put my finger on it, but all of a sudden Marc seemed different— distracted almost, or possibly restless. I was just about to inquire when he reached behind the couch and pulled out a card.

He handed it to me and a goofy grin spread across his face. Marc wasn't a man of many words, especially the written kind. Truth be told, he disrespected cards. He often said that he thought cards were pointless. Needless to say, I was a bit surprised when he handed one to me.

I scrunched my face, trying to express my puzzlement, as I took the card from him. "Who are you and what have you done with my Marc?" I joked.

"You are so funny. Just open it, will ya?"

I ripped open the envelope and quickly scanned the corny preprinted words. Then I read what he wrote. "May you move your stuff in?"

If I was confused before, I was beyond perplexed now. I looked at him and asked, "May I move my stuff in? What do you mean? I already have stuff here."

Let's be honest. Carrie Bradshaw and Mr. Big made dating hard for a lot of people. About six months earlier, I had gotten tired of packing my knapsack every time I planned to stay over at Marc's house, especially if I ended up staying there for a few days in a row, which was becoming commonplace. I wanted to keep a couple of days' worth of clothing and toiletries at his house. But between Marc's commitment phobia and Mr. Big's reaction to Carrie taking it upon herself to move some of her belongings into his apartment, I was a little afraid to broach the subject. I don't know why I was so hesitant to ask him; after all, he had given me a key to his home years ago, although I still never used it without his knowledge. I guess I was just afraid his reaction would mirror Mr. Big's.

I tried to find the perfect time to broach the question. I rehearsed the words in my head. And when I thought the time was right, I forgot my preplanned speech and simply said, "Can you spare a drawer for a girl?" He looked at me like I had fourteen heads.

I tried to clarify. "That way I can leave a few things here without always having to go home and pack each time I come over." As soon as the words came out, I immediately regretted my question. I was about to make a joke to lighten the situation, call him Mr. Big or something. But then he shocked me.

"Sure, of course. I'm actually surprised you haven't taken one already."

I swear the man never ceased to amaze me.

The following weekend, I packed a bag with a couple of days' worth of clothes and toiletries and brought it along with my normal knapsack. When I entered his house on Friday night, I brought my knapsack up to his room, but left the larger bag by the coat closet. I figured I'd have time to actually claim the drawer during the weekend.

The next night, my bag was still by the coat closet. Marc's older brother, Jay, and his wife, Susan, came over to Marc's for dinner. I credited

Susan for Marc and our relationship, although I regretted not allowing myself to meet him the first time she approached me at the Italian restaurant. As the brothers were outside tending to the barbecue, I mentioned to Susan how I had a bag of clothes sitting here, but was afraid that Marc had changed his mind about letting me take a drawer.

"Oh, this is ridiculous!" Susan exclaimed. "I've had enough with his commitment issues already! He is a grown man and it's time he starts acting like one. I'm going to have Jay talk some sense into him."

"But Susan..." I started to interrupt her. I didn't want her to get angry at Marc. After all, I was the one choosing to walk on eggshells.

"But nothing! What are you asking for? You just want a drawer. If that is too much commitment for him, and he can't handle that, well, I have news for you, you don't need him. Where is the bag?" I pointed towards the closet door. "Fine. I will handle this." She got up and grabbed it. With a backwards glance she said, "I'll be right down, and when I am, you will have that drawer."

I took a large gulp of wine as I watched her ascend the stairs to the bedroom, bag in hand. She was gone longer than I expected. When she finally returned, she had a big grin plastered on her face. "Oh, you were upset for nothing. Not only did he have an empty drawer waiting for you, he had two! They are the bottom two on the left side of the closet. I unpacked you, so you are all set. And I am still talking to Jay about his brother!"

It is funny; when you are dealing with a guy that has so many communication and commitment issues, small things have a big impact. Having some drawer space in his home, and knowing my stuff was there, made a huge difference to me. I felt more secure in his feelings, especially as he rearranged his pants and dress shirts to give me some additional hanging space.

My reverie was interrupted as Marc got up and moved over to where I was sitting, bringing me back to the present moment. I stared at the card in my hand, confused. "You don't get it? Do you?" he asked.

"No. Not really."

As he looked deeply into my eyes, he continued. "I want you to move ALL your stuff in. I want you to move in with me."

"You do?"

"Yes, I do," he said and gave me a long, deep kiss. "Do you want to?"

"Do I want to?" I repeated. "Um, let me think about that one for a while," I said as I rolled my eyes for emphasis. "Okay, yes I do!" I exclaimed, and kissed him again. But then it hit me and I turned serious. I inhaled deeply, and then said, "I do want to move in with you. I really do. But I don't want this to be it. I don't want to be your girlfriend forever. I want to marry you. I want to be your wife." I wanted to know that he believed in our relationship as much as I did, and marriage is the tie that binds.

Marc looked at me somberly. "I know you do. And I am working toward it. This is just the first step. We need to do this first. I can't rush into anything. I know me. If I move too fast, I will get nervous and it won't work. But if we go slow and take our time, I'll get used to the idea of you being here full time. I really want this to work out. Okay? Will you move in?"

As a tear rolled down my check, I smiled and simply said, "Okay." I tried to remain cool, rather than dance around the room. I knew what a big step this was for Marc to make, and how difficult it must have been for him. I also knew how desperately I wanted to be a permanent part of his life. With him taking this big step, finally I felt that there was real hope.

The next morning, I was still on cloud nine. Moving in with someone you've been dating for about four years may not be monumental to most people, but when the person you're moving in with has major commitment issues, it is as eventful and unexpected as winning the lottery. I was cherishing every second. I couldn't wait to call my mom and tell her the news. However, I was a little nervous about what her reaction would be when I told her that I was going to be moving in with Marc without a proposal.

Don't misunderstand; my mom is far from a prude. I knew she wouldn't be upset that I would be living with Marc before marriage. But I feared that she would think that this was his way to avoid matrimony. After all, my mom was intimately familiar with the situation, and had lived through it herself when she dated an older and commitment-phobic man.

When I was a little girl, all my elementary school classmates grew up on fairy tales. You know the ones… where the boy and girl meet, fall madly and quickly in love, and then live happily ever after, the end. Well, not me. Sure, my mom read me the classics, but she also made sure I knew that not every story had a happy ending, and that life, as well as romance, wasn't so easy. She told me her dating sagas in lieu of bedtime stories, so I was probably the only girl in Mrs. LaFauci's third grade class who knew the definition of the word 'ultimatum'.

When my mother was twenty–six years old, she was living with her parents in an apartment building in Brooklyn. The apartment next door to theirs changed hands and in moved an elderly, widowed man with his thirty–nine-year-old son, Sidney, who was a corrections officer. My grandmother immediately took a liking to Sidney, and started cooking for him. She would drop off chicken dinners and pots of pea soup at his apartment for him to share with his father. Sidney's dad was equally smitten with my mom. Thinking she was cute, he would constantly bring her gifts of candy and gum. Meanwhile, despite their parent's interest, my mom and Sidney had no desire to get together since they lived so close to one another. Both were afraid that if they started dating, it would be too uncomfortable if their relationship didn't work out. My grandfather would constantly ask his wife, who exactly was courting who, because it seemed that only the parents had interest in the pairing. In fact, my mom and Sidney never even spoke to one another.

Eventually, one night, my mom and Sidney found themselves in a cocktail lounge. As they sipped their scotch on the rocks, they started talking and getting to know each other. It wasn't until Sidney offered my mom a ride home that they realized they were next-door neighbors.

After that night, they started dating. As their relationship progressed and they started spending more time together; Sidney made it very clear to my mom that he wasn't interested in a relationship, and had no intentions of getting married. My mom was okay with it, and continued to date Sidney.

Days turned into weeks. Weeks turned into months, and months turned into years. My mom was at Sidney's side as his nieces and nephews were born, and as his father passed away. At some point during this journey, she realized she wanted more from the relationship than just a boyfriend. Courting Sidney suddenly wasn't enough for her. She wanted to get married to him and start a family. She would discuss this with him, and every time he would answer, "Soon. We will get married soon."

After six and a half years of dating, and countless "soons", my mom broke up with him. "I don't want to force you to do anything that you're not comfortable with," she told him one night in his apartment. "You have to do what you feel is right, and what you want to do. And I have to do the same. I really love you with all my heart, and want to spend my life with you. But I want all of you, and that includes marriage. You don't want that, I know. You have made that perfectly clear to me countless times over the years. But it is not what I want. The way I see it, the best thing for both of us is that we stop seeing each other."

Sidney didn't try to stop my mom. He didn't convince her she was wrong. He didn't fight to try and get her to stay. Instead, he just sat there and let her kiss him goodbye and walk out the door. My mom was devastated, to say the least. She never expected him to just let her walk out of his apartment and his life so easily. It made her question whether he had ever really cared about her at all.

The fear that she had initially about getting involved with someone who lived so close by came to fruition. After their relationship ended, it was so difficult to see him every day around the apartment building. To make matters worse, after his initial shock wore off, he tried to resume their relationship. Countless times Sidney would ask her out to dinner. My mom remained strong and turned him down, knowing if she went out with him again she would be back at what she felt was a dead end.

A month after their breakup, my mom, then a smoker like Sidney, got several cartons of cigarettes, dirt cheap, from someone she worked with who smuggled them into New York from the Carolinas. As in the past, she wanted to split them with him, but more than that, she wanted an excuse to see him in a casual way. The day she got the cigarettes, she called him to see if he was going to be home that evening so she could drop them off. Sidney eagerly said he would be.

When my mom told her mother that she was bringing the cigarettes next door to Sid, her mother went berserk. She started screaming at the top of her lungs, "What is wrong with you? Are you crazy? You are an idiot! You are going to start up with him again as if nothing happened! You have wasted a month, for what? Nothing!"

When it became clear that my mother wasn't listening to her mom, and was going to see Sidney regardless of her mother's opinion, my grandmother took her anger out on her husband. "Harry, stop her!" she yelled. "Don't let her go! She is crazy! She is an idiot!"

Unfortunately, I never had the chance to meet my grandfather, because he died when my mother was pregnant with me. Apparently, he was a very level-headed guy. Calmly he addressed his wife, "Jean, she is a big girl. Let her do what she wants. She is going to do it anyway, whether you like it or not. Do you really think you or I can stop her?" And just as Jean was about to reply, he added, "And can you stop screaming? I am sure Sidney can hear every word! Talk about crazy? You sound like a crazy lady yourself. These walls are paper thin!"

When my mom finally made it over to Sidney's apartment, she was mortified, to say the least. She was sure that her dad was right, and that Sid had heard every word. When he greeted her at the door, she managed to stay cool and collected. "Hi, these are for you," she said casually as she handed him a carton of cigarettes. She didn't tell him that she actually had two cartons. She was planning on saving the second so she'd have another excuse to stop by again in a few weeks.

Sidney tried to kiss her, but she turned her face so his lips landed on her cheek rather than her lips. "Do you want to sit down for a minute?" he asked.

"Um, I guess so," she replied hesitantly. "But I can't stay long. My mom is making me dinner."

"Oh. Okay. I thought I could take you out to dinner tonight."

"Thanks, but no thanks. My mom is making salami and eggs," she answered, although she would have given her right arm to have dinner with him rather than an omelet with her folks.

"How can you turn down salami and eggs?" he joked. "But if I can't buy you dinner, can I get you a drink instead?"

"Um. I guess so," she cautiously replied.

He returned with two tumblers of scotch. As they sipped, they caught up a bit with each other's lives, since they had barely spoken in a month. After a little while, Sidney announced, "I have something for you in the other room. I am going to get it, but I need you to close your eyes and hold out your hand."

My mom did as he instructed, and closed her eyes tightly. She felt him place a small, cool object in her palm. Her first thought when she felt the box was "What did this idiot get me, a cigarette lighter?" because that is what it felt like to her.

"Okay, open your eyes," he instructed.

My mom did and quickly realized he didn't place a cigarette lighter in her palm. It was a small jewelry box. She glanced up at Sidney, confused. "Go ahead. Open it." And she did. Inside the box was a two-and-a-half carat diamond solitaire engagement ring.

As tears streamed down her face, she stammered, "Is... is... this... what I think it is?"

"Yes," my dad replied. "It is. I missed you, and I love you. And I will do what it takes to be with you, and if that means marriage, so be it. Will you marry me?"

My mom jumped up into my father's arms and kissed him and whispered, "Yes." But after a moment, reality hit her and she asked, "Okay, so we are engaged, and I am thrilled. But do you really want to get married, or are you going to want to wait another six and a half years before walking down the aisle? Because I can't do that."

With a smirk, he replied, "No. I want to get married. You go find a place and set a date. Wherever and whenever you want is fine with me. I'll be there."

My mom didn't waste any time. She and my father booked the venue the very next day, finding a place that would marry them two months later. Not taking any chances, she stationed my dad's fellow correction officers at each door's exit to guard them, just in case he changed his mind and decided to run, which fortunately didn't happen.

I believe my understanding and tolerance of Marc's commitment issues resulted from my parents' relationship. I knew firsthand how a commitment phobic man could change and totally embrace the idea of being a husband and a father. My mom always compared my relationship with Marc to hers with my father, and rightly so. She was of the opinion that he was like my dad, and would never take it upon himself to change his mind about marriage without a tremendous nudge or some drastic measure. I honestly tended to agree, although I was hopeful that wouldn't be the case.

As I dialed the phone to share my exciting news, I paused. I didn't want my mother to spoil my excitement by bringing me down to reality.

"Hey, it is me. What's up?" I asked, very nonchalant as she answered the phone.

She took the opportunity to launch into a very detailed account of my dog's condition. Hannah Mae, at ten years old, was undergoing what seemed like a constant string of urinary infections. She was having a rough time lately, and apparently last night had been a bad night for her.

When my mom finally paused for air, I took advantage. "Can I please tell you something?"

"Um... sure." From the tone of her voice, I could tell she was disappointed at the interruption.

"Marc asked me to move in with him last night! I'm so excited!" Without giving her a chance to comment, I decided to beat her to the punch and launch into what I knew would come next. "I know what you're thinking. That this is his way to avoid getting married, but it isn't. We discussed it last night too. I told him that I didn't want to live with him forever and he assured me that this would be the first step for us. I am so happy! Aren't you happy for me?"

I could hear the smile in her voice. "You sound thrilled. And yes, I am very happy for you. I really am. But I have one piece of advice for you."

Shit. I knew that was coming.

"Whatever you do, don't bring all your clothes over to his house at once. Take many trips and move your stuff in a little at a time. If he sees how many pairs of jeans and shoes you have, he will change his mind quickly and never marry you."

Okay, that wasn't the advice I was expecting, but she did have a point. I have an unhealthy addiction to denim.

CHAPTER 11

ALTHOUGH I NEVER SLEPT at my mom's house again after Marc invited me to move in with him on Valentine's Day, I did follow my mom's advice and moved my stuff into his house very slowly. After about a month... okay, after two... I was fully moved into my new home. Marc's once humongous closet seemed small, crowded with the addition of my fifty pairs of jeans and assorted other belongings. (I can't deny it; I have issues.) With a smile, he just kept shifting his stuff and reorganizing his clothes to make more room for me, until finally he ended up with only a small section and a couple of drawers. But if he minded, he certainly didn't show it, though I'm sure he was relieved when I finally stopped arriving with bags of pants, sweaters, suits, and skirts.

Though the closet integration went well, other aspects of our first weeks of cohabitation weren't so pleasant. After only a few days, we both got food poisoning. No matter how much you care for someone, you don't want to share that experience with them, especially so early on. (Though who am I kidding. Food poisoning pales in comparison to my puking on his bedroom floor, after the condom debacle, four years ago!)

I was the first one to exhibit symptoms from what we later figured out was a contaminated sausage dinner. When Marc, hearing alarming sounds coming from the bathroom, found me, I was doubled over in terrible pain, and looking quite a mess. He ran right to my side, grabbed my hair and held it back.

"Not feeling so good?" he asked as he handed me the bottle of mouthwash.

"I've had better days," I grumbled.

"Get back in bed. Lie down, rest."

I listened but remained there for under a minute before needing to make another mad dash. This scene kept replaying like a bad rerun. Marc only left my side to make himself some coffee. When he returned upstairs he found me coming out of the shower.

"Feeling better?"

"I think so," I said, very unconvincingly. "I've got to get ready for work."

"What? Are you kidding me?"

"No, I can make it in." I had issues admitting when I am sick and I stubbornly go in, regardless of how bad I feel. I was unstoppable.

"You can, can you? Tell me how you are going to drive an hour to your office when you've been throwing up every ten minutes since you woke up?"

I didn't have the chance to answer...

Handing me the mouthwash once more, he sternly stated, "This conversation about you going to work is over! I am not letting you leave this house. You are in no condition to go anywhere except back to bed!"

Before he left for work, he ran out to a local deli and bought me several bottles of Coke and a box of saltines. In less than an hour, he returned home, looking quite green.

Marc and I handle sickness very differently. He likes to sleep and I am restless. I have to occupy my brain and either read, watch television, or goof around on the computer. When he arrived home, I gave up my spot in the bed so he could sleep in peace and crawled downstairs to the den, where I snuggled under a thick blanket with my trusty remote control and novel.

Sometime during the day, I managed to call my mom. She was beyond shocked that Marc was able to convince me to stay home from work, a feat she'd never succeeded at. She fretted that we probably didn't have the proper provisions for such a calamity. She knew we were equipped at all times for an impromptu cocktail party, but bottles of wine and spicy cheeses weren't going to help us now.

"Don't worry, Hilary," she told me. "I'll pick up some stuff for you guys and bring it over when I leave work."

At 5:01, the phone rang. "I just left my office. I'll stop at the store and bring you soda, crackers, pretzels, jello, and some chicken broth." I grimaced at the mention of all the food. "Do you want anything else?"

"No, thanks," I croaked, as my stomach did yet another somersault. "That sounds like more than enough."

"How are you feeling?"

"A little better, I think."

"Good. What about Marc? How's he doing?"

"I don't know."

My mom turned on me so quickly my head spun. "You don't know? What do you mean you don't know? Didn't you check on him?"

"No," I replied meekly.

"That is terrible!"

"I know, but…"

"But nothing. He's sick too. You should make sure he is okay."

"He's upstairs in our room and I'm down in the den. I can't make it upstairs like this. Do you know how many stairs there are in this house?" I whined.

"You need to check on him," she commanded sternly. "I'll call you when I get to the house. I'm not coming in, in case this isn't food poisoning. I don't want to catch anything."

And then she hung up. I knew she was right, that I should check on Marc, but the stairs I had to climb to reach him seemed insurmountable. What to do, what to do?

Forty-five minutes later, the phone rang again. "Hi, it's me," my mom said. "I'm pulling into your driveway. I am going to leave the groceries at the front door. How are you feeling?"

"A little better."

"Good. Did you check on Marc?"

"Yes, he's doing a little better too."

"Very good! I told you that you could manage the stairs."

I could have let her comment slide, but I was pleased with my ingenuity. "I didn't! I used my cell to call him instead."

"I guess that's better than nothing, but not by much."

She was right, and I felt bad. Memories of the first time I got sick with Marc came flooding back to me…

We were dating for a little over a year. It was late fall, and freezing. I had slept over Marc's house the night before and woke up on Saturday morning with a scratchy throat. As I normally do when I don't feel well, I tried to ignore my symptoms. Marc's lease on his Mercedes had expired and he was scheduled to trade it in and pick up his new vehicle, a Lexus SC430 convertible. He asked me to go with him.

We chose to ignore the frigid temperatures and drove away from the dealership with the top down. By the time we returned to Marc's house, my scratchy throat turned into a full blown cold, complete with a fever. There was no more denying it, I was really sick. "I better head home," I told him, right before I had a sneezing fit.

"Are you crazy? You are not going anywhere but the couch."

"But I am sick."

"That is exactly why you aren't going anywhere. Lay down. I'll be right back."

I did as instructed and he returned with two Tylenol, a blanket, and a cup of tea with lemon and honey. He sat down on the other couch and grabbed the remote control, finding a chick-flick for me to watch. By the time the movie was over, my fever had dropped and Marc prepared a light but delicious dinner.

"Feeling better?" he asked, concerned after he cleared away our dishes.

"Much." I replied, although I was upset that I was sick. Marc and I had tickets to see Simon and Garfunkel at Madison Square Garden in two days. Then we were flying to Salt Lake City to see Eric and Jaye on Friday morning. It was the first time he was bringing me and I was worried I would still be sick.

"Good. I am going to call up my friend Marty and give him the concert tickets."

"But why?" I asked. "I'm sure I will feel better by then."

"Forget it! You shouldn't be in such a crowded place if you are sick. I don't want to risk you getting worse. The concert isn't worth it. It's more important you get well so you can enjoy the trip to Utah."

"Then go without me," I replied.

"No, it wouldn't be fun without you. If you don't go, I don't want to go."

With that, he picked up the phone and gave the tickets away. I realized something that day. He may not have found it easy to put his feelings into words, but he was able to show me what he felt. I always believed that talk is cheap and actions speak more than words. And his actions showed me how much he cared...

I wanted him to feel the same love I felt that day. Putting my own symptoms aside, I grabbed some DVDs of old Saturday Night Live episodes, the box of saltines and soda that my mom brought over, and climbed the three flights of stairs up to our bedroom.

I flicked on the television and popped the DVDs in the machine. I handed Marc a cracker and he took a tentative bite. I poured him a glass of soda and placed it on the side of the bed. I gave him a small kiss on his forehead and I climbed in bed next to him. Both of us were glad to have each other.

Two weeks after we recovered, I went to my mom's house to work on some tax returns. As soon as I walked in the door I was shocked to see my dog, Hannah Mae. Although only several weeks had passed since I was with her, last she seemed a shadow of her former self. Sure she was happy to see me, but she was very lethargic. Her formerly soft white fur had a yellowish hue to it, and she'd lost an enormous amount of weight.

When it was time for me to leave, I called Marc from the car to let him know I was on my way home. My voice was cracking as shared what I saw. "You wouldn't have even recognized her. I know my mom has been telling me that she wasn't doing well, but I didn't expect her to look like this. I'm worried."

"Why don't you stay there? Spend the night with your mom?"

"What can I really do? I thought of it, but my mom's going out with friends for lunch anyway. I have no idea when she'll be home and besides, I'd rather be with you." I said, selfishly.

When my mom came home from her afternoon out, she found blood throughout the entire house. Realizing that Hannah Mae hemorrhaged, distraught, she rushed her cherished pet to an emergency veterinary clinic. Despite her panic and worry, my mom didn't alert me to the situation right away. She knew that I was having dinner with Marc's family for the first time since I'd moved in with him. She didn't want to spoil my evening.

She waited until the following morning to fill me in as I was driving to work. I felt horrible. I was upset that she had to handle the situation alone, and guilty that I chose to spend the night with Marc when I could have been there for both of them.

"I'm waiting for the vet to call me with the test results. As soon as I know something, I'll call you." For the past few months, my mom had shuffled Hannah Mae back and forth for tests, but they never found anything more than signs of a urinary tract infection. This time I didn't need test results; I immediately had a bad feeling.

I was barely in my office an hour when my mom called. My heart raced in my chest as I reached for the phone. "The vet says Hannah Mae is very sick. She doesn't have an infection. She has cancer of her urethra."

I expected that she had cancer. I wasn't shocked by the diagnosis. But I was not prepared for what my mom said next. "They said that her bladder is on the verge of rupturing, and if it does, she will suffer an agonizing death. We have to put her to sleep. Like now."

I screamed, "No!" Co-workers came running into my office. One held me tight as I cried on her shoulder while listening to my mom. "Hilary, I am sorry. But we have no choice. We have to do it. Can you leave work now?"

Crying, I answered yes. My mom told me to meet her at her office, so we could drive to the clinic together. As soon as I got in the car I called Marc. "Hi," I said my voice breaking, followed by sobs.

"What's wrong? Are you okay? Do you need me to get you?" Marc sounded panic-stricken.

"I'm on my way to my mom's office," I told him. We have to put Hannah Mae to sleep." I filled Marc in with everything I knew, and he listened quietly as I continued to sob. When I was done, he asked if I wanted him to meet me there and go along too.

"Nah, I think I should just go with my mom," I said completely touched that he wanted to be there with me.

"Okay. If you want me to meet you somewhere, let me know. If you want to stay at your mom's house tonight, stay there. Whatever you need to do, just do it! Don't give me another thought."

"Okay," I whispered as tears ran down my face.

"Hil, it will be okay," Marc said softly, lovingly, and reassuringly. "It is the best thing for her. Let's face it, she wasn't well for a while. You don't want to see her suffer. Stay strong for her, and for your mom."

"I'll try."

"Good," he answered. "I love you. I am hanging up. Be careful driving, and don't speed."

My mom was waiting in her office's parking lot. As soon as I pulled in, she opened her passenger door and I hopped in. In silence, we drove to the clinic. The woman behind the desk quickly ushered us inside an exam room, where the vet, a kind young man, explained more about Hannah Mae's condition and detailed what was going to happen next. Then the veterinary assistant carried my dog into the small room where we stood. Hannah Mae seemed so happy to see my mom and me. Her tail was wagging and she had many kisses for us both. My mom and I sat on the floor playing with her for a few precious minutes before the vet said that it was time. "Are you sure you want to stay here?" he asked us solemnly. My mom looked at me, worried I wouldn't be able to do it, but there was no doubt in my mind; I wasn't going to let my pup die alone.

"Yes," I said, and my mom nodded her head to the vet as well.

"Okay, I'm going to give her two shots," he explained. "The first will tranquilize her. She'll immediately get very tired, and appear to just fall asleep. Then I will give her the second to stop her heart. Don't worry, she won't feel anything."

Just as the vet described, it happened. Within seconds of receiving the shot, Hannah Mae's eyes got heavy, and she sat down. Then she curled her little body into a ball, just as she did every day when she fell asleep, except this time she would never wake up again.

My mom and I were hysterical. Tears streamed down our faces as we continued to pet the lifeless body of the dog we loved with our hearts and souls.

Devastated, neither of us was able to return to work, so we spent the rest of the day together, crying and reminiscing. We went out to dinner together, and when we were through, I returned to my new home and to Marc. As soon as he saw me, he took me into his arms and held me tight as I cried. He was so loving and tender. He stroked my hair as I clung to him. The cat, circled around us, sensing something was wrong. I bent down and picked him up. He nuzzled close to me and rubbed his face against mine as if he was kissing me, a move that, until that moment, I thought was only reserved for his father. He, too, was trying to comfort me. If I'd had any doubts in my mind about moving in with Marc, I knew right then and there that I was right where I was supposed to be. I was home.

Though sickness and Hannah Mae's death were difficult to deal with, those first few weeks of living together we were surprised to find that everything else was easy. It was as if we'd lived our whole lives together. We had so much fun just doing the simple and mundane tasks of daily life—cooking, cleaning, and going grocery shopping. Life was just easy. In the kitchen, Marc and I found a comfortable groove. We worked so well together as a team, and we took turns being each other's sous chef, as we chopped, peeled, and sautéed. Marc would cook during the week, since he came home earlier than I did, but on weekends I would be the lead cook.

"Did I ever tell you about the fire?" I asked Marc one night as I was frying up some chicken cutlets.

"No, I don't think so," he answered. "Do I need more wine for this story?"

"Probably," I said and chuckled. "I was about four years old, because my grandmother was still alive. She lived with us. My mom was going to make french fries with dinner. Her mother told her that she made them wrong. So my grandmother tells my mom the 'right way'. Of course, my grandmother forgot a few key steps, and the potatoes caught on fire. My mom freaked out and threw water on the flames."

"Oh no, she didn't."

"Oh yes, she did. The kitchen was ablaze. My grandmother, who was in another room with me, got so scared she jumped up to help my mom. The only problem was she was going on impulse and adrenaline. She momentarily forgot that she'd had her leg amputated, so she fell on the floor, which made me scream louder. My mom called the fire department and literally threw me outside. She told me to go to our next door neighbor's house. She had no idea if Elaine was even home, which of course she wasn't. But I was too scared to go back to my house, so I sat on the porch, freezing, with no coat on."

"You must have been petrified."

"I was. My dad got home right before the fireman arrived. He saw me on Elaine's stoop, hysterical. I just kept muttering 'fire, fire'. He told me to stay and he rushed in the house, grabbed the fire extinguisher, and put out the fire."

"Your dad was the hero," Marc said as he engulfed me in a tight hug.

I nodded yes and I held on to Marc. I felt so safe in his arms, just as I always did. I never worried when I was with Marc. I always knew he would look out for me and protect me. He reminded me so much of my dad in so many ways.

*   *   *

As the months passed, our ease and comfort with each other extended to running errands as well. A normal shopping trip always seemed to take twists and turns, becoming an adventure. Once, in order to save time, we split up and went to two different stores on the same strip. I finished before Marc, and when I met up with him, he showed me a large wallet which he found in the parking lot.

"Look at this. I checked it and it's full of cash, credit cards, blank checks, insurance cards and a driver's license." Handing me the license he said, "Take this and call information. Get a phone number for the owner while I pay for our stuff."

I did, but the wallet's owner had an unlisted number. The operator explained that she wasn't allowed to release it. "I guess we should just give it to the manager?" I suggested.

"No. How do we know that he won't keep it? There is a lot of money in there. I know!" he exclaimed. She lives only about fifteen minutes away. Let's head over. If she's there, we will give it to her, and if not, we will leave her a note to call us."

"I bet she must be freaking out now, wondering where her wallet is," I told Marc as we drove.

"I know. Money's one thing, but did you see how many credit cards she had in there? Calling the companies to cancel them alone will take her a week."

"There is her house," I said as I pointed to a mid-sized Tudor home on the tree lined street.

Marc saw I was holding the wallet. "Leave it in the car," he directed. "I want to make sure that we are at the right house before we go and hand off her wallet to the wrong person."

Marc knocked on the door and a man answered. Marc asked if the woman, whose name was on the license, lived there.

"Yeah she is my wife, what do you want?" he grunted.

"Can she come out? We found something that belongs to her," Marc calmly replied. The man yelled for his wife and I retrieved the wallet from the car.

"Donna?" Marc questioned.

"Yeah," she grunted. I couldn't help but wonder if she and her husband met in charm school.

Handing her the wallet, Marc explained, "We were just at Trader Joe's and we found this."

"Oh. I was just there." she said absently, as she took the wallet from his outreached hands. She turned around and walked into her house, slamming her front door.

Dumbfounded and resentful of her reaction, I turned to Marc and asked, "I guess it was too much to expect for her to say thank you? A little appreciation would have been nice, given that we went out of our way."

"Don't try and understand people. You never will. It doesn't really matter if she appreciates what we did or not. We did what we thought was best. I don't regret doing it. In fact, I'd do it again in a second."

As we drove away, I smiled to myself. I realized that I'd just witnessed a different side of Marc. Most people, me included, would never go out of their way to help a stranger. They would take the easy way out. He didn't. And he didn't care about the woman's lack of reaction, unlike me. He only cared about doing the right thing. This showed me that while he may have had a difficult time opening up and expressing his feelings, he had a big and compassionate heart. He truly cared about people, even strangers, which I think is one of the most admirable qualities anyone can have.

Cooking and shopping aside, the best part of us living together, by far, was when we started redecorating Marc's house, so it became *our* home instead. Slowly but surely, my style and taste was reflected there too. We painted the walls bright happy colors, as opposed to the beige that was everywhere. New area rugs were purchased, as well as new dishes and stemware. The wine glasses were more of a result of me breaking the old ones, but still, change was fun. I would always tell Marc that I colorized not only his home, but also his life.

In what felt like a blink of an eye, spring ended and summer arrived. As the days got longer, and the warm weather appeared, so did the house guests. When you live on the beach, you have a never-ending supply of friends and family showing up for long weekends all summer long. Marc and I joked that we were running a hotel. We even went so far as to decorate the guest rooms with room numbers and signage, like what you would find in a hotel room. The closets had signs in the inside that said, "We are not responsible for lost or stolen articles." The doors to the rooms had signs that said, "We provide our guests with a smoke-free environment."

Along with each guest came the questions...

Hailing from Florida, Marc's cousin Marta and her family were the first to arrive that summer. As soon as she walked into the house, she spotted the walls that Marc and I recently painted. "Marc, I love the living room! The yellow is so vibrant. Not, that it wasn't nice before, but now it looks so homey. I bet it was Hilary's idea. Right?" asked Marta.

"Yeah, she picked it out," Marc replied with a smile.

"She's done good. And speaking of good decisions, when are you finally going to decide to marry her?"

Marc let that one slide, but a week after Marta and her family left, Eric and Jaye arrived. Jaye was still sporting the rhinestone ring from our New Year's Eve's faux engagement. Since she also wore it when she visited in January, I couldn't decide if it was a new permanent accessory or if she wore it just to bust Marc's chops a little bit more. Regardless of her motives, it seemed to me that she was never without that ring.

"It's great to see you two so happy together," she said as we sat on the deck, enjoying a nice glass of white wine. She removed the ring from her finger, held it up to the light, and then held it out to Marc. "Do you need this ring? Because if you do," she paused for emphasis, "just let me know... it's yours if you want it. You do need one, right?"

Marc rolled his eyes at her. But as usual, she was unstoppable. "Come on, Marc. Get your act together already and marry this girl! What are you waiting for? She isn't going to stick around forever. I won't let her!"

The next day, I had to go to work, but Marc spent most of the day with Eric and Jaye. When I got home, Jaye couldn't wait to fill me in on her day. "Eric had a conference call this afternoon," she said, "I stayed on the beach with Marc. We got to talking. I told him I think it's great that you moved in, and that he seems to be happier than I have ever seen him before. But I told him not to take the situation for granted. I wanted to make sure he has no intentions of just living with you forever."

"Nice, thanks," I answered. "Do you think he got it?"

"Who knows with him, but I did tell him that if he loves you he needs to decide what he wants. He needs to marry you or let you go. Staying in limbo forever isn't the solution for anyone."

I knew Jaye was right, but I didn't want her to scare him.

That night after dinner, as we sat outside sipping coffee and smelling the fragrant ocean air, Eric said, "A couple of months ago I went to a team building retreat. One of the things that we did was go around the table and share our deepest fears. It was really interesting. Not only did you learn a lot about everyone, it also forced you to admit things to yourself that you may not want to. Want to do it?"

Always eager, immediately I said yes, but then instantly regretted it.

Jaye rolled her eyes, "Aren't you tired of this game yet?" she asked Eric. To me and Marc she said, "Every time we have dinner with someone he plays this game. It's really getting old."

"Oh come on, you love it. I know you do," Eric teased his wife. "I'll even let you start."

"Oh yippee, lucky me," she said, sarcastically. "Fine. It's easy. I'm a mother. My biggest fear is something happening to my son." Jaye, in a lot of ways, reminded me of my mom. She came off as strong and tough, but she was extremely sensitive and caring. She loved with her full heart, and thought of herself last. Her son was only a year younger than me. He was a toddler when she divorced his father. Until she married Eric, when he was in his early teens, like my mom, she filled the role of both mother and father for him. She always did, and continued to, put his needs and well-being above her own. Like my mom, she would do anything for him, and like me, he knew it.

"That wasn't so hard, now was it?" Eric joked. "Marc, why don't you go next."

If possible, Marc seemed less enthusiastic than Jaye. "We really are doing this? Okay, fine." He took a deep breath. I figured he was going to say something flippant. But he shocked me. "I fear failure. I know that I am always made fun of because I am so cautious, conservative, and slow. I know I overanalyze everything. But I can't act any other way. I need to be as certain of the outcome as possible because I don't like to lose. I can't lose. I only can act when I feel comfortable and confident enough that my decision is the right one, and winning and success is the only option. I am this way both professionally and personally." When he said personally, he reached under the table and gently squeezed my thigh.

I gave Marc a sad smile. "Can I go next?" I asked, feeling brave. And for the first time in my life I expressed my deepest fear. "I am afraid of being all alone in the world, with no one caring about me. I have been afraid of this ever since my dad died. I was so young. Fourteen. I was just a kid. If dealing with his death wasn't hard enough, I was petrified about something happening to my mom too. I barely let her out of my sight. I felt like somehow if I was with her I'd be able to protect her. She worked close to the house, but if she got stuck in traffic and came home late, she'd find me in a panic. I'd basically be on the verge of calling the police. I knew that if something did happen to her, I'd have no one. I'd be alone."

Tears started to run down my face, but I continued. "I never felt bad about being an only child before my dad died. In fact, I liked it. I was good at it. I even played Monopoly by myself," I tried to joke, but my voice cracked. "After he died, I really wished I had a sibling to share the experience with. It was so isolating. No one understood what I felt like, what my life was like. My friends couldn't relate. In fact, someone at school told my guidance counselor that I was going to commit suicide because I looked sad. Seriously? My dad just died, should I have been laughing?

"My cousins were all much older than me. They had their own children and families to deal with. I just had my mom. She did everything possible to help me through, and she did. She gave up a lot of her own life in the process, and I feel bad about that. But still, even now, I worry about being alone. One day something will happen to her and I am afraid no one will care about me..." My words trailed off as my tears took over.

"Come here," Marc said as he stood up and opened his arms to me. "It's okay. You don't have to worry anymore." He stroked my hair and kissed me. "I love you."

A moment later, Jaye and Eric joined the hug.

"We love you too, Hilary," Eric said.

"You never have to worry," Jaye added. "You are so special to me. I will always be here for you, no matter what."

In Marc's arms, and in the arms of our friends, finally I felt some of my fear subside.

After Eric and Jaye returned home, Marc and I had less than two weeks alone before the next guest checked into the hotel, err, I mean our house. I loved the hustle and bustle of having so many people at the house, though I could have lived without the constant washing of the beach towels and the vacuuming of the sand. Sometimes I felt more like a chambermaid than a girlfriend.

The next arrival also hailed from the sunshine state—Marc's childhood friend, Jeffrey. Jeff had been Marc's brother's best friend since the second grade. He teased Marc that he knew him since he was sperm, which was pretty much true, since Jay and Jeffrey were seven years older than Marc.

Many older brothers usually don't want to pal around with their younger siblings, but this wasn't the case in Marc's family. Jay loved Marc from the day he was born, and made sure to include him in everything he did. When Jay discovered music as a teen, he made sure to share his love with Marc. In a roundabout way, Jay was responsible for Marc becoming a musician, because if Jay didn't introduce Marc to bands like The Beatles, Pink Floyd, and Led Zeppelin, Marc might never have had the motivation to pick up a drum stick.

Whenever Jeffrey came over to the house to see Jay, Marc would tag along. Over the years, as the boys became men, their age difference mattered less and less. The three all remained extremely close, and if you saw them out together you would have sworn that they were all brothers.

Jeffrey married young and had a son soon after. Marc frequently babysat his boy. Sadly, the marriage didn't last too long, and when they split up, Jeffrey moved from New York to Florida. A few years after the breakup, he gained sole custody of his son.

Although he got engaged several times after the divorce, Jeffrey never remarried. It seemed he preferred playing the field. He was an out-of-control flirt, who went a little crazy whenever there was a woman around. He was the kind of guy who was constantly grabbing you so he could hug you tightly and caress any part of your body he could get his hot little hands on. Since Marc had known him his entire life, I felt comfortable humoring him and playing along. Besides, Marc seemed to enjoy watching the show!

One evening after dinner Jeffrey wrapped his arms around me. "What is wrong with my friend?" he asked me, right in front of Marc.

"What do you mean?" I asked flirtatiously, trying to egg him on.

"Why the hell isn't he married to you already? There is obviously something wrong with him." Jeffrey asked, as Marc just smiled.

I, on the other hand, encouraged Jeffrey's line of questioning. "I don't know. But I do know you ask very good questions. Why do you think he isn't married yet?"

"Insanity is the only thing I can think of. Yeah, that's got to be it. It's the only reason he would risk letting you getting away. But if he isn't smart enough to do the right thing, it will be his loss, not yours. I'll tell you what. If he doesn't marry you by the end of the year, I will." Jeffrey grabbed me and twirled me in his arms. Jeffrey's son had just had a baby, so he added, "Not only will you become a wife, you will also be an instant grandma. Now who can beat that?"

As tempting as it sounded, I didn't have any sweeping desire to become a thirty-year-old grandmother... though it would have made for a great conversation starter.

Two weeks after Jeffrey left, Marc's dad, Marvin, and his girlfriend, Renea, arrived. One of the first afternoons, while Marc was puttering around and Renea watched television in the den, I lounged on the beach with Marvin and Marc's older brother, Jay. Jay and I were both reading our books when out of nowhere Marvin asked, "What's going on with my boy?"

I wasn't sure if his question was directed at me or his son, but I answered anyway. "What do you mean?"

"He isn't getting any younger, you know. When is he going to come to his senses and marry you already? I don't get it. I thought I raised a smart kid. I don't know why he is acting so dumb. What is he waiting for?"

"You got me," I said. Turning to Jay, I asked, "I'm sure he talks to you. What do you know?"

Jay smirked but said nothing.

"Come on Jay. Spill it!" I commanded.

"Yeah Jay, tell us," Marvin chimed in. "What do you know? I sure hope you're trying to knock some sense into him, because he needs it!"

"Whoa... calm down, the both of you." I don't think Jay was expecting his dad and me to ambush him. "Yes, I talk to him constantly about it. Believe me, I'm working on him, and he is coming to his senses. Slowly but surely, I am watching him change. Hilary, I know you see the difference in him too. But you can't pressure him." Turning his head, looking deeply first into his father's eyes and then mine, he continued, "It will make him freak. Trust me, that's the last thing that you want. He has to do it on his own, and in his own time." And since everything with Marc and his brother reverted back to either music or movies, Jay continued, "You need to take a lesson from the Beatles. Let it be, let it be." And then he sang the full song on the beach to me and Marvin. As I listened to him sing, I realized that while everyone in Marc's life was pestering him about marriage, if there was a person out there, who had the ability to help convince him to make the next step, it would be Jay. I hoped Marc would trust his older brother's advice and listen to reason.

CHAPTER 12

"MY MOM CANCELLED DINNER for tomorrow night," I told Marc as I hung up the telephone. "She still has a little bit of a cold, and she doesn't want to take a chance of giving us anything before we go away." It was a few days before Christmas, and Marc and I were getting ready to make our annual pilgrimage to Florida to spend a few days with his family, before dashing off to spend the balance of the week with Eric and Jaye in the Florida Keys.

"Okay, does she want to go out to dinner instead?" Marc asked.

"No. She doesn't want to be with us. That didn't come out right, did it?" I chuckled. "She's afraid that if she's with us we'll catch something from her. She is right, the last thing we need is to get sick on vacation. That wouldn't be fun."

"Yeah, I guess so," Marc answered quietly. He seemed disappointed. While Marc got along well with my mom, and loved to have dinner at her house, I had never seen him pout when our plans with her were cancelled. It was out of character.

Perplexed at his reaction, I asked, "What's up? You seem so sad that dinner was cancelled."

"What do you mean? I am not," he answered defensively. "I just thought it would be nice to see her before we left, is all."

"We'll have dinner with her when we come back. It really isn't a big deal. She only lives twenty minutes away. We can see her anytime." With that, the dryer's buzzer sounded, and I ended the conversation by heading up to the laundry room to fold our clothes and finish packing.

I tried to wrap my head around Marc's reaction. There was definite disappointment there and I didn't know why. Why did he want to see her so badly? Did he have something he wanted to discuss with her? Like our future, perhaps?

*   *   *

In every couple, one person is more of a planner. They are more organized. They may keep elaborate to-do lists or detailed calendars. They may have rituals, like putting something in the same place as not to forget it. To be blunt, one person is more anal than the other. Throughout out our relationship, hands down, Marc had been that person. He had pre-lists for his to-do lists. I usually flew by the seat of my pants. I hardly ever wrote myself notes or utilized a calendar. I felt that if I couldn't keep something in my head, how important could it be? Other than the fact that I lost my car keys on my desk daily, and had shown up for eye exams on the wrong day, my method always worked fine for me.

Whenever we travel, Marc has a major check list. It includes everything from the obvious, like taking our wallets, to the obscure, like unplugging the water coolers. Everything that has to be done is on that list.

The night before our trip to Florida, Marc, ever the planner, prepared the cat's breakfast bowl, pre-ground our morning coffee, and set up the coffee machine. He even laid out a plastic bag for us to peel and take two oranges with us. The morning of our flight, I peeled the oranges and went to put them in his laptop bag. "No, just throw it in the fridge," Marc said, "We aren't leaving for a while. We might as well keep them cold. I'll grab them before we leave."

We took a cab to the airport. Though it was close to Christmas, there was no traffic. We were shocked to find that there were no lines at security either. As I removed my jacket and shoes, Marc reached for his cell phone, which he always clips to his belt when we travel. Panic swept across his face. "Where is my cell phone?"

"What?"

"My cell phone... where is it?"

"What do you mean? You don't have it? Did you leave it at home?" I couldn't believe this was happening, especially to Mr. Organization.

"Shit! NO! I had it in the cab. I put it on the seat when I took the money to pay out of my wallet. I must have left it on the seat.... how did I do that?"

"It's okay," I replied, trying to stay calm and sound like the voice of reason. "The driver is probably still in the airport. I'll call the cab company." I reached for my cell phone and dialed the number, but nothing happened. "Oh, no!" I exclaimed. "There's no reception." I started walking away from the scanners, but my call still wasn't going through. Not knowing what else to do, we walked off the security line. I redialed. Again, nothing happened. Before we knew it, we were standing outside the airport, trying to make a phone call that just refused to go through.

At this point I handed Marc my phone, thinking he could perform magic; he is technologically blessed, I am not. "What is the point of having a cell phone if it doesn't work?" Marc muttered as we both got more and more frustrated. "What are the chances I forget my phone and yours dies? This is ridiculous!"

Not knowing what to do, I started asking limo drivers, cabbies, and passengers if I could borrow a cell phone. Well, you can imagine how happy my fellow New Yorkers were to hand me their mobile phones. An airport worker, who was watching us, told us where to find a pay phone in the terminal. Marc and I ran over to it. By now, twenty minutes had passed. It took me a while to remember how to use a pay phone. (When was the last time I used one, the eighties?) I managed to figure out where to put the money in just as Marc rebooted my phone. I don't know why neither one of us thought to do this sooner, but he actually got through to the cab company before I did. The driver had found his phone, and was going to return to the airport with it. The only problem was that he was twenty minutes away already.

Marc and I were instructed to wait where he dropped us off. We stood there freezing, waiting for the driver to reappear. As soon as he arrived, Marc tipped him heavily and reclaimed his phone. We returned to security, and fortunately again the lines were still short. We were able to quickly pass through, making a mad dash to the gate where our plane was already boarding.

With no time to grab a snack before the flight, Marc turned to me and said, "Good thing we brought those oranges." As soon as the words were out of his mouth, the realization hit him. "You listened to me and put them in the fridge, right?"

As I sheepishly nodded my head yes, Marc said, "Oh great! I forgot those too!"

I couldn't stop myself from saying, "Next time you need to add take oranges to your list!"

As the plane lifted off and Marc drifted to sleep, all I could think about was how out of character this trip had been so far, and we hadn't even left the state. Why was Marc suddenly getting forgetful? He obviously had something on his mind... was he worried about Jaye pressuring him like she did the year before? Or, more likely, was he at a crossroads regarding our relationship?

*   *   *

"There they are," Marc said, pointing. I followed his finger and saw Marc's dad and his girlfriend standing by the baggage claim in the West Palm Beach airport, as we made our way through the terminal.

Not even out of the airport complex, Marvin explained to his son, "I need you to look at my garage door opener. It's not working right. Oh, and I also think I need to install a new water filter."

"Um, Okay. Anything else?" Marc questioned.

"Nah." Marvin replied. "That should do it." Then after a pregnant pause, he continued, "Well, actually no. On second thought, I think the florescent light in the garage is also on its way out. I probably should be changing that too, you know, while you are fixing the garage door, and all."

"Let's just stop off at Home Depot first, that way we don't waste the full day," Marc told his dad. Being Mr. Fix-it, Marc always had chores to take care of the first day we arrived in Florida, and it was clear that this year wouldn't be any different. But since he was quick about tending to them, before we knew it we were lounging poolside with his dad at the senior development where he lived.

After a few hours in the sun, Jeffrey, who lives very close by, came over for a visit. Marvin returned to his house so that we could spend some time alone with Jeffrey. As always, he flirted unmercifully with me in front of Marc. "Come here, you," he said, as he grabbed me in a humongous hug. I tried to break free after a few minutes. Jeffrey wanted no part of that. "Where are you going? Don't move. Well, move. Move in closer. Yeah, yeah, yeah, that's more like it. Marc doesn't mind, do you, Marc?"

I humored Jeff and snuggled up. While Jeffrey's hands on approach didn't actually bother me, his routine was getting a little old. Sure it was funny and all, but there was only one guy whose arms I wanted around me, and his name wasn't Jeffrey!

Marc smiled. "No, it's okay. Knock yourself out. Enjoy yourself while you can." While Marc was nonchalant about the exchange, the three of us caught the attention of the other pool goers, whose eyes became glued on us. Suddenly, I felt like we were part of a reality TV show, as we broke up the resident's monotonous conversations about where they ate dinner last night and where they were going to have dinner tonight.

"Okay, I don't mind if I do!" Jeffrey answered as he held me tight. After a few minutes, he allowed me to break free. He suddenly got somber and serious, as he turned to me, pointing at his watch. "Hey, look at this."

"Did you get a new watch?" I asked. "It is a very nice one."

"Nope, that's not it," he answered smugly.

Confused, I asked, "If I'm not looking at your watch, what I am I looking for?"

"The date that is on the watch, silly... check out what day it is! In about a week, it will be New Year's. New Year's! You know what that means, don't you?"

Perplexed, Marc and I answered in unison, "No."

"Oh Marc, I'm not surprised you forgot. But Hilary, how could you have? I am hurt. Seriously hurt. But don't worry. I will get over it. I am good that way. I don't hold grudges, or take things too seriously."

"What are you talking about, Jeffrey?" I asked.

"Our deal... remember it now?"

A smile crept on my face as I replied, "Oh, of course. How can I forget that?"

"Deal? What deal?" asked Marc, sounding a little upset that he wasn't in on our little secret.

"The deal we made at your place this summer, my friend. Remember? I told her that if you don't propose to her by New Year's Eve, I will marry her myself!"

Marc said nothing.

But I chimed in, "So I guess I may become an instant grandmother after all."

*   *   *

On Christmas morning, as soon as Marc and I returned from working out at the development's gym, Marvin reminded us that we were invited over to Marc's cousins Ira and Marta's house that afternoon for a little holiday gathering. Ira is actually Marc's first cousin; he is Marvin's brother's son. But Marc knew Marta long before she married Ira. In fact, Marta and Marc used to live with each other.

When Marc was a freshman in college, his parents sold their house and bought a new one a few blocks away. The new house was a two-family residence, and the first tenant that they took was Marta and her mom. Because of her vibrant and warm personality, Marta immediately became part of Marc's family, and became great friends with Marc and his siblings.

When she first moved into Marc's house, she was in a serious relationship. When it ended, it was Marc who introduced her to his cousin, Ira. They hit if off instantly, and were married a short time later. If you think that a commitment-phobic man wouldn't enjoy playing matchmaker, well, you'd be wrong.

There was something so special about Marta. She has such an easygoing personality and is beyond hysterical. You immediately are comfortable around her. She is one of those people that you just meet and feel like you have known your entire life. So when Marvin reminded us that we were heading over to her house, I was thrilled.

Ira and Marta had just moved into a new home. It was on a large parcel of land, complete with a stable and horses. Not the type of home you'd imagine someone having in South Florida.

As soon as we arrived at their house, Ira handed us two glasses of wine and Marta took us on a tour of the inside. After the tour was complete, glasses in hand, Marta and I broke away and went for a walk around the property. I was dying to see the horses.

"So how are things going with you two?" Marta asked as we stood admiring the animals.

"Really good," I answered. "I thought when Marc first asked me to move in with him, things would be awkward. You know how he is. But that didn't happen. It has been very easy and comfortable, right from the very beginning. You saw us together in the summer. And since then, things seem even better. I didn't even realize that was possible. I am so happy. Actually, I am happier than I honestly thought possible. And want to know the best part? I am sure that he is, too."

Marta turned away from the horses and grabbed my arm. "Oh, Hilary, I am so glad you are so happy. Really, I am. But is this all you want?"

"All I want? What do you mean?" I asked.

"You know. Don't you want something more? Don't you want to get married one day?"

"Yes, sure I do."

"Does Marc know that?"

"Yes, of course he does." I suddenly didn't like where I knew this conversation was heading.

"He does?" She sounded surprised. What did she know that I didn't?

"Yes. He does." I replied, enunciating every word for emphasis.

I hoped the conversation would end there, but it didn't. She pressed on with the determination of a marathon runner only a few feet away from the finish line. The conversation started to feel like an inquisition. It is a good thing I liked and respected Marta, because I was getting tired of this. "Do you talk about it with him?" she asked.

"Yes, of course I talk to him. Why wouldn't I?" I was thankful that I was wearing sunglasses so she didn't see me roll my eyes. "He knows how I feel and what I want."

Marta pulled her sunglasses down so that I could clearly see her eyes. I saw that although I was getting upset, she didn't mean me any harm. She was being sincere, and cared about both of us. Her intention wasn't to hurt me, but to get to the truth. "And what does he say?"

I took a deep breath. I didn't really want to say it out loud. But I did, because I didn't know if she already knew the answers from Marc, or if he told her something different than he told me. "He tells me he is happy. He tells me that he knows that I want marriage. And he tells me he is getting closer to the idea of marriage, but he is just not there yet." I could have added more, but I wasn't yet ready to be that honest with Marta—or, more importantly, myself. I didn't want to tell her that I feared he would never be ready. I didn't want to disclose that I didn't know what I would do when and if he finally admitted it.

Marta was now wearing her sunglasses on top of her head, so I was able to see her eyes cloud over. She exhaled deeply. "Oh, Hilary, I am sorry. I hate to be the one to tell you this. I really do. But I feel that I have to. You are still young, but you are getting older. We all are. It is a fact of life. I don't want to see you waste your life waiting for Marc to commit to you. It is never going to happen."

I felt like I was being sucker punched as she continued. "Marc is never going commit. He is never going to get married, ever. It has nothing to do with you. He loves you, I know he does. But marriage… that is another story. People don't change. He will never be a husband. And to expect him to be something that he is not is wrong, and selfish. He won't be happy and neither will you. What is the point in that? I know having you live with him is hard enough for him. I am actually surprised that he asked you to move in with in in the first place, and that he has been able to stick it out for this long. But I guess it is still new for him. I don't think he feels quite so threatened or trapped yet. But what if that changes? Especially when the talk of marriage comes up, what will happen then?"

I am not sure if she was looking for me to respond, but I didn't. Since she barely paused, I guess she was okay with my silence, or expected it. "I don't want you to be blindsided by some moves he may make. I don't want to see you hurt, but I fear that is exactly what will happen, one way or another. Marriage isn't for everyone. And if you are okay with just being in a relationship with him under his terms, then fine. But it will only work if that is all you want for the rest of your life. If you want something more, I am sorry, but you need to leave. You need to move on with your life, not only for your sake, but for Marc's sake too. You need to stop wishing and waiting for him to do something he never will be able to do. That is no way for either one of you to live. I really like you. I want you to be happy, and I want Marc to be happy too. I don't want to see you waiting on a happy ending that is never going to happen." With that, she fell silent, and opened her arms to hug me.

I was thankful for the embrace so I didn't have to say anything in reply. I had no words. And even if I did, I wouldn't have been able to speak without crying. There was no way I was going to break down and cry now. I didn't want Marta to know how hurt I was.

The hardest part was not that her words stung. The real pain I felt was internal, because in my heart, I knew she was right. Some of what she said to me I already knew, but I wasn't brave enough to say the words to myself. But to make matters worse, since she had been so close to Marc for so many years, I figured that he had opened up to her and confessed his fears and intentions. Was this why he had been acting so strangely? Was he nervous about talking to me? I wondered if he'd told her that he planned on ending the relationship because he was afraid of a true commitment. Based upon how our relationship was progressing over the last few months, I didn't think that was likely, but what did I know? He wasn't the easiest man to read. Nothing really would've surprised me at that point.

After about a minute or so, I broke free from her embrace. I wasn't about to let her know how confused, upset, and hurt I really was. I wanted time to digest everything she'd said and everything that I felt. I had to decide what to do next, but whatever that was going to be, tonight wasn't the night to make any decisions. Determined to act as if everything was perfect and I wasn't affected by the conversation, I simply said, "Thanks for confiding in me. I really appreciate your honesty, and needed to hear everything you said." Then I glanced at my watch and asked, "Shouldn't we head back to the house? Won't your other guests be here soon?"

"Yeah, they will be. You're right, we probably should head back."

We walked back in silence. When we entered the house, I passed Marc but didn't say anything. I simply smiled at him and walked into the kitchen with Marta. "What can I help you with?" I asked. "Give me something to do."

"Um, okay. Do you want to chop up some veggies?" she asked.

Boy, did I want to chop some vegetables. For as long as I could remember, whenever I'm upset, all I wanted to do was throw myself into mindless tasks. Cleaning, cooking, organizing, it didn't matter. All that mattered was that I keep my mind and body busy; otherwise I drove myself crazy.

I tended to be high strung, and I got aggravated and stressed easily. I always had. One of my favorite things about Marc was how he had always been able to diffuse my tension and calm me down, seemingly effortlessly. He had a special way about him. On my own, when I was upset or frustrated, I didn't think clearly, causing myself to get more agitated. Marc, on the other hand, was rational and logical. He was able to hit my reset button. Not only did he make me feel better, he helped me channel my frustrations into something productive, regardless of what my issue was.

Before I knew it, Marta and Ira's house filled with family and friends. It seemed that everyone and their uncle were in Florida from New York for the holiday week. I breezed through the rooms, kissing and hugging people hello and making small talk, while avoiding Marc and Marvin as much as possible. And every opportunity I could, I worked my way back in the kitchen so that I could continue to wash, dry, and put away anything that I could.

"Hilary, are you here?" Marc called out as he wandered into the kitchen.

He looked down and found me on the floor, on my hands and knees, with a bottle of cleaner and a roll of paper towels. "What are you doing now?" he asked. "I have barely seen you all night. You've been busy helping her since we got here and now... are you washing the floor?"

"Nah, I just noticed that someone must have spilled some wine. I didn't want it to stain, so I'm just wiping it up."

"From the looks of it, someone must have spilled the entire bottle. Come on, enough already. Get up. You've already gone above and beyond. Anything else that has to be done can wait. Marta can take care of it in the morning." He leaned over and extended his hand. I took it and rose to my feet.

He hugged me and exclaimed, "Whoa. Fantastic?"

With a smile I asked, "I smell fantastic?"

"No, you smell like Fantastik."

"It's just a hazard of the job, sir!" I joked, working hard to keep up my act. I wasn't about to let on to him what Marta and I chatted about earlier.

"Ah, it's okay. I can handle it. Come hang with me for a while." Marc guided me to the back porch, where his dad and the remaining guests were sitting. He sat down, positioning me so that I was sitting on his lap. I was happy and comfortable there, but I was too distracted to keep up with the conversation around me. I don't think Marc noticed, and if he did, I think he probably just assumed I was tired from all my hard work.

When it was time to go, Marta gave me an extra-long hug goodbye. We didn't say anything further to one another about our earlier conversation. We didn't have to. As we hugged, it was abundantly apparent to both of us that this might very well be the last time we saw one another, and we were both sad.

CHAPTER 13

"JEFFREY WILL BE HERE in about fifteen minutes to pick us up and take us," Marc announced as he walked into the kitchen, where Marvin and I were thumbing through a pile of newspapers and drinking coffee.

"You sure you don't want to borrow my car?" Marvin asked.

"Yes. There's no need, but thanks." Marc replied, putting his cell phone back in his pocket. After the earlier cell phone snafu, he was being extra careful with his little gadget. "He'll drive us to Eric's parents' house. He hasn't seen Eric in a while. Besides, Eric already rented a car and will be driving to the Keys. We are flying home from Fort Lauderdale, so we wouldn't even be able to get you your car back."

I closed up my newspaper and folded it back together. Rising from my seat, I walked over to the sink and rinsed my coffee cup and put it in the dishwasher. "I guess I'll go and pack us up."

"Thanks," Marc replied, "I will help you."

"Marc, let the little girl take care of the packing. She can handle it. Besides, if you are leaving and not coming back, I need you to look at my dryer. It's has been making a funny noise lately and the clothes are taking a long time to dry. I was going to call the repairman, but since you're here..."

I smiled and suppressed my giggles as I watched Marvin lead Marc to the garage, where the washer and dryer were. Marc didn't say a word to his dad, but I knew he was stewing. We'd been here for days and the dryer didn't just happen to go on the fritz moments before we were heading out. I knew doing more repair work, after everything he'd already fixed around the house, was the last thing Marc wanted to do right then. Call me selfish, or call me juvenile, but after my conversation with Marta the night before, I sent up a silent prayer that the project wouldn't be a quick fix. Marc deserved some pain and suffering too. Besides, I had to call my mom and tell her about last night. I needed advice, big time. And some venting wouldn't hurt either.

She didn't utter a word as I gave her a play by play.

"I understand why you are upset. I'd be too," she said. "But I wouldn't take everything Marta said to you as gospel, if I were you. She may know something; but chances are, she is just telling you what she thinks. Marc is so closed mouthed about everything, especially his feelings. Do you really think he went spilling his deepest thoughts and feeling to her?"

"When you put it that way..."

Cutting me off, my mom said, "But Marta was right about something... you have to take a good hard look at your relationship. You have to be prepared that it might be like this forever. You also have to be prepared that one day he may just call the whole thing off. That was my biggest fear with your father. I always worried that one day another girl would turn his head, and he'd break up with me and marry her right away. That happens, a lot, you know."

"Yeah, I know."

"You're on vacation now. There is really not much you can do or say at the moment. Enjoy the rest of your vacation. Try to have fun, but also try to sort your feelings out. When you get home I suggest you have a long, hard chat with Marc and make sure you are both on the same page. Hopefully, you are."

Talking to her, as always, calmed me down. An hour later, I found myself with Jeffrey and Marvin sitting comfortably in the den, watching *Judge Judy*. Judy was just about to give her verdict, and we all sat up a little in our seats as we knew she was about to slam the plaintiff who was suing her sister, when Marc entered the room, waving his screwdriver as if it were a white flag. "I give up. I can't find anything wrong with the dryer. No matter what I do, it's not getting hot. I checked and cleaned the filter. I removed a ton of lint from the vents. I tightened everything up and I have no idea what is wrong."

"So what should I do?" Marvin asked.

"Get the phone book out and find the number for a real repairman. Or better yet, just replace this damn thing. I think it needs to be retired. Either way, I am done with it. While this was a lot of fun, I can't keep playing with it. I am going to clean up now. We've got to get going. I told Eric we would be there by now."

Marc must have been on speed as he cleaned up, because within moments Jeffrey was tossing our bags into the trunk of his car. He threw his keys to Marc and grabbed a hold of me. Once again, he was in full flirtation mode, as he asked, "How about you drive and I sit in the backseat with Hilary? This way we can cuddle up all nice and cozy and you can enjoy the driving experience of this fine vehicle."

"I think I have had enough fun already for one morning," Marc said as he tossed the keys back at Jeffrey.

"Fine, can Hilary sit up front with me at least then?" Jeffrey asked, sounding like a little boy.

"Whatever makes you two happy," Marc replied. "As long as we get going..."

Marc may not have minded, but I did. I knew that Jeffrey was only playing, but I was not in the mood. I dashed into the back seat. I wanted to be alone and again think over everything that Marta had said to me the night before. And if I couldn't be alone, at least I could be alone in the back seat of the car.

Jeffrey and Marc made themselves comfortable in the front, and we made our way towards the interstate. As he approached a traffic light, Jeffrey turned his head to Marc and asked, "Hey, Marc, before we go down to Fort Lauderdale, what do you say we stop off at my place. I have some appliances that need fixing. Maybe you can look at them?"

Trying to sound all tough, but laughing at the same time, Marc replied, "Just drive the damn car!"

Before we knew it, we were pulling into Irvin and Lois's driveway. Eric was outside, puttering about with his dad, when we arrived. He enthusiastically greeted us and brought us inside. We found Lois and Jaye cleaning the kitchen following their lunch.

Lois rushed over to give Marc and me a big hug. When she pulled away, she checked out my left ring finger with the subtlety of a baseball announcer calling out the final homer in the ninth inning of the World Series.

Jaye, who was still sporting the rhinestone faux engagement ring, turned to Lois, and loudly for everyone's benefit, said, "Don't worry, Mom. I have this ring handy, just in case Marc should happen to need it over the next few days." Then, as if she thought her hint might have been too subtle, she added, "You heard what I said, Marc, right?"

Marc rolled his eyes and resumed his conversation with Eric and Jeffrey. I smiled at Jaye, but my enthusiasm was gone. I was worried there would be a repeat of last year, especially after everything Marta had said. I tried to brace myself for a very long few days.

All I wanted to do was get back in the car and drive down to the Keys. The quicker we got there, the quicker we could get home.

The boys had already packed up the rental car while Jaye and I were in the house, so all we had to do was hop in. On the way to Islamorada, Eric drove and Marc and I sat in the backseat. As Eric made his way to I-95, I rummaged through my bag to pull out the information on the condo I'd found on the internet. All business, I told Eric the address and explained we had to reach the real estate office by five o'clock in order to get the keys.

"We really cut it close," Jaye replied while glancing at her watch.

"I am sure they can leave keys for us some where if we run late," Eric answered. "I am sure we aren't the first people to come late."

Eric and Marc were very similar. Not much fazed either one of them. Unlike me, they didn't worry or get upset easily. Also, they both found the humor in every situation. This was one of my favorite characteristics about Marc. Many times, when I would be stressed and on the verge of tears, he would find a way to make me laugh.

"Speaking about being late," Marc said, "Did you hear what happened to William at the convention in September?" William was a business associate of theirs.

In unison, Eric and Jaye answered, "No."

"His flight was scheduled to land late; so when he made his reservation, he requested a late check-in. But there was a storm somewhere or other, and his plane was delayed three hours. He ended up landing around one o'clock in the morning, local time. Since he came from the east coast, it was three o'clock his time. He was exhausted; all he wanted to do was fall into bed. When he finally got to the hotel they told him that since he was late, they gave his room away."

"How could they do that?" Jaye asked.

"Guess they can do what they want," Marc continued. "They did arrange for him to stay the night at a hotel across town. He was furious. Right before he left, he asked if he'd been charged for the room if he never arrived, even if they didn't have rooms available."

Marc paused for effect before continuing. "You're going to love what the man said. He told William, 'Of course you would have been charged. We do have a twenty-four hour cancellation policy'."

Everyone laughed, but not me. I didn't think Marc even noticed, which troubled me since usually I was the one who laughed the hardest at his jokes.

Marc changed the subject. "Did I tell you? Jeffrey has a friend who has a home in Islamorada. He passed along the names of a few good restaurants. Also, he told Jeffrey where he keeps his spare key, in case we want to go over there to check out the house."

"Really? He doesn't mind four strangers wandering in his house?" Eric asked.

"Weird, I know, but he doesn't. Jeffrey told me that not much bothers him."

"That sounds interesting," Jaye replied. She loved real estate and remodeling homes.

I semi listened to the various ongoing conversations while staring out the car window, because I knew that I had a decision to make. I knew I could either spend the next few hours in the car, and the subsequent days sulking and being upset by Marta's words and what they represented, or, as I did the night before, put on my happy face and just enjoy the vacation. It wasn't a difficult decision, really. I knew that if I made myself miserable, all I would do is hurt myself, have a bad time, and bring everyone down. That was the last thing I wanted to do. Especially since this could very well be the last time I would vacation with Eric and Jaye. I knew it would be hard for me to shake my feelings, but I was determined to try.

I think Marc must have sensed something, because at that precise moment, he squeezed my leg. I turned to him and he smiled at me. "You okay?" he whispered.

"Yes, I am now," I simply replied, smiled, and nuzzled against him.

Eric and Jaye were oblivious to us in the back seat. Jaye was busy filling us in on the comings and goings with some friends of theirs in Utah. Marc and I knew them fairly well from when we had stayed out west. She was in mid-sentence about one of the lady's new job, when she exclaimed, "Oh no, I forgot to take the soup!"

Marc and I looked at each other and shook our heads, bewildered. "Soup?"

"Last night I made the most delicious butternut squash soup, for Christmas dinner." She explained, "I know we're in Florida, and it is hot, but it just seemed to fit. There was a ton left, so I packed it up in Tupperware to bring with us. But I forgot it at Lois's."

"Oh, I wouldn't worry about that," Marc answered. "I don't think there is any butternut squash soup in either of our futures anytime soon." I didn't have to put a game face on. His comment sent me in hysterics and it felt great to laugh.

"I'm confused," Eric said. "Besides it being a million degrees here, what is so funny about soup?"

"Not any soup. Butternut squash soup," Marc clarified, as he started to laugh with me.

"Okay..." Eric tried again. "I still don't get it?"

"Hilary had a bad experience with butternut squash soup recently," Marc answered.

"I did, did I? If memory serves me right, you didn't fare so well with it either, big shot!" I answered, punching Marc in the arm.

"Is anyone going to fill us in with what happened?" Jaye asked.

"Sure," Marc replied as he squeezed my leg yet again. "You know how Hilary loves to make soup, right? Well, she found a recipe online for butternut squash soup. Isn't that what happened?"

"Yes, I found a recipe online. And I followed it to the tee."

"Yeah, she sure did," Marc added. This earned him an elbow to his stomach.

"The recipe said to puree the squash and the broth in the blender, which I did," I said. "But as soon as I turned on the machine, there was an explosion. Soup went everywhere. I figured I must have not had the top on securely, so I rinsed my hands and shook the soup off of me. I put the top back on and tried to make sure I had it on very tightly. Once again, it exploded and soup and squash chunks flew in every possible direction. I figured the blender was busted. So I called Marc to fix it. He is good at fixing stuff, you know."

Marc picked up where I left off. "She didn't call me, exactly; she was screaming and cursing like a maniac. I calmly came to see what was wrong, and I found her in the kitchen, literally covered from head to toe in soup."

"It was quite an attractive look," I added.

He continued, "Yeah, you looked positively lovely. As I was saying, she was covered in soup, telling me the blender top wasn't working."

"Which of course, he didn't believe."

"They never believe us, do they?" Jaye asked. "So, what did he do?"

Eric sighed, "I think I have an idea."

"Yeah, I think you know, Eric," I answered as Jaye chuckled. "He paid me no mind, as if I didn't know a broken blender top when I saw one. In one swift and sure motion, he just covered the machine and turned it on! And it exploded yet again! This time, he too was covered in butternut squash, as was the rest of the kitchen. Whatever spots I missed, he took care of!"

"Yeah, I am glad you're still amused," Marc snarled. This time it was his turn to poke me. "She was almost victorious, yelling, 'See, I was right! I told you it's broken!'"

"Was it?" Jaye asked.

"No. Of course not." Marc replied, as he rolled his eyes. "The blender was fine, but the soup was boiling hot."

"Oh, no," Jaye replied, as she turned around in her seat to face me. "You mean you didn't know you couldn't put something hot in a blender?"

"No, I had no idea. Does everyone know this but me?" I asked.

"Yeah, I think so," Eric said, "Even I knew this one."

"And he can barely make toast," Jaye added.

CHAPTER 14

THE HUMOR OF THE butternut squash soup fiasco set the pace for the rest of the road trip's conversation as we headed south to the Keys. We were laughing and joking the entire way. We seemed to have made good travel time, and made it to the real estate office with time to spare. The agent was extremely nice and helpful, and told us about several restaurants in the area, including one we could walk to from the condo. That sounded heavenly to all of us, especially after spending the entire afternoon in the car.

The condo we rented was only a few blocks away from the real estate agent, and nestled in a quiet area off the beaten path, directly on the beach. The building was beautiful and recently renovated. It was five stories high, and our apartment was on the fifth floor.

We emptied out the rental car and made our way to the building's elevator. When we opened the condo's door, we were pleasantly surprised at how nice it was. There was a large kitchen with all new appliances. This would have been very handy if we had any intention of actually cooking, which we didn't. There was also a very comfortable living room which overlooked the ocean. Off the living room was an enormous balcony, which also faced the sea. In addition, there were two bedrooms, complete with king-sized beds and their own bathrooms. We instantly knew we would be very comfortable.

Eric had made sure to load up on wine and vodka before we met up with them in Fort Lauderdale, so we were able to enjoy a bottle of wine on the balcony before dinner. We decided to walk to the restaurant the real estate agent told us about, which was so close that we reached it in moments.

The restaurant specialized in seafood and was a throwback to years past. There was dark wood paneling on the walls, adorned with replicas of fish. The wood tables that filled the dining room were worn and cracked, but overall the restaurant had a very warm and homey feel. It was cheesy and cozy at the same time. The restaurant was packed with locals, but surprisingly, we didn't have to wait long for a table.

The hostess was extremely friendly as she sat us at a nice sized round table in the center of the dining room. The menus were huge, and Marc and Eric were thrilled to see Grouper on the menu. Both boys are obsessed with the fish, and instantly decided they were going to have Grouper Francaise before Jaye or I even glanced at our menu.

Eric ordered a bottle of wine, and by the time the waitress returned with it, Jaye and I selected on our entrees. I picked the Cajun mahi-mahi, and Jaye ordered a lobster. We also decided to start off with appetizers of raw oysters and clams on the half shell.

Jaye, like Eric, grew up in Canada. She was raised in Newfoundland, and lived right on the sea. Her father made his living as a fisherman, and her family was extremely poor. She was the youngest of four children and the only girl. She even remembered a time, when she was a very small child, that they didn't have indoor plumbing. Every time she ate lobster, she was flooded with memories of her childhood, and always shared the same story with us.

"I am still amazed at how lobster is considered a delicacy," she mused, as we all expected. "When I was a little kid, my brothers and I would help my dad catch lobsters for dinner, and my mom would cook them outside in a large pot of water. We would moan and groan every time we ate them, which was pretty much every day, because they were so easy to catch. We always thought of lobster as a poor man's food. To think that the rest of the world thought of them as a delicacy, it still surprises me."

As soon as she was done with her trip down memory lane, Eric raised his wine glass and exclaimed, "To vacation!" We all clinked glasses and echoed his sentiment, then sipped a delicious and oaky cabernet.

"Can you believe it is almost New Year's Eve already?" Jaye asked.

"No, I can't," I replied. "Where did this year go?"

"I have no idea," Jaye answered.

"Time really is going fast," Marc answered.

"Speaking of time flying, is it too early to make hotel reservations at the beach for this summer?" Eric asked. "I know the reservations fill up quickly, and I want to make sure Jaye and I can secure a room at the hotel."

"I think we can arrange something," Marc answered with a smile. "Right now we're wide open. The only reservation we have is around the Fourth of July. My dad is coming out that week for his birthday."

"Well, those vacancies won't last long, Jaye. We can't delay; we need to jump on the planning. Chop, chop! Look at it. We aren't even in January yet, and the hotel already has bookings. I can't imagine what our chances would be if we wait until February. This calls for immediate attention," Eric joked.

Eric, like Marc, always makes me laugh, and I was laughing away when Marc inquired, "When you are you guys planning on coming, anyway?"

"Probably in early August," Eric answered. "We have to go to Canada for my annual family reunion. So we're thinking that we'll stop off in New York for a few days, either before or afterwards. In all seriousness, we probably won't know our plans until very close to the trip."

Marc replied, "Okay, that makes sense. Early or middle August shouldn't make much difference." I took another sip of my wine. Then, as casually as if he were discussing the weather, Marc added, "I hope that I'll be lucky enough to be married to Hilary by the summer."

What????

I almost spit the wine across the table. Lucky for Jaye, I had quick reflexes. We might be married by August? What was he talking about? How is this possible? Did I get engaged and miss it?

I wasn't the only one bewildered by the comment. Jaye jumped back in her chair. "What did you say, Marc? Did you just say Hilary and you might be married by the summer?"

And with a shit-eating grin, Marc simply replied, "Yep," and took a leisurely sip of wine.

"Oh my God," Eric exclaimed as the waitress appeared with our appetizers. As she placed the seafood on the table, he turned to her and announced, "I don't believe this!" Pointing at Marc and me he continued, "Our friends here just got engaged!"

Her face lit up, she clearly was thrilled. I guess engagements, if that is what you would call this, don't happen every day at this restaurant.

"Congratulations!" she sung as she topped off all our wine glasses. "Drink up, drink up. Don't worry; the next bottle of wine will be on the house! I am going to go tell the owner!"

Eric, Jaye, and Marc were all smiles. Marc didn't say anything to either confirm or deny Eric's assumption, so talk of our engagement continued. I felt like it was last New Year's Eve all over again. Except this year the roles were reversed. I was the one caught off guard, and not sure what to feel. Part of me was jumping-for-joy happy, but other part was nervous. Sure, Marta's warning kept playing in my head, but that wasn't what was bothering me. Why would Marc, Mr. Commitment Phobic, casually announce our engagement to our friends before discussing with me? This wasn't how an engagement was supposed to happen. Was it?

As everyone spoke at record speed around me, I was quiet, desperately trying to process what had happened. Was Marc playing a game with our friends to avoid an uncomfortable scene like we had last year? It seemed like a plausible option, but if that was his plan, why didn't he fill me in first? How cruel would it be if this was all a joke and I wasn't in on it?

Or could Marc be telling the truth? Could he really intend for us to get engaged, and actually think that we might be married by the summer? Has he been wrestling with this thought for a while and just come to the realization that he wants this now? Or did he make his decision before we left New York? Could that be why he wanted to have dinner with my mom so badly before we left? I liked that idea a lot, and hoped it was the case, but I still couldn't understand why he announced this to Eric and Jaye before discussing it with me. Shouldn't the bride be the first one to know?

I desperately wanted dinner to end. Why did we order appetizers anyway? I needed to get Marc alone so I could get to the bottom of what was going on. My eyes darted around the table. Marc and our friends looked so happy, laughing and joking about our upcoming nuptials.

Marc must have sensed my confusion, because he turned to me and whispered in my ear, "Enjoy the moment. All is good." And then he gave me a long, deep kiss, right there at the table.

I did a double take. This night was getting more surreal by the second. Marc doesn't even like to hold hands, let alone kiss in public. And now, in the middle of a crowded restaurant, in front of his best friends, he was basically making out with me?

When he released me from his embrace, I was dizzy. My head was spinning from all the thoughts popping into my brain at record speed. If I was going to get through this night, I had to stop worrying about what was going on. So, I decided to just go with the flow. Maybe I was kind of, sort of, possibly engaged. Or maybe I wasn't. But either way, I wasn't going to be able to find anything out right now, so I might as well enjoy my "engagement".

I looked into Marc's eyes, and I saw love and joy radiating from him. I realized that in the end, it didn't really matter if we got married or not. I was thrilled that I trusted my gut, defied conventional dating wisdom, and gave Marc and my relationship the time and space to grow and flourish, although many other people probably wouldn't have if they were in my shoes. I was thankful that I got to know the man Marc really was, the man that even he didn't realize he could be. And if somehow Marc was serious, I knew that by the time our engagement was announced, I'd be an expert at celebrating. After all, practice makes perfect, and who else had this much practice?

Just as she'd promised, as soon as she brought our entrees the waitress appeared with another bottle of wine and four fresh glasses. "From the owner," she said with a big smile. "I told him the exciting news, and he was thrilled to be part of the special night." Then, like a scene out of a movie, as soon as she removed the cork with a pop, at the top of her lungs she called out to the crowded dining room: "Excuse me!" Some diners stopped their conversations, but the majority continued as if she hadn't uttered a word. Not to be deterred, she announced again, "I said, EXCUSE ME." A hush spread through the restaurant. The waitress proudly announced, with as much enthusiasm as if she'd known both Marc and me our entire lives, "Something amazing and romantic happened here tonight. This beautiful couple just got engaged!" Then she turned to us and asked, "Can you please stand up?"

I expected Marc to be hesitant, but he wasn't. He sprung from his seat, grabbed my hand, and pulled me up. "Everyone, please join me in congratulating them," the waitress said. Then she began to clap.

And with that, the restaurant went wild. People were whooping, cheering, and clapping. I had never seen such an outpouring of excitement from strangers. It was surreal. I looked around the room for a hidden camera. It definitely didn't feel like real life.

From across the table, I saw Eric start clicking his water glass with his fork. Within seconds, he was joined by practically everyone in the restaurant. Marc and I didn't pick up on the hint until an elderly man from across the room yelled out, "Hey! What are you waiting for, son? Kiss the pretty lady, already. I'm not getting any younger, you know!"

Marc didn't need to be told twice. He grabbed me and pulled me close. Once again he kissed me long, deeply, and most importantly, unselfconsciously in front of everyone in the restaurant, to the delight of the diners, which made them cheer even more.

Eventually the fanfare subsided, and Marc and I sat down once again. Eric raised his glass, and just like the year before, he said "Congratulations! To the happy couple! I hope your marriage is a long and happy one!"

CHAPTER 15

"SO WHAT THE HELL happened tonight?" I asked Marc as soon as we were safely alone in our bedroom.

"What do you mean?" he asked coyly as he slowly removed his sneakers and socks, then slowly sat down on the bed.

My nervous energy was getting the better of me. I paced around the room. Exasperated, I asked, "What do you mean, what do I mean? I will ask slowly. What... happened... at... dinner... TONIGHT?"

Marc patted the space next to him on the bed, gesturing for me to sit down, which I did, although I couldn't stop my leg from bopping up and down. Casually he replied, "Dinner was good, wasn't it? I loved my grouper. How was your fish?"

I shook my head in disbelief. "Fish? You're asking me about the fish? Have you completely lost your mind?"

He tried very hard to suppress his laughter. "No, I didn't lose my mind. You wanted to know what happened at dinner, didn't you? So I told you about my fish and asked you about yours. Isn't that what people do? Did you want to know something else?"

Despite my frustration, I couldn't help but laugh. "Yes. I want to talk about everything that happened except for the fish."

"Something else happened?" he asked.

I sighed deeply. "You are getting on my last nerve, mister! Do you think you can be serious for a minute?"

"I don't know, but I guess I can try."

"Good, try hard. I need you to focus. Can you please tell me what's going on? Why did you tell Eric and Jaye that we may be married by the summer?"

"Oh, that's simple. Because we may be."

"May be what? Married?"

"Yes." He replied, still grinning from ear to ear. *Who is this man?* I wondered.

"Did we somehow get engaged and I missed it?"

"No."

I rubbed my head, trying to fend off the headache I was sure this conversation would bring me. I couldn't help but wonder if I was the only person in the world who had discussions like this. "Can you please clarify? No, I didn't miss it, or no, we are not engaged? You are killing me, you know."

"Yes, I know I am. But that is why you love me. I am just so funny," he said, still beaming.

"Yeah, you are a regular riot. Now can you please answer my questions?"

"Fine... Be that way if you must. No was the answer to both of your questions. No, you didn't miss it, and no, we are not engaged. But don't worry, we will be engaged soon."

Why did I allow myself to get my hopes up? Would I ever learn? I'd heard the word "soon" before. After all, it was the magic word my dad used to put off my mother for six and a half years. I knew the drill and I didn't want to follow in their footsteps. I didn't want to have to break up with Marc for him to realize that he wanted to spend the rest of his life with me, like my mom had to do with my dad. The smile faded from my face. "Soon? What exactly does soon mean? Is soon a month, is soon a year, or is soon five years? Why are you doing this to me? Wasn't last year enough? Do I have to celebrate our engagement every year for nothing? I don't need practice, you know. It's starting to become cruel."

I got up and was going to head into the bathroom. But Marc didn't let me. He grabbed my arm and pulled me back down on the bed. He pushed a lock of hair away from my eyes, and tucked it behind my ear. When he did, he saw that my eyes were full of tears. "Why are you getting so upset?" he asked, clearly confused. "I thought you would be happy."

"I was happy. But now I don't know what to think. 'Soon' can be anything. I never know where I stand with you, and it is getting tiring and frustrating. I should have listened to Marta last night."

"Marta? What does she have to do with anything?"

I regretted mentioning her name. I didn't really want to get into that conversation, but what choice did I have? "Yesterday she told me that you will never get married. Ever. She said that we were just wasting each other's time. And she pretty much encouraged me to move on."

"She did what?" A look of shock spread across his face.

"Didn't you wonder why I spent pretty much the entire night in the kitchen? Since when do I love to clean that much, especially on vacation? I was upset. I tried really hard to put her words out of my head today. And I think I did a pretty good job of it... that is, until the "married" comment. But it's my fault. I shouldn't have let myself get so wrapped up in everything tonight. I should know better. I should be wiser by now. One day maybe I'll smarten up."

Before I could say anything further, Marc grabbed me and pulled me close. He kept me in his embrace for a few minutes. As soon as he let go, he started to speak. "I need you to listen to me. I have no idea why Marta said those things to you, I swear I don't. I haven't discussed my feelings with her at all. The only person I really speak to is my brother. I think that she was just vocalizing what she thinks. But her beliefs are wrong. Dead wrong! That is not how I feel. At all."

"Really?"

"Yes, really. Why didn't you tell me what she said last night, or this morning?" Marc asked in a soft and caring voice.

"I don't know," I answered. "I thought about telling you, but I didn't really see the point. I didn't want to have an awkward conversation and ruin our vacation. I figured we could talk about it when we got home... or not."

Marc fell silent for a moment, and then asked, "So do you still want to know what 'soon' means?" I nodded my head. "Soon means as soon as we get home."

"Really?"

"Yes... really. Would I lie to you?"

I wanted to say I didn't know, but I suppressed that urge. Instead I said, "No, but tonight was so weird. You were talking about marriage out of the blue, in front of Eric and Jaye. It was so out of character and so hard to believe."

"Yeah, I know. It wasn't easy for me to do, either. But I did it tonight. And I am doing it now, again. I have every intention of marrying you. I love you. See, I said it again." He was glowing.

"I love you too." I replied. Then I clarified with a small smile, "And I believe you. I think." Then I added, "Eric and Jaye will be in New York for the trade show a week after we get home. Will we be engaged before then, or after?" I needed to be sure.

"Before... definitely, before." With that, he leaned over and kissed me.

I was about to pester him with more questions as he lay down on the bed. He grabbed my arm and pulled me down with him "Okay, enough talking for now. Time for bed, it has been a very long day, and I'm tired."

How he could even think of sleep at a time like this was beyond me...

I quickly realized that sleep wasn't forefront on his mind. And even though we'd made love many times before, this time felt different to me. I think it was because finally I felt I had a secure place in his guarded heart. And I liked it.

When the sun started streaming through the condo's windows early the next morning, waking me, I had to blink my eyes in rapid succession, trying to clear sleep and the cobwebs from my head. Did Marc really, kind of, sort of propose, or was it all a dream? As I rolled over to face Marc, who was still fast asleep and snoring loudly, I realized I didn't have to pinch myself. He really did say all those things last night, and the more I thought about it, the more I believed him.

By the time Marc and I got out of bed, Eric and Jaye had a pot of coffee brewed. Marc and I filled our cups with steaming hot coffee and made our way to the balcony where we found our friends sipping coffee, and speaking in hushed whispers. As soon as they spotted us, their conversation came to a standstill. It was clear that I wasn't the only one perplexed about last night's chain of events, because as soon as Marc and I sat down, with not so much as a good morning uttered, Jaye began her inquisition. "Marc, I think you must've been drinking during the day yesterday. Were you drunk last night?"

Confused, he replied, "No, I wasn't drunk. Why would you think I was drunk?"

"Because you're being drunk is the only way I can think to explain the crazy things you said. You sure were on a roll!"

Marc and I exchanged a sly glance. Playing along, he asked, "Unusual behavior? Crazy things I said? What do you mean?"

Eric and I sat quietly, drinking our coffee. Jaye was getting agitated. I loved how she worried about me. "You said you and Hilary will be married by the summer. That is crazy talk for you. Why would you say something like that?"

"Oh, that." Marc answered as he took another sip of coffee. "I said it because it is true. We will be."

And then the unexpected happened—Eric and Jaye both were speechless, which was out of character. I had never seen either one of them at a loss for words, let alone both of them at the same time.

"Are you two okay?" I asked. "Marc, go check their pulses. They aren't speaking or moving. Are they even breathing?"

"Barely," Eric answered. "I think we are in shock. At least I know I am."

"I'm not," Jaye announced, doing a complete three sixty. "I told you that Marc was serious last night, didn't I, Eric?"

"No," Eric answered as he rolled his eyes at his wife.

"Pfft. I knew that you guys were engaged! I am so happy for you both!" Jaye got up and hugged us both, and then went into the kitchen for more coffee.

"Got to love that wife of mine," Eric smirked. "She just can never admit that she's wrong. Ever. She knew you were engaged, yeah right. She kept me up all night trying to figure out what happened. I need a nap, and it isn't even nine AM!"

By mid-afternoon, I couldn't contain myself one second longer. I'd been staring at the same page for ten minutes, not reading a word. I closed my book with a little too much force than was needed, and rose to my feet. I told the group, "I'll be right back. I just have to go back to the condo for a second."

Marc offered to come with me, but I told him no. I wanted privacy. Not wanting to take any chances of someone sneaking up on me in the condo, I went into our bathroom, closed the door, and punched my mother's phone number into my cell phone. After two rings, she answered.

"What's wrong?" she asked as way of a greeting.

"Sheesh," I replied. "Why do you always assume something's wrong?" I asked.

"Gee, I don't know. Maybe because whenever you call me in the middle of the afternoon, especially while on vacation, there usually is."

"No, that isn't true," I said, though I knew she was right.

"Then how would you describe what happened yesterday morning when you called me in whispered hysterics after you were reeling from your conversation with Marta? Nothing was wrong then too, huh?"

I moved my phone away from my ear and brought it to my face where I smirked at it and rolled my eyes. As soon as I returned it to my ear, she asked, "Are you back now? Your silence tells me I was right, which I already know. But go on. What do you have to share?"

In what felt like one breath, I relayed everything that had happened the night before as well as this morning. I expected my mom to be happy and excited for me. But instead she said, "Oh, that's nice."

"What do you mean, that's nice? Aren't you excited for me?"

"No. Not really."

"Why aren't you happy for me? You love Marc."

"Yes, I do. I think he is a very great guy, and I would love to see you married to him. But I will be happy and excited when there is something to actually be happy and excited about. Right now, there's nothing."

"How can you say there's nothing? I told you how he said we'll be engaged when we get home from Florida."

"It sounds great. And when you actually do get engaged, then I'll be happy. But right now, there's a lot of talk and no action. How are you so sure that what he said is going to happen will actually happen, especially after all the drama last year?"

"Are you saying he's lying?" My defenses were on high alert.

"No, I'm not saying that at all. Don't get so defensive. I don't think he'd lie to you, nor do I think he would intentionally hurt you. It's clear that he cares deeply for you. But you have to face the facts. He has commitment issues. I know it, you know it, and he knows it.

Why does my mom always have to make such valid points? I wondered as she continued. "Until he actually makes the move, you and he both have no idea if he will actually be capable of doing it. I know you don't want to think about that, and I don't blame you, but you should. You need to have your eyes wide open. I don't want to see you disappointed or hurt. Try not to get your hopes up. Okay?"

"Okay." I hung up soon after. I'd had enough of a reality check to last me for the rest of the week. What is it about mothers anyway? You never want to admit they're right, but let's face it, they usually they are. Oh, how I prayed that this time she would be wrong.

By the time the sun set and we left the beach, we were all golden brown. We showered and Eric made his famous grapefruit martinis. As we drank, we discussed where to go for dinner. "How about that restaurant in the real estate office's parking lot? What was it called again, Hil?" Marc asked.

"The Village Café," I answered. "The agent said it was great. Want to try it?"

"Yes," Eric answered as he poured out the contents of the shaker into four martini glasses.

"I really don't like you guys driving if we are going to be drinking. We aren't familiar with this town; I don't think it's a good idea," Jaye, the voice of reason, chimed in. "Why don't I call a cab for tonight? I saw a phonebook in the closet earlier."

A half hour later, there was a car sitting outside the condo waiting for us. The driver, Gary, was probably in his late sixties, with long gray hair that he wore in a ponytail. He had on an orange and yellow Hawaiian shirt, opened down to his belly button. The stereo was on full force, and Marc and Eric's favorite band, Led Zeppelin, was blasting through the speakers.

Marc, Jaye, and I sat in the back, and Eric sat next to the driver. "Sorry, let me just lower this music," Gary said as he reached for the volume control knob.

In unison, Marc and Eric yelled, "No!"

"You guys like to get your led out too?" he asked. "Excellent! I think we'll have a good time together."

When we reached the restaurant, Jaye went to pay the driver. "No, no, no," he replied as he shooed away her dollar bills. "I am picking you guys up in a couple of hours. Just pay me everything tonight."

"But..." Jaye started.

"No buts. I am not worried I am going to get stiffed; after all, you guys need to get home, don't ya? Go on, enjoy your meal, and call me when you're ready to head back." With that, he rolled up the window and drove away.

"Wow, people are so nice here," I commented.

"And trusting," Marc added, "not like back home."

In the restaurant, after ordering a bottle of wine, Eric told the waitress, "Guess what? Our friends here just got engaged!"

"Wow! Congratulations! How exciting!" she exclaimed. "Make sure to save some room for dessert. We have a killer key lime pie and dessert will be on the house, to celebrate."

"Thanks so much," I said. As soon as she was out of sight I turned to Marc and said, "So I think I understand this sort of engagement now."

"What?" he asked.

"All part of your master plan to get free stuff," I joked. "Right? Fess up."

"Yeah, that's exactly it. You found me out, I am willing to marry you to get a free slice of pie."

Eric once again raised his glass. "To the happy soon-to-be married couple!" We clinked glasses and took a sip.

"I know what I am having!" Eric exclaimed as soon as he opened his menu.

Marc followed suit opened his menu, and immediately closed it. Just as Eric did, Marc exclaimed, "I know too."

In unison Jaye and I guessed, "Grouper Francaise?"

As we waited for our entrees to arrive, Jaye, still sporting the rhinestone faux engagement ring, removed it from her finger and passed it to Marc. "I think you can do better than this, but just in case, do you need this?" she asked.

"No, I think I can do without it, but thanks for asking."

"So do you already have a ring for Hilary, Marc?" she asked.

"No, not yet, I want her to pick out what she likes."

Jaye beamed.

"There's no need for that," I announced. "I already have one."

All eyes turned to me. "How do you have one?" Marc asked, clearly caught off guard.

"I have my mom's. She stopped wearing it years ago, after my dad passed away. She always told me that I can have it anytime I wanted. When we get engaged, I want her ring. That way, I'll always have the three people I love the most with me at all times—my mom, my dad, and you."

"Oh, that is so sweet," gushed Jaye.

"Good going, buddy!" Eric exclaimed. Turning to his wife he added, "Why couldn't I have found a girl who had her own ring? You made me buy you one."

"And I was worth every penny," she said, "wasn't I?"

"I don't know about that," Eric replied, but the twinkle in his eye showed that he knew just how lucky he got in the wife department.

Marc, ignoring the banter, asked me, "Are you sure? You don't want me to buy you your own ring? You can always use your mom's diamond for something else, you know."

"Yeah, I know, but this is what I really want. I always have."

"I had no idea."

"Why would you. We never almost got engaged before, did we? Oh, yeah, we did once, but that didn't really count."

Dinner arrived and was even better that the night before. As promised, as soon the busboy cleared our dinner plates away, the waitress returned with plates of key lime pie. "Congrats again!" she exclaimed as she dropped off the sweet and tangy pie, and added, "On the house!"

When we were finished, Jaye rang Gary to pick us up.

As he drove us back to the condo, Gary asked, "Where are you folks from anyway?"

"We are from Utah, and our friends are from New York." Eric answered.

"I'm from New York too." Gary said. "I taught high school English on Long Island. As soon as I retired, my wife and I moved down here. Problem was I couldn't spend that much time alone with the missus, if you know what I mean. Wives! They could drive you insane! That's why I started driving this here car, to get a break from her."

Wonderful, I thought to myself. Finally Marc is coming to terms with marriage and commitment, and now he'll be talked out of it by a former English teacher turned cabbie!

"Now whenever she gets on my nerves I just tell her I have to do a pickup," Gary continued. "I get in my car, blast my tunes, and drive. Sometimes I actually have a pickup to do, but most times I just drive a few blocks to get away from her incessant chatter. You guys married?"

"We are," Eric answered smiling, "and our friends in the back, they just got engaged last night."

"Engaged, you say? Wow! Congratulations. Marriage is the best thing in the world. I wouldn't trade my wife for anything. Not even a million dollars. Just promise me one thing. If you ever meet my wife, never tell her I said that. It would ruin my image."

I guess everyone is a comedian after all.

*   *   *

The remainder of our trip flew by and followed the same easygoing pace as the first few days. Every morning we had coffee on the balcony, then went for a long walk on the beach, followed by a huge breakfast at a local eatery. The afternoons were spent lounging by the sea or exploring the town.

One afternoon we found ourselves wandering through Jeffrey's friend's house, still shocked he told us where the spare keys were. Another day we decided to walk through the residential area where we were staying. "Look over there," I called out, pointing to a parcel of land between two homes that had what appeared to be every type of fruit and vegetable growing. "How are there crops in the middle of a block?"

"I have never seen so many bananas in my life," remarked Marc.

"I've got to try one," Eric said as he walked up to the tree and picked one off.

"Get one for me too," Jaye instructed and Eric complied. Not to be left out, Marc also reached for one.

"Oh my, this is the best banana I have ever tasted in my life," raved Jaye.

"I know," Eric mumbled as he took another gigantic bite.

"Mmm.. It is so fresh," Marc added.

"Hey, give me a bite," I said to Marc.

Puzzled, he asked, "Why? You hate bananas."

He is right. There is nothing that I hate more, food wise, than bananas. Even as a little girl, I couldn't stand them. My dad once took me to dinner and ordered seven-layer cake for desert. When the waitress brought it to the table, I was shocked to see it contained bananas. I was so repulsed, and carried on so much about how gross it was, that even my dad, a man who never met a cake he didn't love, had to skip dessert.

"I know, but everyone is raving about them. I have to try it too. Maybe my taste has changed."

"Whatever." Marc answered as he placed his banana by my mouth and watched me take a small, cautious bite. A smile slowly spread across my face. "You like it?" he asked.

I nodded my head.

Triumphant, he turned to Eric and Jaye. "First I get her to eat salmon, then lamb chops, and now bananas. Am I talented or what?"

"Funny, Mister. Just for the record, I didn't used to eat salmon because I once got sick off of it. As for the lamb chops, my parents ate meat so well done that every time my mom cooked one, it was pretty much cremated with no taste. Just because you are a good cook doesn't mean you are a miracle worker, you know." As I took another bite of banana, I wondered if maybe it did. He really did have a way in the kitchen... and he really did help improve my eating habits over the years. But one thing he must have forgotten: his mad cooking skills didn't have anything to do with my lamb turn-around. His next-door neighbors, Ann and Warren, were responsible for that one. But I let it slide.

Every night, as dusk approached, we enjoyed either a martini or a bottle of wine on the balcony, and then got into Gary's waiting car. To Marc and Eric's delight, Led Zeppelin always was playing and he had a funny tale to share with us. To Jaye and my astonishment, pretty much every night we found ourselves back at the Village Café, toasting to our "engagement" and watching our boys eat grouper Francaise.

We must not have been the only one amazed at this. On our final night there, the chef, Francis, sent us home with his recipe.

CHAPTER 16

RETURNING TO WORK is never easy after a long vacation, no matter how hard you try to stay connected while traveling. This trip was no different. Even though I made sure to check my email every day while we were away, as soon as I walked into my office and saw my overflowing desk, all I wanted to do was cry. I didn't know which pile to attack first, there were so many of them, and everything looked so pressing.

To make matters worse, my head was not in work mode. Now that we were home, I couldn't stop wondering if Marc and I really were on the verge of engagement. I didn't want to discuss the possibility with anyone; I was afraid of jinxing it. The only people who knew that something was possibly going to happen between Marc and me were my mom, and of course Eric and Jaye.

Since I am normally an open book, it was difficult to discuss my vacation with my co-workers and friends. How could I talk about our trip without slipping about the big news? I knew the best solution to stop my worrying head, and control my loose lips, was to bury myself in my work. Fortunately for me, there was plenty of it.

Years ago, when I first started dating Marc, I was right in feeling that I finally found myself a career as opposed to a job. I had been with the same company for over six years, and as the company grew, so did my role. When I started, I left a position in a public accounting firm. I was a CPA and hated it. I used to wake up every morning and wonder how long I had left before I could either retire or die from misery. Not only did I find the actual work incredibly boring, I hated that I was never in the same place for any period of time. I was constantly going to clients, all over the New York tri-state area. And to make matters worse, since

I was the junior member of the firm, I had no control over where I went. I was never able to keep any type of appointment, and worse, I was never able to make any type of impact for my clients.

I wasn't surprised that I didn't enjoy accounting. I didn't have any sweeping desire to get into the field in the first place. When I graduated from high school and had to pick a college major, I wanted to pick something artsy, or something related to communications or journalism. But I was worried about getting a job after graduation. My cousin, who was fifteen years older than me and a partner in a CPA firm, suggested accounting. He pointed out that I was good in math, and made the winning argument that accounting was a good career choice for a girl. For whatever reason, I listened to him. It didn't take long to regret it, but I was in too deep. I didn't want to switch majors and extend my college tenure, so I stuck it out. When I graduated, I didn't even want to look for a job. I was content to continue waiting tables.

I thought my mother was going to kill me when I told her this. But rather than yelling at me or causing a fuss about how foolish I was being, she went shopping and bought me several gorgeous suits. Of course I fell in love with their strong lines and beautiful cuts. I knew I couldn't wear them to Friendly's to make a Happy Ending Sundae or a Fribble, so I decided to give the accounting world a try. The way to my heart always had been through my closet...

While I loved the outfits I wore to work, that was pretty much all I loved. I resolved myself to the fact that I would never enjoy doing accounting, and tried to make it through the days by amusing myself any possible way, which was no easy feat.

Then one day, my mom was at work, and her firm's accountant, whose office was in the same building as the law firm my mom worked at, approached her to see if I was happy with my position. She explained to him that I hated it, and asked if his firm was looking for anyone. He told her they weren't, but his friend, John, was. He gave my mom John's contact information.

I had no interest in calling this man. The prospect of switching jobs didn't really appeal to me, especially since I doubted that I would ever find anything in the accounting field even remotely rewarding or interesting. But after a little thought, and pep talks from my mom, and friend Cassie, I called John, and arranged an interview.

The day I was to meet him, I woke up with the worst cold imaginable. My throat was so sore and I couldn't stop sneezing and blowing my nose. I ignored my symptoms and went to work, as I usually do when I am ill. I was a hot mess. All day long I couldn't figure out how I would leave early to make my interview, or even if I should go to the interview, given my condition. But as my health deteriorated, I decided to use my cold as an excuse to leave my office early. My boss didn't mind. I think he was actually relieved that I wasn't going to infect the entire building.

When I got home from my interview with John, my mom couldn't wait to hear how it went. I replied simply, "Forget about it. I will never hear from him again."

"Why?"

"Take one look at me. I am a wreck! I refused to shake his hand; I didn't want to make him sick. Then I used up half a box of tissues. I was with him less than an hour. Who in their right mind would hire someone who looks like this?"

I must have looked even worse than I thought, because she didn't argue. "Don't worry about it," she said. "After all, you weren't even looking for a new job."

Fortunately, John saw past my disheveled appearance, and gave me a shot. He hired me as the assistant controller of his beverage alcohol distribution company. I went from being the junior person at the CPA firm, who wasn't allowed to make any sort of decision, including what color pen to use, to being responsible for managing a staff of three part-time people.

I didn't have a clue what to expect, but from my first week, I loved my new role. I never expected that I would love to get up and go to work in the morning, or that accounting could actually be fun. But it was. And since it was a small company, I had the opportunity to get involved in all areas of the business.

As the company grew, so did my role. I was promoted numerous times, and now I was in the role of Director of Finance and had a team of twelve full-time employees reporting directly to me. It was extremely rewarding but quite stressful at the same time.

All twelve people, it seemed, had some sort of issue while I was in Florida. On my first day back, my office seemed to have a revolving door. The hours ticked by at a record pace. When the dust finally settled, I was amazed to look at my clock and see that it was almost seven.

Only during my hour-long commute home did I allow my mind to wander back to the Keys. But every time I started thinking about the possible engagement, I forced other thoughts into my head, or just raised the volume on the radio. By the time I pulled into the driveway, the radio was on the maximum volume.

I knew Marc was equally as slammed at work, and I also knew that nothing would happen before the weekend. There was no sense in driving myself crazy. Marc's brother Jay's advice from the summer kept on ringing in my head: "Just let it be."

Work was no easier for me the next day. My to-do pile seemed to have grown exponentially. Coffee cup filled to the brim, I cranked up my iPod and started to dig into the piles.

I found my groove and was actually able to make some headway by lunchtime. Proud of myself, I was just about to take a walk down the block and grab a slice of pizza when the receptionist buzzed me. "Hilary, Brendan from Texas Distillers is on the phone for you. Can you take him?"

"Sure," I replied, thinking sadly pizza would have to wait.

Brendan was one of my favorite clients. He is a beverage consultant, and has worked for many of our clients during my six year tenure at the firm. His current venture was a client based out of Texas that specialized in ready to drink cocktails.

"Hey Brendan, how was your holiday?" I asked enthusiastically.

"Excellent. My son just turned five last month, so he was thrilled about Santa coming. It was priceless watching his expression as he opened his presents Christmas morning. Especially since my wife and I went completely overboard."

"You? Overboard? Why, I can't imagine that," I chuckled.

"Yeah, I know. Shocking, huh? How about you? How was your holiday? Do anything special?"

"Yeah, my boyfriend and I headed down to Florida with another couple. It was beautiful, and we had a really good time."

"Nice! So, want to get back on a plane?" he asked.

"Get back on a plane? What do you mean?" I was totally confused.

"I was going over all the reporting with the accounting team in Texas last week and try as I might, they just don't understand it. I spoke to the

CEO and he wants to fly you down to meet with them. I am heading down there next Thursday, so he wants your trip to coincide with mine. So what do you say, Texas on Thursday? Don't worry; you will only have to be here one day. You'll grab the early flight, and we'll get you to the office by 11:00. You will spend the day with the team; then we'll do dinner at night. I'll drop you off at the airport first thing Friday morning. You'll be home in time for dinner!"

Okay, this was not what I was expecting. There was no way I was prepared to head out of town now, especially with everything going on. Also, I haven't traveled for work in over a year. The last trip was to attend a trade show not to see a client. Why now, of all times, was this coming up?

"Gee, I don't know," I replied. "I have to discuss it with John."

"Of course you do. Can you try to speak to him today so we can book the flights and everything? We'll take care of everything, the flights the hotel, food, everything. Be sure to tell John that they are very anxious for you to come."

"Okay, Brendan, I will," I said as I hung up the phone.

My mind was reeling. I knew I had to speak to my boss. And I already knew what his answer was going to be. Of course he would want me to go. I needed to think quickly about how I could get out of this trip. But before I went to John's office, I called Marc.

"Hey, it's me," I said as soon as he answered the phone. "I need help," I explained.

"What is wrong?" he asked, sounding worried. Yes, I know I tend to be a bit melodramatic.

"I've a problem, and I don't know what to do. I just got off the phone with a client. They need me to fly down to Texas next Thursday for the day, and I can't go. I don't know what to tell John."

"Why can't you go?" He asked not understanding the problem.

I started with the surface issue. "We have company. I can't leave. Eric and Jaye are coming, remember?"

"Yeah… so what?" He asked. "You are only going for one day, right?"

"Yes, but…"

"But what? You just spent a week with them. They're in for the show. They'll be busy. I'll be busy too. You'd be at work anyway. So what is the big deal? You miss a dinner? Who cares? Go do your thing…

Have fun. Besides, Texas is beautiful this time of year. I think it is great you are going."

"You do?"

"Yes, I do. I'll talk to you later. I have to get on a conference call."

Ugh, I wanted to scream. Why was he so anxious to get rid of me? Why didn't he see the issue?

I knew I didn't have a choice. I had to go downstairs to John's office. Marc may not have helped me get out of the trip, but, I may have been able to pull a few tricks out of my sleeve.

I gently knocked on John's open door's frame. He looked up from his computer monitor and I asked, "Got a sec?"

"Sure. What's going on? I've barely seen you since you returned."

"I've been crazy busy, just the way you like me. I just got a call from Brendan. They want to fly me to down to Texas next Thursday to meet with their accounting department."

"Okay," he answered, with not so much as a shrug of his shoulders.

"I really don't think it is a good idea for me to go."

"Why not?" he asked clearly puzzled.

"I told you how swamped I am. Flying down to Texas is a colossal waste of time. I am going to spend two days traveling for what, a meeting that will last a couple of hours at most? What's the point of that? It's a waste of everyone's time and money. I can set up a conference call and do everything remotely. Isn't that so much more efficient?"

"You make a good point," he replied.

This was easier than I thought. Damn, I am good! I should've known John would see it my way. He is a smart man after all.

I started to get up and head to the door, looking for a quick departure before he could change his mind. "Great, I'm going to go and call Brendan now and tell him that I'll set up a conference call."

"Whoa. I didn't say to do that."

"But you said I made a very good point."

"I did, and you are right. It is a waste of time. But they are the client, and they're covering the airfare and the hotel, so who am I to say no? Besides, it doesn't matter if you and I feel that this meeting is a waste of time or not. *They* feel that it is necessary, and since they are the client, they deserve to have what they want. We are a service company, after all."

Crap!

"Yeah, I know," I replied, trying to think quickly. "But also it's the beginning of the year. I've so much to handle." I started rattling off all the pressing projects I was in the middle of while counting them on my fingers. As I got to my second pinky, I asked, "Don't you think it would be better for us if I focused on all this instead?"

"Of course," he replied. "But you are going to be gone for two days, not two years. There is nothing that you listed that can't wait for two days."

"But…" I started.

He cut me off before I could utter another syllable. "But nothing. Go back upstairs, schedule the trip. I get it, you don't want to go. Sorry, unless there is a valid reason why you can't go to Texas next Thursday, you are going."

With that, he picked up a report that was on his desk and started reading. I was dismissed, battle clearly lost.

He wanted a valid reason? I had one of those alright.

I was petrified to leave town right now. It was too close to when Marc said we would be engaged. How could I leave the state? What would happen happened if I missed my engagement?

I know that I wasn't thinking clearly, but given the circumstances, honestly, could you blame me?

CHAPTER 17

PRECISELY AT NINE O'CLOCK on Sunday morning, my cell phone rang. I didn't need to look at the display to know it was my mom. "That woman sure doesn't waste any time, does she?" I muttered under my breath. I shouldn't be getting angry with her; after all, it wasn't her fault I was in a foul mood. She didn't do anything to contribute to my misery. And I couldn't blame her for being anxious to speak with me. I knew that her curiosity was getting the best of her. While she may have been very negative initially about the possibility of Marc and my pending engagement when I called her from Florida, her hopes started to rise once we returned home. The more I filled her in about everything that happened on our vacation, the more I think she believed that Marc really was on the verge of proposing, and she was delighted.

All week long, I had confided to her that I was sure that if Marc was serious about popping the question before Eric and Jaye arrived back in New York, he would do so on Saturday night. It was the only day that made sense. I couldn't imagine him doing it during the work week. By the time we both came home from work and managed to make and eat dinner, we were barely able to keep our eyes open, yet alone plan our future together.

I knew Friday night was out of the question as well. We had long scheduled dinner plans with friends. And on Sunday, we were having an early dinner with Marc's entire family. His sister Ilene's son, Adam, a college senior, was finishing his winter break, and was heading back to school in California on Tuesday morning.

I was actually excited about the family dinner, as I always was. I loved spending time with Marc's family. As an only child I always longed to be part of a large, happy and loving family, and Marc's family was just that. When I came into Marc's life, I wasn't worried about how his siblings and their spouses would take to me, but I was concerned about the kids. Most of them were teenagers, and I was sure that they would all be so wrapped up in their own lives that they wouldn't be interested in warming up to their uncle's new girlfriend. I couldn't have been more wrong. From the first time I met them, they made me feel like a part of their lives.

As my relationship strengthened with Marc, so did mine with the kids. I would play games with the boys and go shopping and for manicures with the girls. Marc, who was the kind of uncle I always wish I had, loved that I was so easily able to become close with his nieces and nephews, who meant the world to him.

What he wasn't prepared for was the day when I came home from work and asked him how happy he was that his niece, Marla, got accepted into her first-choice college.

"What are you talking about?"

"Marla's acceptance letter that came today," I clarified.

"It did?"

"Yeah, didn't you know?"

"Nope," he replied with a pout and then asked, "How do you know?"

"She called me."

"Great, just great," he answered, feigning jealousy. "My niece has exciting, breaking news, and does she call me, her uncle who she knows since the day she was born? No. Of course not! Why should she? She has you now." He sighed, and added, "Oh, how easily I was replaced."

I gave him a million-dollar smile and said, "Don't be jealous, Marc!" But I knew he wasn't... he was proud and happy.

The still-ringing phone broke my reverie. "Hello, Mom."

With no time for pleasantries, she practically sang into the receiver, her excitement and enthusiasm getting the better of her. "So what's going on?"

"I am cleaning the fridge, if you really want to know."

"You're what?" she asked, sounding shocked. I don't think she expected that reply.

"You heard me. I'm cleaning the refrigerator."

"Oh, shit," she sputtered. "If you're cleaning at nine o'clock on a Sunday morning it can't be good." Worry crept into her voice. "What happened?"

I dragged out my reply for emphasis. "Absolutely... positively... nothing!" I couldn't stop the frustration and anger from bubbling up in my voice, although I managed to keep the tears away.

"Where is he?" she whispered. It was almost as if she was afraid that Marc could hear her. "Can you talk?"

"Marc is down the basement working out. He can't hear me."

"Do you want to come home?"

I paused twisting a long lock of hair behind my ear as I willed myself not to cry. "Yes, I want to so badly, but I am not going to. I am going to stay here. I can't leave now. God, I am so frustrated."

"I can only imagine. Can you please tell me what happened last night?"

I took another deep breath and poured myself yet another cup of coffee. I think I was on my sixth one already. But it didn't matter. I needed the caffeine to power what I knew would be an all-day cleaning frenzy. Scrubbing was the only thing that I knew to take my mind off my disappointment and anger.

"I told you already. Nothing happened."

"I got that part. I want to know what really happened. When I spoke to you yesterday morning, you sounded so happy."

"Yeah," I muttered, "I was." It was amazing how long ago yesterday morning seemed now.

I put my roll of paper towels and my bottle of cleanser down on the kitchen counter and sat on the stool by the island, so I could share my tale. "We had a great day. Nothing special happened. It was just a normal kind of day. We had some coffee. I read the paper and Marc worked on his laptop while we had coffee. Then I called you."

Trying to keep the conversation light, she answered, "Yeah, I remember that part."

"Oh. So, after you and I hung up, I worked out with Marc. When we finished, we had a steam shower before breakfast. It was really a cozy morning. I actually thought he was going to pop the question after the steam, but that didn't happen."

"Okay, that sounds good so far. Go on."

"After breakfast, we went out for a while. We ran a few errands. We hit Costco, Bed Bath and Beyond, and I dropped off some skirts that I needed shortened at Tony the Tailor."

"What happened when you got home?"

I took another sip of coffee, as I contemplated brewing another pot. But since my heart was already racing, and my leg jittering, I thought it was probably best I skipped it. "Then Marc's friend, Boya, stopped by. You know the one who helps him do work around the house?"

"The guy from Trinidad?"

"Yeah, him."

"What is he doing in that house now?" I knew that she really wasn't interested at this point, but she was trying to keep me talking. She knows that although I'm usually a chatterbox, when I am very upset I clam up and barely utter a word, keeping my emotions and fears deep inside, rebuilding my protective walls.

Although I knew her game, I kept talking. "He wants to redo the bathroom upstairs, the one by the living room. He wants to get rid of the tub and put in a stall shower, replace the tiles and make an entrance to the bathroom from the guest bedroom, so it has more of a suite feel."

"That sounds nice."

Absently, I replied, "Yeah, I think it will be." I knew bathroom fixtures was the furthest subject of interest on both of our minds.

"So what happened next?"

"While they were discussing the bathroom, I baked chocolate chip cookies. It was early evening by the time his friend left."

"And?" I must have been driving my mom crazy. I was stretching out the day so long, but I had a method to my madness. I was trying to replay every moment to see if there was any crucial event I missed that prevented Marc from asking me to marry him.

"We started to get organized for the night. Marc was going to grill filet mignon, so we seasoned them up. I prepared some veggies and cut up cheese for us to nibble on as an appetizer. Then Marc built a huge fire."

"Sounds like a lovely evening so far."

"It was. When I came into the den with the cheese, the fire was already blazing, and Marc had soft music playing on the stereo. He even lit a ton of candles. It was like a scene from a movie, it was so romantic. He opened a bottle of wine and told me that it was a very old burgundy. Apparently he has had it for about fifteen years and was saving it for a special occasion."

"Guess I know what you thought the occasion would be."

I shook my head, remembering. "Yep. I sure thought I did. What could be more special than our engagement?" My mom remained silent.

She didn't want to rub salt in my wounds. "So when he said that, my face lit up. I was so happy. He poured me wine and we raised our glasses. We clicked them, but he didn't offer a toast. He said nothing, but that isn't unusual for him. I wanted to say something, but I wasn't feeling creative, so I just said to us."

"We lounged around and chatted about nothing. I was anxious, but not concerned at first. I guess I thought he might ask me any time, so I figured that he was building the anticipation, you know, not wanting to rush the night or the engagement. After all, we had a beautiful evening ahead of us, right?"

"Yeah, well, it sure sounds that way. Did you?"

"Um hum." I answered, remembering. "It was really nice and romantic too. The filets were amazing. He cooked them perfectly. They were charred on the outside and ruby red on the inside. When we had dinner, he opened another bottle of wine, and again explained how it was a special one that he'd been saving. We ended up grabbing the air mattress we have in the basement and brought it upstairs and placed it right by the fire. I told you it was a romantic night, right?"

I am sure my mom was able to read between the lines. "Eventually a few hours later, we fell asleep in each other's arms. It was a great night. But it didn't end the way I expected. He didn't utter one word about marriage. Not one single solitary word. Nothing! Nada! Zip!"

My mom was silent, so I continued. "What was the point of such a romantic night if he wasn't going to do anything?"

"I thought you told me that you have romantic nights all the time?"

"Yeah, we do, but this time I was sure, based on everything that he said in Florida, it would be different."

"I don't know, maybe you guys fell asleep too soon."

"Mom, please," I said, exasperated. "We fell asleep hours later, not the instant our heads hit the pillows on the air mattress. There was plenty of time to ask me to marry him if he wanted to. "

"Maybe you're jumping to conclusions. Maybe he'll propose tonight," she said hopefully.

"Last week you were sure he was just putting on an act for Eric and Jaye, and now you think that he'll just pop the question sometime today? We're having dinner with his family tonight. Believe me, he will never propose in front of them."

"But…"

I cut her off. "But what? Why are you so hopeful anyway? I have to face facts. It didn't happen last night. It isn't going to happen tonight, it's not going to happen tomorrow. It is never going to happen. I was a fool to ever believe it would."

"Hilary…"

She tried to interrupt my rant, but I cut her off again. "Don't 'Hilary' me. This is my own damn fault. I was a fool to believe that Marc just miraculously changed his mind about marriage in Florida. I mean, come on. What dream world was I living in? I should have listened to Marta when she said that he would never want a commitment. I should have listened to you when I called you from Florida and you warned me that you feared this talk of marriage was just Marc's way to avoid a repeat of last year with Eric and Jaye. But did I listen? No, because I was a fool. Maybe one day I'll learn to listen to you."

Those are usually words my mom loves to hear, but this time, she said nothing. Her silence spoke volumes. She didn't want to be right. Not about this. She knew how upset and hurt I was, and there was not a doubt in my mind that her heart was breaking for me, just as mine was in a million little pieces.

"Hil, try to calm down. I really think that you should come home. I think that it will be the best for you."

"No, I'm not leaving," I said, adamantly.

"If you change your mind…"

But I cut her off, "Yeah, I know. I gotta go now. I hear him coming up. I don't want him to see me crying."

"Okay, but remember, if you need me, I'm here."

"I love you, Mommy," I replied before I hung up. I was so thankful to have such a great relationship with my mom, and to be able to express my feelings to her.

By the time Marc came into the kitchen, my tears were gone. I had my trusty bottle of cleanser in my hand and was feverously attacking the fridge.

After I made sure that every shelf sparkled, I made my way to the other appliances. I polished and shined the stove, dishwasher, and garbage disposal. Everything was so sparkling clean, I was able to see my reflection in the stainless steel finishes.

Once the kitchen was complete, I made my way through the rest of the house. I changed all the beds, even the clean guest bed linens that weren't used since I changed them in the summer. I did countless loads of laundry. I mopped the floors and vacuumed. I even used an old toothbrush to scrub the grout in our shower. By the time the sun began to set in the evening sky, there wasn't one crack or crevice in the entire house that wasn't spic and span.

Marc didn't know what to make of my cleaning frenzy. He never saw me attack imaginary grime with such vengeance before, except possibly at Marta's house on Christmas night. I don't think he even made the connections that my cleaning spree was related to me being upset and hurt. In fact, I think he was amused, watching me work my way through the kitchen. But as the hours ticked by, with me refusing to relinquish any cleaning products, I think he grew a little concerned, or more accurately, confused. He tried to get me to stop me many times, but I just couldn't sit still. So he did what any concerned, worried and caring man would do. He lay down on the couch and took a nap!

Finally as dusk fell, I squeegeed the last mirror in the house. The timing coincided with when Marc woke up from his nap. With the cat still resting on his chest, he called out, "Are you still cleaning?"

"Yep!" I said. "I've accomplished a lot today."

"I can only imagine. You've been at it since you woke up. I guess I need to cancel the cleaning lady this week."

"Yeah, that's probably a good idea."

"Well, can you wrap it up now? We have to be at the restaurant in about an hour. Want to freshen up a bit?"

I took a glimpse of myself in the mirror I'd just cleaned. While the house was spotless, I was a complete and utter mess. My hair was standing in every possible direction. My clothes were disheveled, with smudges on them, and I smelled like I'd bathed in a mix of Mr. Clean, Windex, and Fantastik. "Hmm... that's probably a good idea. I'll be down soon."

I slowly made my way up to the master bathroom. Exhaustion hit me as I cursed the number of stairs in this town house. I was sore in places I didn't realize I had muscles. I stripped out of my filthy clothes, turned on the shower full force and as hot as possible, and stepped inside. The steam engulfed me. I wanted the water to wash away not only the grime that was attached to me, but also the sadness and disappointment that I felt deep down in my core.

I stayed in the shower until my skin began to wrinkle. As I blow dried my hair, I stared at my reflection in the mirror and muttered, "At least I clean up well." I stalled as much as I possibly could. I tried on at least five pairs of jeans before I ended up wearing the first pair I put on. It wasn't that I was worried about how I looked; I was simply just dreading the family dinner. I wasn't in the mood to be social tonight. I wanted to be left alone so I could wallow in self-pity and mope, or possibly clean more, although I doubted I could find anything in this entire house that wasn't already sparkling and gleaming. I began to wonder if I'd made the right decision to stay here today, rather than heading home to my mom's.

As I walked downstairs, a thought popped in my mind. At least no one in Marc's family knew about what happened in the Keys with our almost engagement. I knew I hadn't uttered a word, and I was positive that Marc hadn't either, except maybe to his brother, Jay. The fact that I didn't have to worry about anyone bringing it up or questioning us about it was the only thing that made the thought of dinner slightly bearable.

"Hey, you look like a new girl!" Marc said with a smile as I joined him in the den.

"Yeah, isn't it amazing what a shower can do," I replied sarcastically. "I am going to feed Alex," I said as I started to turn around.

"No need," he replied. "I already did it."

"Oh, okay. I'm just going to..." I had no idea what I was going to do. I just felt the need to do something. Anything...

But before I could continue, he interrupted me. "No. You've been running around like a crazy person all day. Come. Sit with me for a minute."

I walked over to the couch where he sat, and eased myself down. I made sure to sit as far away as I could possibly while still being on the same piece of furniture. "What time do we have to be at the restaurant?" I asked, trying to make small talk.

"We should probably leave here in about fifteen minutes."

Neither of us uttered a word. We both sat there in uncomfortable silence. I didn't know about him, but I was lost in thought. I was desperately trying to give myself a pep talk and will myself not to let my emotions show, not now or later tonight. Marc was absently petting the cat, which, as always, was right at his side.

I noticed that Marc had a distant look in his eyes. I couldn't tell if he was troubled or upset about something, or if he was just in a pensive mood. I figured I was probably reading too much into his facial expressions because of my fragile emotional state. He probably had his mind wrapped around what to have for dinner. You know… the big, important decisions in life.

It was weird. I sat next to him, as I had done for the past few years, but something felt different. It was strange. Foreign… Marc and I had always been able to enjoy each other's company in comfortable silence, but this felt different. I had never been at a loss for words around him. Conversation and joking around always had come easily to us, right from the very first night we met in that Italian restaurant. But idle chatter seemed ridiculous at that moment, and I wasn't in the joking mood. I desperately wanted to talk to him, but I didn't know what to say, or how to start the conversation. And even if I did, how could I bring up what was really on my mind when we had to leave the house in fifteen minutes?

Marc took a deep sigh. I turned and faced him, but he didn't notice. He was focused on the cat, or so it appeared. I was sure my suspicion was right. Something was troubling him, I was positive about it. *What the hell*, I said to myself. I may not have been willing to tell him what was on my mind rightthen, but I sure was ready to find out what was on his. "What's with the sigh?" I asked. "Are you okay?" I think I sounded more put out then worried, but hey…

"Yes. No. I don't know," he muttered.

"All righty then... thanks for clarifying," I tried to joke. But he didn't so much as crinkle his face, yet alone smile. Instead, he did sigh again. This time, even louder than the first.

"You keep sighing. Is something wrong or not? You don't usually sit and sigh."

"You're right, I know, I don't."

"Yeah, well I know that. We have met before, you know." I was trying to lighten the atmosphere, but it didn't seem to be working. Marc appeared to be growing more troubled by the moment. "Are you going to tell me what's bothering you, or do you just want to sit and sigh until we leave for dinner? Or maybe we should just cancel dinner." That would have been my vote.

"No, we can't. It wouldn't be fair to Adam. He is going back to college in two days, and I didn't get to spend any time with him during his break. I promised him that I would see him before he goes. I don't want to disappoint him."

Now it was my turn to sigh. I am sure glad Marc didn't want to disappoint his nephew. How admirable. I wished he was as worried about not disappointing me as he was Adam. Did the promises he made in the Keys mean nothing to him? I knew that he wouldn't pick up on the sarcasm I wasn't trying to mask, so I replied, "Yeah, you wouldn't want to disappoint him, now would you? You are a wonderful man, I know."

Marc placed the cat on the floor and swiveled around on the couch so that he was facing me. He looked me directly in the eye and said, "We probably should talk before dinner." And then as if he was having a conversation with himself, he replied, "Yeah, we really need to talk."

Now I got worried. I was able to discount the sighs; maybe he was tired or something. After all, watching me clean all day had to be draining for him. But saying how we needed to talk was not Marc's style, not one bit. When he has something to say, he just comes right out and says it. He never announces it. In fact, he always makes fun when someone says "Can I ask you a question", or "Can I tell you something". Now, he was doing exactly what he was famous for mocking?

"Yeah, sure." Speaking slowly to mask my concern, I continued and asked innocently, "What do you want to talk about?"

"Um, well, actually, I don't know where to start."

"How about the beginning, it is a clever concept, huh?"

"Yeah, well, okay. But this is harder than I thought it would be."

I was getting a little impatient. What was up with him anyway? He was the one who wanted to talk, so why couldn't he just speak? "I'd help you start, but I don't know what's on your mind. Why don't you just spit it out? How bad can it be?"

I caught a long look in his eyes and I realized it could be very bad. But if it was, I liked the idea of him spitting it out even more. It would be like ripping off a Band-Aid.

"We really need to talk about what happened in Florida."

Shit! I knew it. I should have listened to my mom. I should have listened to Marta. I should have listened to my inner voice. I should never have believed that all of a sudden, over a bottle of wine with Eric and Jaye, in an old-fashioned fish restaurant, Marc totally changed his feelings about marriage. One day, maybe I would learn not to get my hopes up. How I wished I had never let those protective walls down in the first place. If I kept them erect, my heart wouldn't be breaking now.

"Okay. Let's," I replied softly, trying to sound calmer and kinder than I felt.

He once again fell silent. It was like he knew what he wanted to say but didn't know where or how to find the words. Finally, after what seemed like forever, he started to speak. "Things got a little crazy that night in that restaurant."

"Yeah, I know." I was determined to say as little as humanly possible, regardless of how hard it would be. He was the one who announced our engagement to our friends, and pretty much all of Islamorada, not me. If he'd changed his mind about us getting married, or worse, never meant it in the first place, I wasn't going to make it easier on him to hurt me. He was a big boy, and he would have to come clean on his own.

"I really got caught up with everything that night."

"Yeah," I replied. "You weren't the only one who did. We all did." My mind was racing. Caught up with everything? What does that mean?

"Yeah, that's true." And again he fell silent. Seriously, he was killing me. I wished he would just come out with it already. By now it was crystal clear to me that regardless of what the reason was, Marc and I would not be engaged. Not tonight. Not ever. I was mentally preparing myself. I would be disappointed, but prepared nonetheless.

"Marc, if you have something to say, can you please just come out and say it already? This beating around the bush isn't helping the situation."

"I know, I know. You are right. I know. I just don't really know how to say it."

"Try, please?"

He inhaled again deeply and rubbed his temple. "Okay, here goes. You know before you moved in, I never lived with anyone before, right?"

"Yes, I know."

"I don't mean just another woman, I mean anyone. I never even had a roommate, ever. I didn't know what to expect. So when you moved in, it was extremely difficult for me, to say the least, but I knew we had to do it. I thought that over time, things would have gotten easier for me, but..."

But? But what?

I looked at him. I really looked at him. I saw his defensive body language, as if he was bracing for a confrontation. I saw that his eyes were dark and stormy. I heard the regret in his voice, and instantly knew that the situation was worse than I'd originally thought. Not only did he not want to marry me, he was breaking up with me!

CHAPTER 18

AFTER A FITFUL SLEEP, I awoke the following morning still trying to process and understand what had happened last night. My emotions were all over the map. But I couldn't dawdle around the house trying to analyze my feelings. It was a Monday morning, and like it or not, I had to go to work.

I called my mom from my car as I drove to my office, the way I did every morning. I normally looked forward to our chats, as my commute was over an hour long on a good day. Talking with her always put me in a good mood and helped prepare for the day ahead. But after everything that had happened last night, I didn't really want to talk on the phone, especially with her. It was too hard.

My mom answered the phone on the first ring. I wasn't surprised. I knew that she would be anxious to talk to me after yesterday morning. I knew she was worried about me, and I didn't blame her. I would be, too, if the roles were reversed. She didn't offer a greeting when she picked up, she just immediately questioned, "How are you?"

"I'm fine. I'm just fine and dandy."

Her motherly antennae were on high alert. "That's funny, you sound anything but fine."

I didn't want to get into anything with her. Not now. I couldn't. "No, really I'm fine."

"You are not. Don't lie to me. I can tell. I can hear it in your voice. Talk to me."

"Mom, really, I am okay. I don't want to talk about it. Please."

"You know you'll feel better if you let it out. Come on. I know you're disappointed, but I'm worried about you. Please talk to me."

"Seriously, I'm okay. I will get over it," I answered, sounding calmer than I felt.

"Why are you doing this? Why are you shutting me out? I love you. I only want to help you."

"Yeah, I know. And I appreciate it, really I do."

"Good, so talk to me," she practically begged.

"Mommy, please," I answered as I merged onto the highway. "I don't want to. Not now. I can't. Please don't force me to. I will talk to you later, I promise. But I just can't do it now. I am driving and I have a day from hell ahead of me. I have three meetings with John and clients today. Not to mention I have to get ready for my trip to Texas, which I need like a hole in the head, especially now. And if that all that wasn't bad enough, I also have to conduct interviews for a new accounts receivable person. I need to get through today, somehow. I have to focus on everything that has to be done; I don't have time to wallow in my emotions."

"Okay, fine. Whatever you say..."

We chatted about nothing of importance for the next few minutes, and I told her that I'd be at her house later for dinner, as planned.

"Marc too?" she asked.

"Yes, Marc too." Marc and I had scheduled this dinner with my mom weeks ago, when she had to cancel right before we left for Florida. We made these plans and we were going to keep these plans, no matter what had happened yesterday. "Yes, we will both be there. I am going to hang up now. I will call you when I'm on my way home."

The beautiful thing about work was it was an excellent distraction. While I wasn't nearly as busy as I pretended to be, I was quite swamped nonetheless. Which was perfect, as it stopped me from fixating on last night's conversation with Marc. I made it out of my office at a reasonable hour and I called my mom on my way home.

Her tone was icy. I could tell she was angry as she said, "I have been trying to call you all day. I must have left five messages with Claire. Didn't you get them?"

"Yes, I got them. I told you I was going to have a day from hell, and I did. I didn't have time to go to the bathroom today, yet alone talk."

"Please. Do you think I am stupid? You had five minutes in the day to have called me back. I am worried about you."

"Don't be. I told you I was fine."

"Whatever."

"Listen, I am almost home. I'm going to take a quick shower and change. We should be at your house in less than an hour."

"Maybe we should cancel."

"What do you mean cancel? Why should we cancel?" Canceling was the last thing I wanted to do. I really wanted no, needed—to see my mom tonight.

"Oh, I don't know, maybe because you're upset and you are not talking about it."

"But Mom, there really isn't much to say."

"You don't want to talk to me fine. Don't. I am not going to force you. But you will feel better if you let it out. I know it and you know it too."

"I guess you're right," I replied. "But I am still processing everything. Can you please just respect this?"

"Yes," she quietly replied. "I can respect it, but it doesn't mean I agree or like it. So you are still going to come over?"

*   *   *

"Hey, Loretta," Marc greeted my mom with a big smile as she opened her front door.

"Hello, Marc," she answered, her tone Arctic cold. I don't think Marc picked up on it, but I sure did. As soon as we entered the hallway, she grabbed me and hugged me tight. Whispering in my ear, she asked for what felt like the millionth time today, "Are you okay?"

"Yes, Mom, I am fine." But just like the eleventy million times she already asked me today, she still didn't believe me.

"We brought some wine," Marc told her as he held out two bottles of Cabernet.

"Oh great, thanks." She took them and carried them into the kitchen. Marc and I trailed behind. "I sure can use a drink today, but I already started," she answered as she picked up her tumbler of scotch.

"Rough day, Loretta?" Marc asked.

"You could say that," she retorted. As she handed Marc a corkscrew from one of the kitchen drawers she said, "Marc, why don't you open the wine for you and Hilary, I am going to stick with the scotch. Hilary, go get two glasses, and then let's go into the den."

I walked into the dining room, opened up the china cabinet where we kept the wine glasses and pulled two out, which I handed to Marc. As he filled them with wine, I took a deep breath, and thought to myself this was going to be one strange evening.

We all walked together into the den. My mom had quite the spread waiting for us... a large serving tray filled with cheese, crackers, chips, dip, and assorted vegetables.

"Wow, Loretta," Marc said. "There is so much! There are only three of us, you sure went all out."

Normally, my mom would smile and joke with him. She would tell him that she wanted to make sure we didn't want for anything. But not tonight! Tonight she was angry, and she wasn't good at masking her emotions. "I made what I wanted to. If you don't want it, don't eat it."

I reached for a chip and dipped it. "Yum, I love onion dip, Mom," I said, popping it into my mouth.

"I know, that's why I bought it. I would do anything for you. All I want is to see you happy." I looked at Marc as he casually reached for a chip, and realized he was totally oblivious to what she was trying to express. In fact, I didn't even know if he'd picked up on her attitude.

"Mmm, the dip is good, Loretta," he agreed.

My mom smiled a small, almost invisible grin. In fact, it was actually more of a grimace.

"So, how was work today?" I asked as my mom reached over and nibbled on a piece of pepper jack cheese.

"Fine."

"What happened with Meredith today?" I asked, trying to make conversation. My mom was a legal secretary. She works for a single practitioner attorney who shared office space with a small firm. Meredith worked for the other firm. She had been there for about twenty years, joining the firm right after high school. When the founder retired, his son took over the firm. Rumor had it that he had to promise his dad that he would keep Meredith on no matter what, and he had. The problem was that Meredith was very insecure, and jealous of all the other secretaries in the firm. Every time they hired a new secretary, Meredith started trouble, until the new hire ultimately quit or got fired for fighting with her!

Since my mom worked for a different firm, she was immune to Meredith's shenanigans. This was quite fortunate, because some of the stunts that Meredith pulled over the years had been quite outlandish. My mom always had a good Meredith story to share.

"Nothing," my mom replied.

"Did the new girl quit already?"

"No, she's still there. But nothing happened." The expression "the apple doesn't fall far from the tree" sure held true for me and my mom. Just like me, my mom can talk to anyone about anything. I was convinced she could carry on a conversation with a shoe. But the moment she got upset or angry with someone, she clammed up. This was exactly what she was doing now.

"I'm going to get the salad ready," my mom announced as she rose from the couch. She grabbed her scotch before heading into the kitchen.

"Aren't you going to help your mom?" Marc asked as soon as she left the room.

"Aren't you going to tell my mom about last night?" I countered.

"Yes, I told you I would," he answered, showing no emotion. "And I will."

"When? She knows something is up. Can't you see how she is acting? She has been calling me all day. She's driving me crazy."

"I will tell her after dinner."

"After dinner?" I wanted to make sure I heard him right.

"Yes. That's the way these things are done." Did he suddenly become an etiquette expert or the new Mr. Manners? I wondered, as I watched him casually reach for a carrot slice. He smeared it in the dip and as he bit down on it, exclaimed, "I really like this dip. I don't know why I never buy it."

I rolled my eyes and headed into the kitchen. Leave it to him to be focused on food at a time like this. Men!

"What can I do to help?" I asked my mom, who was filling a bowl with all the salad fixings that she'd clearly prepared earlier that evening.

"Nothing, I don't need your help. Why don't you go back to the den and keep your boyfriend company." The way she said "boyfriend" made it sound like a bad word. How I wanted to scream out that he wasn't my boyfriend, but I guessed that was going to have to wait until after dinner, because apparently that was how these things were done.

Every time I tried to help her, she shooed me away. I didn't know what to do, so I went into the bathroom to buy a few minutes. Staring at myself in the mirror, I had a silent conversation/pep talk with myself to try to help me make it through the meal. I flushed the toilet for good measure, and then joined my mom who had just finished up the salad preparation.

"Grab the snacks from the den and tell Marc to sit down in the dining room." Again, the way she said 'Marc' made it sound like a four-letter word—which, I guess, technically it was.

I walked into the den and saw Marc casually sipping his wine, as if he didn't have a care in the world. He was apparently oblivious to the tension in the air. "My mom has the salad all set. Come on," I said as I started picking up the snacks. Marc carried half of them into the kitchen. My mom was in the bathroom when we got there, so silently we put the leftover food away in the fridge.

She emerged a few seconds later and I grabbed the salad bowl and carried it to the dining room. She was right behind me with four different containers of salad dressing. We all took our usual seats at the oblong table. Marc sat at the head, facing the den; I sat to his right, closest to the kitchen door; and my mom was to my right. "Hand me your bowl, Marc," she said, and he obediently did. As she filled up his bowl, she faked a look of shock. "Oh my. I put olives in the salad. I forgot that you don't like them."

I knew she hadn't forgotten about Marc's dislike of olives. She forgets nothing, which really can be quite a pain in the ass. Marc may have been oblivious, again, but I saw right through her. She was trying to send Marc subtle hints of her disappointment. But I was the only one who noticed. "Don't worry about it," he answered. "I'll give them to Hil." And as soon as my mom filled my bowl, that was exactly what he did.

We began to eat our salads in silence. It was deafening to me. I knew I couldn't make it through a meal in silence like this. My mom wasn't about to start a conversation, and since I had been shooting Marc daggers with my eyes, every time he was about to open his mouth, I knew he wasn't about to, either. So if this meal was going involve any conversation, I knew it was up to me. "Did I have a day today," I mused.

"I know, you were very, very busy today," my mom commented. Her tone was killing me.

"Oh, yeah, you had all those interviews, didn't you?" Marc asked. "How did they go?"

"Not so great. Interviewing is a torture test, I swear. I was hoping to have found someone today so I won't have to do more tomorrow, but no such luck. It is so nerve wracking."

"I know about nerve wracking days," my mom said. "And Hilary, can you please pass the dressing?"

As I reached over, Marc asked, "So what happened?"

"I don't even know where to start. Oh, I know. Let's start with how many people schedule interviews and don't show up to them. Do they even call to cancel? No! Why would they do that? I mean, really, how rude and inconsiderate is that?"

"It must be disappointing," my mom commented. "Some people have no idea how their actions affect and hurt others, now do they?"

I looked at Marc. Oh, God bless him, he had no clue that she was commenting on anyone besides job seekers. Her snide remarks were going right over his head, or so it appeared.

"But then the ones that showed up. UGH! What a bunch of characters! Let's see. Where to start?" I paused, pondering. "Oh, I know. First there was the guy who brought a fresh copy of his resumé with him," I said as I rolled my eyes.

"What's wrong with bringing a copy of his resumé?" Marc asked

"Nothing is wrong, if he had any of the same work experience shown on it. He totally redid it so that nothing on the first version was on the second. I am all for constantly tweaking, but bringing in basically a brand new resumé is too much, don't you think?"

"You do have a point there," Marc replied, picking yet another olive out of his salad and putting it into my bowl.

"I don't know if I see anything wrong with that," my mom said. "If he had a change of heart about what he said—I mean, wrote—isn't it better that he just fixed it, rather than proceed with a façade? Wouldn't it be worse if he lied and got your hopes up for nothing?"

I had to give my mom props for all her double entendres today. The woman was on a roll.

"Yep, but coming clean at the interview?" I looked around the table. It was working, we were all talking. And yes! We were almost done with salad. "But do you want to hear about the best interview of the day?"

Marc answered, "Sure."

My mom, with less enthusiasm, replied, "I guess so."

"Okay, so this kid comes in. He just graduated from college in December. Clearly this was one of his first interviews. I do my whole shpiel about the company, and when I mentioned we were in the alcoholic beverage business, his eyes lit up, and do you know what he said?"

I paused for a second to see if anyone took the bait and would offer a guess. When my question was met with silence, I exclaimed, "He said, 'cool, I like to party!' Can you believe that?"

I should have known my mom would have had a reply. "At least he's honest," she offered as she rose from her seat and started to gather up our salad plates. I got up from my seat to help her. As I did, I shot Marc a look which I hoped he understood: *help me here.* I don't think he picked up on it at all. He just grabbed the wine bottle and topped off our goblets. I was thankful he'd brought the second bottle, though we hadn't yet come close to finishing the first.

"Hey, Loretta," he called out. "Do you want to switch to wine?"

"You know, I never like to mix, but I think I will risk it tonight."

From the corner of my eye, I saw him go to the china cabinet and grab a glass for her. She turned to me and whispered, "What is the worst that can happen. I get sick? I already feel like shit, knowing you are so upset." I sighed deeply in response as I loaded the salad dishes into the dishwasher.

"Here you go," my mom called out as she placed a big tray on the dining room table. "I made your favorite, Marc."

Marc glanced at the heaping plate and smiled wide. It was potted chicken, cooked in a light tomato broth, with potatoes, string beans, and carrots. Personally, I never cared for it, but Marc goes wild for it every time she prepares it. Knowing how much he enjoys it, without fail, my mom always makes it when we come over.

"Wow, Loretta, this is amazing," Marc announced as he savored his first bite. "Each time you make it, somehow it seems better than the last."

With a hint of a smile, she said "I am so glad that you enjoy it." I was waiting for another gem but she didn't follow up with any. She fell silent.

I was afraid the silence would continue, so I racked my brain for a humorous story to tell. "Hey, did I tell you what happened to me last week at work with my stress ball?"

My mom and Marc both shook their heads. "Good. It's pretty funny. When Danny went on vacation last month, he picked up a stress ball for me as a souvenir, 'cause he knows I'm always stressed at work and that I can never sit still, especially while I am on the phone. It was the best... present... ever! I started using it immediately. Every time I took a call, I would squeeze the ball. It was great! I was on the phone with Elliot the other day..." I turned to my mother and clarified, "Mom, you know Elliot. Remember he was the guy that once bought us lunch when he saw us in the pizza place."

"Oh, yeah. I remember him. He seemed like a very nice man," she answered as she took a sip of wine.

"So I was on the phone with him, and thank God it was him, because as I was sitting there squeezing my ball... in mid-sentence I couldn't help it. I screamed out, 'oh shit!'"

"Very professional," Marc interjected.

I chuckled, "Yeah, I know. Not my finest moment. But I couldn't help it. Elliot, knowing me so well, asked what I did this time."

"Even your clients know you're a klutz," Marc joked.

"Yeah, I am world renowned for the messes I get myself into." I took a sip of wine.

"Sorry to interrupt. Loretta, can I have some more chicken?" Marc asked, and my mom obliged. The man really loved this dish. I, on the other hand, was struggling to eat, as the knots in my stomach grew.

Picking up where I left off, I continued, "I kept muttering 'oh my God, oh my God'. But finally I found my words. I told him that as I was talking to him I broke the stress ball. There was sand everywhere, and when I say everywhere, I mean *everywhere*. My desk, my keyboard, everything was covered in sand. I was blabbering. I asked him what I was going to do. Calmly, he told me, 'first, you're going to pull yourself together. Second, you're going to clean up. Then third, you are going to call me back.' I think he may have hung up on me, but I'm really not sure."

Marc was enjoying the story, and laughing. My mom was picking at her chicken. Like me, stress and aggravation wreaks havoc on her stomach. I continued with my tale as I moved the chicken around my plate. "So my team must have heard my scream, because several people came running into my office. One girl brought an air can. Another brought a roll of paper towels. One of the guys took apart my keyboard to clean it. As we all feverishly tried to clean up my desk and the surrounding area, Steve, ever the jokester, paged the office and announced, 'we have a spill on aisle four'."

I was laughing at this point. "But that wasn't the best part," I continued. "Eventually I called Elliot back, and when I did, you know what he told me?"

I paused for effect, but no one had a guess. "He told me that he always knew I was a ball breaker, and now had the proof!"

I glanced over at my mom, and she was genuinely laughing this time. Score one for me. It was the first time all night that she looked like she was having fun, which made me feel better, because thankfully dinner was done.

I helped my mom clean up. As I walked into the kitchen with the last dinner plate, I glared at Marc. In a hushed whisper, I said, "Dinner is done. Are you going to finally speak to her?"

He flashed me a pearly white grin and simply said, "Yep."

Moments later I emerged with a tray of assorted cookies, as my mom carried a carafe of coffee. She offered a cup to Marc, which he declined. I accepted. Marc took a bite of cookie, and then placed the remainder on his napkin. He turned to me and said, casually, "Hilary, last night at dinner, did you happen to see the rings my sister was wearing?"

"Yes. I saw them."

"They were my mom's diamonds. Ilene redid her engagement ring and wedding bands to use my mom's diamonds after my mom passed away."

"I know," I said. "Your sister once told me."

I glanced over at my mom and saw her give Marc the stink eye. I could only imagine the thoughts that were swimming in her brain. I was sure she was thinking, first, you break my daughter's heart, and now you have the audacity to talk about your sister's engagement ring in front of her and me.

If Marc picked up on the daggers she was shooting him with her eyes, he ignored them. "Isn't that nice, Loretta?"

He would have had to be blind to miss her exaggerated eye roll as she answered, sarcastically, "Oh, yes. It is just lovely."

"Yeah, I think so too," he answered, undeterred by the sudden chill in the air. "You know, Loretta, Hilary wants your diamond."

"I know," my mom answered, staring straight at him with anger in her eyes. Clearly, she was ready for war. "She can have it any time she wants."

"I think she wants it now," he answered softly.

Still upset, she replied, "Like I said, she can have it anytime she wants it. She can have it now if she wants it now. Actually, as far as I am concerned, it's hers. She can do anything she wants with it. She can make earrings with it. She can make a necklace with it. She can even make a ring out of it. She can do can do anything she wants with it."

"I think she wants to make a ring out of it, Loretta."

Clueless, and still angry, my mom spat back, "If she wants a ring, she can make a ring. Like I said, it is hers. She can do anything she wants with it, anytime she wants to."

"Good," Marc said, as his smile deepened. "So she can make an engagement ring out of it?"

"A what?"

"Can she make an engagement ring out of it?" Marc repeated before clarifying, "Because we are engaged."

I watched my mom's face as it transitioned from shock to sheer joy. But no words came out of her mouth. She was completely and utterly speechless. I jumped up out of my chair and hugged her. Marc got up next and hugged her next. And then Marc kissed me.

We both sat down and waited for her to form words, which proved to be more difficult than anticipated. "You??? You??? Agh, agh, arr, are what?" she stuttered. "You are engaged? What? When? How?"

I smiled first at Marc, and then turned to face her, "Yep, you heard him. Marc and I are engaged," I sang.

"What?" She asked again, clearly disbelieving my words.

"Yes, we really are engaged." I grabbed Marc's hand.

"What? When?" In my life, I have never heard her struggle so hard for words.

"We got engaged last night!"

"What do you mean last night?" she asked, her communication skills having returned. "You didn't tell me this. How did you not tell me? All day, I was worried sick. You stinker," she exclaimed, and then started to just talk in circles repeating everything she already said. "You stinker! How could you do this? How could you not tell me? Is this why you were avoiding me? You are engaged? You stinker!"

"Yes," I answered. "Do you know how hard it was to avoid you all day? You called me like twenty million times."

"I wasn't that bad."

"Oh, yes you were." I got up and hugged her again. "I couldn't talk to you today because I knew if I did, I would slip and tell you the news. But I promised Marc I would wait until we were here tonight to tell you so we could do it together."

"Really?"

"Yes, really," I replied with a smile.

"I still can't believe you kept this from me all day. How did it happen? I need details!" she demanded. "I thought you guys were going out to dinner with Marc's family last night."

"We did," I answered, as Marc sat there with a shit-eating grin on his face. "It was pretty crazy. When I spoke to you in the morning, I really was upset. I was so hurt and angry that I spent the entire day cleaning. Then, right before dinner, Marc asked me to sit down with him. He was acting all weird, sighing, rubbing his temples. It took a while for him to actually get words out of his mouth. When he did, he started talking about how things got out of control in Florida. So I immediately thought that he regretted saying to Eric and Jaye that we would be married by the summer."

I turned to Marc and saw he was still smiling. "So then he starts telling me how before I moved in with him, he never lived with anyone, not even a roommate. He said how difficult it was for him to have me move in, and how he thought that over time, things would have gotten easier for him. Then he paused, and said *but*."

My mom was literally on the edge of her seat as I continued the story. "As soon as I heard the word 'but', I feared the worst."

Marc let out a laugh. "Feared the worst, Hil? Loretta, catch this one... she thought I was breaking up with her!"

My mom didn't say anything. She just sat there, wide eyed, waiting for us to finish the story.

"Yeah, I did think you were breaking up with me," I said to Marc, gently punching him in the arm. "Is that so farfetched? Really? Especially with the way you were acting and all?"

Sheepishly, he answered, "I guess not."

"Can I continue?" I asked.

"Proceed."

"I did think he was breaking up with me. I really did. I thought that things had gotten too heavy for him, with the marriage talk, and all. I wanted to be wrong, so I asked him, but you are happy, right? He looked at me as if I'd lost my mind. Given the situation, I don't think that was a crazy question, do you?" I asked my mom.

She shook her head, agreeing with me, which I knew she would do. I continued, "Well, he thought it was crazy."

"Yeah, I actually said to her, 'what kind of crazy question is that?'" Marc clarified.

"I said, 'I don't know, are you happy?' But he didn't answer. I started to get more nervous. My heart was beating so hard. My stomach did flip flops as I waited for him to say something, anything. Finally, he asked if he could continue. So, I said okay, as I braced myself."

Marc, clearly enjoying himself, added, "So, I had to start all over!"

"And he did," I continued. "He started at the beginning. Once again, he said, 'Before you moved in with me, I never lived with anyone, not even a roommate. It was very difficult for me to have you move in. I really thought things would have gotten easier over time, but I never expected it to be this easy. Now that you are living with me, I can't imagine living any other way except with you by my side.'"

I looked at my mom, and she was beaming. Marc was beaming. And I was beaming as I finished the story. "And then he asked me to marry him!"

I looked first at Marc, and then at my mom, who had tears running down her face. I hugged her again as I asked, "So are you happy for me?"

"I am beyond happy for you. I am thrilled for both of you. You have no idea how happy I am! I love you! And I know you two are perfect for each other!" She turned to Marc and said, "Come here, let me give you a hug." And when she did, she whispered, "I love you too. Take care of my baby."

Marc replied, simply, "Always. I love her, Loretta."

And I knew he meant it with all his heart. I never was so happy, or had felt so secure, in my entire life.

CHAPTER 19

THE MORNING AFTER we shared our wonderful news with my mom, she went into work late. She first wanted to stop off at the bank where she kept her diamond ring to get it out of the vault. She came over to our home later that evening for dinner, and proudly and happily handed the ring—the ring that her husband had given her so many years ago—to her future son-in-law, with tears of joy in her eyes.

Two days after we shared our news with my mom, Jaye and Eric arrived for the annual trade show. As Marc had promised in Florida, we were engaged for their arrival. Of course, they were delighted. I flew to Texas the following morning for my business trip. As I stared at the passing clouds, I kept feeling the need to pinch myself. I was that happy.

I had been home from my business trip for about a week, and no one besides my mom, Jaye, and Eric knew about our engagement. I couldn't help but wonder if Marc's silence about the announcement meant he was having doubts. I knew I should have stopped thinking the worst by now, but I couldn't help it. Worrying was in my nature. I took after my mom, whose father once joked that she should become a professional worrier, where given her talents, she could earn a fortune.

Marc and I were in the waiting room of his eye doctor, awaiting his yearly exam, when I broached the subject. "I've got a question for you," I announced as I put the magazine down that I was thumbing through. "Are you ever going to tell anyone about us?"

Marc looked at me, puzzled. "What do you mean?"

"Um, our engagement," I clarified. "Are you going to tell your family about it? No one knows anything yet."

"Oh, yeah. Sorry. I guess we should have done it already. It's just been crazy with the trade show and all." Before I could say anything further, he took his cell phone out of his pocket and started dialing. "Hey, Jay, it's me," he said to his brother. "I'm actually close by your house right now, at the eye doctor's. Do you have any plans for dinner?" He paused for a second, listening to his brother. Then he replied, "Good. Hilary is with me, we should be done in about an hour. Where can we meet you?"

Marc put the phone back into his pocket and turned to me with a huge smile. "So is tonight soon enough for you?"

Just as he did with my mom, Marc didn't mention anything to his brother or sister-in-law during the entire dinner. This didn't surprise me; this was how these things are done, after all. It was only when the waiter brought over our check and some complimentary biscotti that he brought up the subject. It was no surprise that he made the announcement in the same roundabout way that he did with my mom.

"Susan," he asked casually, "Do you have a jeweler that you can recommend?"

"Yeah, sure," she said. "What are you looking for?"

"Hilary's mom is giving her the diamond from her engagement ring. We want to have it reset."

Susan's reaction, coincidentally or appropriately, mirrored my mom's. "What do you want to make?" She turned to me. "Are you looking for earrings, a necklace or do you want to make some sort of a ring?"

I turned to Marc. I wanted him to share the news with his family. "We are looking for a ring, actually," he clarified.

"Oh, that's nice," Susan replied nonchalantly, "any particular kind?"

"Yeah, as a matter of fact, yes. We are looking to make an engagement ring."

Susan asked, "Why?" (You've got to love how Marc keeps getting asked why. Everyone sure had nailed his issues.)

Marc, as proud and excited as he was at my mom's house, exclaimed, "Because, obviously, Hilary and I are engaged."

Tears streamed down Susan's face as she got up from her seat to hug me. Jay pretty much flew across the table to grab ahold of and embrace his baby brother. They were both clearly thrilled and a lot in shock.

Marc's sister, Ilene, was in Florida with her husband and daughters visiting their dad and Marta at the time. Marc didn't want to wait until she returned to New York to share the news, especially since he'd already told his brother.

Marc called me at work the next day. "I phoned my dad's first," he reported, as soon as he hung up with his sister. "I figured I could tell everyone at once. I thought she would be at the house or at least by the pool with the kids, but she wasn't. He told me that she went to Marta's with the girls. So I first told my dad."

"Was he shocked?"

"What do you think?"

I chuckled in response.

"He kept saying, 'that's my boy! Finally you came to your senses!' Oh, and he mentioned that he should have listened to Jay on the beach. Do you have any idea what that means?"

I never told Marc about our conversation that day. "Yeah, I have an idea of what he means. I'll tell you later. Tell me about Ilene's reaction!"

"So when I reached her, she was in the car with Marta and the girls. They were going shopping or something. The connection wasn't the best, so I pretty much just blurted out that we got engaged. I don't think Ilene either heard me or believed what she heard, because she asked me to repeat it like seventeen times."

"Really?"

"Yep... finally she must have realized I was telling the truth, because she started screaming at the top of her lungs that Marc and Hilary got engaged. All four of them went wild. I have never heard such loud screams in my life. I almost went deaf from all the yelling. They finally calmed down when they almost hit a tree."

I hung up the phone with Marc a few minutes later, beaming. Now that our family knew, our engagement felt so real. I couldn't wait to tell my office friends that I was getting married. I got up from my desk, and was just about to make way through my office so I could tell my colleagues, some of whom I have known since before my first date with Marc, when the receptionist buzzed me.

"Hilary," Claire called, "There's a Marla on the phone for you." She paused for a moment. "I almost didn't put the call through. I thought it was a wrong number."

"Why?" I asked, confused.

"Because she didn't ask for Hilary Rick, she asked for Hilary Grossman."
A smile spread across my face as Claire continued. "It took me a minute,
but then I realized she was looking for you. When asked where she was
calling from, she told me to tell you it was your niece! Congratulations,
Hilary! I am so happy for you! You and Marc make such a cute couple!"

Chapter 20

Seven Years Later

IT WAS THE BEGINNING of December, and one of Marc's longtime friends, Marty, was throwing his annual holiday party. Marc had known Marty for a million years. They both grew up in Belle Harbor and worked in the same pharmacy together many, many years ago. But, more than that, they shared a huge love of music. Marty was a guitar player, and he and Marc played in various bands over the years.

Marc and I love Marty and Carol's holiday party. For the past few years, however, we'd been unable to attend, as it always seemed to fall on the same night as my office's holiday party. Oh yes, I am still at the same company; however, I am now the CFO. So, this year, when we learned we didn't have a conflict, we were thrilled to say the least.

There was one thing about this party that made it so special… the people. Marty and Carol always mix up their guest list and include people from all aspects of their lives, past and present. Their house is filled with Marty's fellow musicians and Carol's flight attendant friends, as well as a sprinkling of childhood friends, family members, and anyone in between. Since most of the time no one really knows anyone except for the hosts, the guests tend to be super friendly, mixing and mingling with each other. By the end of the night, when Marty assembles a band of party goers, everyone is friends, singing and dancing together.

Marc and I were not in the most festive of sprits as we approached their front door. His father, Marvin, had passed away just a few weeks before, after suffering a massive stroke, just as my own dad did so many years ago. Marty greeted me first, with a big hug when we entered the house. I started to hand over the bottle of vodka we brought. But instead of accepting it, he told me to bring it to Carol, who was in the kitchen, as she was just about to start making the first batch of her famous cosmos. As soon as I started to walk away, I saw Marty grab ahold of Marc and embrace him with such love and compassion. Even after all these years, I am still blown away by how close Marc is with all of his friends, most of whom he has known since childhood.

After chatting with Carol for a few minutes and helping her set up a tray of cocktail franks, I joined Marc in the living room. It looked to me like he was trying to make his way into the kitchen to join me and greet Carol, but he was stopped by a woman who sitting on the couch.

"Marc? Marc? Is that you?"

Marc turned to her, looking a bit puzzled. Instantly I knew that he couldn't place her face. He looked over at me for help, but I had never seen this woman before, so he was on his own. She rose to her feet. "You don't remember me, do you?"

"Sorry, afraid not," Marc answered honestly.

"Oh, that's okay," she said as she patted her midsection. "I did change a little after all these years. It's me! Patty! Remember me? We worked with Marty and Carol at Ark Drugs like a million years ago! Remember?"

Marc started to nod his head. "Oh, Patty, yeah, I remember. You used to work the registers, right? How have you been?"

"Excellent," she said with a smile. "How about you? I haven't seen you in like forever. What have you been up to?" Since I was now standing directly at Marc's side, she couldn't help but notice me. Still warm and friendly, she extended her hand and said, "Oh, hi, I am Patty."

"Hi," I answered with a kilowatt smile, extending my hand. "I am Hilary."

As she shook my hand, Marc put his arm around my waist and clarified, "My wife." There is something about how Marc says that word. *Wife*. It is such a little word, but so powerful. It is not so much the fact that he says the word, but the way he says it... with such emotion, such pride, and most importantly, such love. It is almost as if he feels he is the only man in the world who has a wife.

When we first got married, considering how commitment phobic he was, I figured it would be a difficult word for him to use. I thought he would avoid it, struggle with it, and that it would get it caught on his tongue. But I was wrong. It never did. He embraced it from the get-go.

The first time I heard him say the word was when we were in the airport in Aruba, returning home from our planned elopement. We passed through customs and immigration, and one of the officers asked Marc who he was traveling with. Marc turned to me first, before looking at the officer, smiled wide with twinkling eyes and replied, "My wife."

I will never forget that moment as long as I live. And afterwards, he made sure to use the word "wife" every chance that he got. It is pretty ironic, considering the fact that I was the one who was pro marriage initially, that I was the one who needed to get used to saying the word "husband". Who ever thought the word would get stuck on my tongue?

Just as shocking to me is how quickly he took to the idea of wearing a wedding band. When I first broached the subject, and told him how important it was to me that he wore one, he fought it with all his might. He pointed out that he doesn't wear any jewelry, not even a watch. I used all my powers of persuasion to convince him he wouldn't feel the ring on his finger. He didn't really believe me, but he humored me nonetheless. Not wanting to be too bitchy about it, I assured him that if he tried the ring and hated it, I would understand and not expect him to continue wearing it. I just wanted him to give a wedding band a chance. To his shock and amazement, he didn't mind the ring at all; in fact, he seemed to like it.

A few months after we were married, I came home from work and found Marc sitting on the sofa with the cat on his lap, looking very sad and upset. When I asked him what was wrong, he confessed that during the day, while helping several guys from his office load up a truck with computer equipment, he lost the ring. He made the guys take apart the truck, but despite their efforts, they just couldn't find it. He felt terrible, but more so was worried that I would think he lost it on purpose.

I assured him I didn't, but I did point out that I thought he was probably overjoyed at the prospect of not having to wear a ring anymore. He looked at me like I was crazy, and swore that I was wrong. He insisted that we go to the jeweler the next day and get a replacement, which we did. He found his original ring about a year later, under his desk. He now jokes that he has two: one as a spare, in case he ever loses his ring again. (Which he totally did!) The second time he lost his ring while working outside. Don't ask me how, but days later I found his band in the grass.

"Your wife? Really?" Patty's face filled with shock and astonishment. She looked as if she was trying to piece together a puzzle. "You... got... married?"

Grinning widely, Marc replied, "Yes, believe it or not, I got married."

Patty was shaking her head. "I can't believe it. You? Got... married?" She repeated it slowly once more, as if she had to hear it once more to really believe the words.

Marc was so used to this reaction. He simply smiled at her as he nodded his head.

"Wow!" Patty exclaimed. "None of us ever thought you'd get married."

"I know, neither did I," Marc answered.

Not wanting to be left out, I chimed in, "Neither did I!"

"Huh," Patty muttered. "Amazing! What made you change your mind?"

Marc gazed into my eyes and said, "It was just something that happened. She made it easy."

Easy is the word that Marc always uses to describe what happened to make him change his mind about marriage. *Easy* is also the word he uses to clarify what made our relationship different than all the other relationships he'd had in the past. Unlike me, he says, the other women he dated tried hard to control him and control the relationship. They wanted him to conform to their needs and desires. They suffocated him. They expected him to spend all of his weekends with them, and them alone. They became jealous of the time he wanted to spend with his family. They were demanding and too needy. But I was different.

In the beginning, I gave him time to sort out his feelings. I didn't play games with him, nor did he play games with me. We were honest with ourselves and each other. I didn't push myself on him. I let him set the pace for our relationship. I gave him the space he needed, and he didn't feel caged in. The more space I gave him, the less distance he wanted between us.

As time went on, and as our relationship deepened, I didn't feel threatened about how close he was to his family, especially his nieces and nephews. Instead, I encouraged him to spend time with them, and in the process, I became not only closer to him, but to them as well. Now, most of the time, they will reach out to me first with the exciting news of their lives. Marc always pretends to be jealous, complaining that he used to be their favorite, and how easily I replaced him in their affection. But it is all an act. He loves that we now all have such a good relationship.

Also, I didn't stop him from doing the things he loved, like construction projects around the house. Instead, I became part of the process. From early on, when he had a project that he was working on, I wanted to help, regardless of how minimally I was able to contribute. My assistance started out small, of course. I would run to the hardware store or get a tool from the garage. But over the years, he taught me a lot. Just like I did with music, I learned my lessons well. (Apparently I am a good screw-er!) I now am able to help him with all projects around the house. This turned into a major bonding experience for us over the years, as we remodeled most of the house together, making not only home improvements, but memories that we will cherish always.

My favorite project still is when we enlarged the once humongous closet to make it even bigger. They say mothers are always right, and my mom was correct when she warned me not to take my entire wardrobe over to Marc's house at once. I did have too much stuff. But instead of encouraging me to stop buying clothes or requesting that I clean out some of the pieces which I no longer wore, Marc did what every girl dreams of… he built me a bigger closet, and I helped.

Finally, I never put unrealistic expectations on him, but more importantly I always tried to be his partner. I remember towards the end of the first summer we spent together, Marc and I were getting ready to go to the beach. He reached into the shed and took out two Lafuma zero gravity beach chairs. I reached for one, as I always did, and said, "Give it to me. I'll carry it."

Marc shook his head no, as he always did, and started to walk towards the beach. But this day, he stopped in his tracks and faced me. "Every time we go to the beach you offer to take a chair and every time I say no. You know I'll take the chair and yet you still offer, and mean it. Every other girl I have ever dated would have just expected me to carry the chair for them. You are different."

When Marc and I first started to date, I would run errands for him. Little things, like dropping his clothes off at the cleaners, picking up and wrapping presents for others, or exchanging his shirts for different colors or sizes at Polo. Many times I would have my mom accompany me on these trips. She would always ask if he would do things like this for me. "Of course," I would tell her. But of course I lied.

But now, that is a totally different story. Marc goes out of his way each and every day to make my life easier for me. Since I get home from work later than he does, he always cooks dinner during the week. He drops our clothes off at the cleaners, and he is constantly on the lookout for products that he knows will put a smile on my face. He even schedules my hair appointments!

Marc still finds it hard to express his feeling in words, but I don't mind. He may not tell me often that he loves me, but I don't need him to. He shows me, every single day. And I am a firm believer that actions speak louder than words.

But let's face it, there are some days where you really need to hear the words, and when I have those days, Marc doesn't let me down.

Knowing that I was having a very difficult day at work, within moments of me calling him up for advice, he fired off this email to me.

From: Marc @ work
To: Hilary @work
Date: Thursday, June 28 2008 11:38 AM
Subject: Opinions

Remember, regardless of what some people think and what their opinions are, you know you are really good stuff and many people know it! Never let others fog up your clarity. You are smarter and better now, and as you can see, you're a lot happier! I love you.

Marc and I are still extremely close to Jaye and Eric. Even though we live across the country from them, we make sure to see them at least three times a year. Without fail, whenever we are together, the conversation always drifts back to Marc and my early years. As we reminisce, Jaye never is afraid to remind Marc that he was an asshole. But she also doesn't hesitate to tell him that she happy and proud that he has become such a better man.

And as for me… that sad, insecure only child who wore a back brace, the one who lost her father when she was fourteen, is gone. There isn't a trace of that girl left. I no longer worry about being alone. I now have brothers and sisters and nieces and nephews. More important than anything, I have someone who loves me for me. Someone who helped me find my inner strength and confidence. I have someone who is always there when I need him, someone who always puts me first. Someone who makes me laugh even if I feel like crying, and someone who makes every day and every night special. I have the most amazing best friend in the world, one I also call my husband.

And the best part is… Marc is just as happy as I am.....

THE END

ACKNOWLEDGMENTS

The people in this book were, and always will be, the most important characters in my life. I love you all... And I am so thankful you helped me find my "happily ever after".

Mom, thank you for making me the person I am today, and teaching me that not every romance is a fairytale. You always will be my best friend.

Marc, thank you for not only embracing the idea of me sharing our story, but for all your encouragement and support during this process. I know it hasn't always been pretty. You are one amazing man and I love you more than words can say.

A huge thank you to Christina Baker Kline. Not only did she transform a rough cut into a beautiful gem, she taught me so much in the process. I never write a word, even a casual email, without hearing Christina's voice.

To my first readers—Tania, Susi, Beth Ann, Darcie, Leslie, Yvonne, and Denise—you guys rock!

To everyone who has read my www.feelingbeachie.com blog. Not only have you guys become my friends, you gave me the courage and confidence I needed to write this book! Thanks guys!

To all the book bloggers out there—THANK YOU! You are amazing. You really know how to welcome a new kid! You have no idea how much your hard work, praise, and constructive criticism means to me... Special shout outs to Ana, Maryline, Simona, Samantha, Jess, Chrissy, Isabella, & Annabel—you all have become dear friends!

To my amazing publisher—I am so thrilled to be part of the Booktrope family. Katherine Sears and Kenneth Shear—thank you so much for letting me be one of the "cool kids". Speaking of Booktrope—drumroll for my dream team... Greg, Jennifer, & Samantha!!!

Greg Simanson, you are a genius! Saying that you created a cover of my dreams would be an understatement. Every time I look at it, it takes my breath away...

Jesse James Freeman, I can't thank you enough for introducing me to Jennifer Gracen. You were so right... we connected instantly and have become fast friends!

Jennifer Gracen, thank goodness for you. I love to joke that I am a writer who can't spell. Thanks to your tireless work, I don't have to worry...

And last but certainly not least, a huge round of applause to the wonderful and talented Samantha March. Mere words aren't sufficient to express the gratitude I feel for you. You have done so much for me... You are such a pleasure and so much fun to work with. I am so excited and honored to have you as my book manager! Huge hugs!

MORE GREAT READS FROM BOOKTROPE

Biking Uphill by **Arleen Williams** (Contemporary Fiction) Sometimes the best family is the one we build ourselves. A heartwarming story of enduring friendship.

Grace Unexpected by **Gale Martin** (Contemporary Romance) When her longtime boyfriend dumps her instead of proposing, Grace avows the sexless Shaker ways. She appears to be on the fast track to a marriage proposal... until secrets revealed deliver a death rattle to the Shaker Plan.

Waiting for You by **Heather Huffman** (Romance) Karise's life takes an unexpected turn after she meets Aidan–but is she ready to accept the true love she's been waiting for?

Autumn Getaway by **Jennifer Gracen** (Contemporary Romance) Newly divorced mom meets a chivalrous and handsome man at a destination wedding. Can she overcome her fears for a second chance at love?

Just Friends with Benefits by **Meredith Schorr** (Contemporary Romance) When a friend urges Stephanie Cohen not to put all her eggs in one bastard, the advice falls on deaf ears. Stephanie's college crush on Craig Hille has been awakened 13 years later as if soaked in a can of Red Bull and she is determined not to let the guy who got away once, get away twice.

Caramel and Magnolias by **Tess Thompson** (Contemporary Romance) A former actress goes undercover to help a Seattle police detective expose an adoption fraud in this story of friendship, mended hearts, and new beginnings.

Discover more books and learn about our new approach to publishing at www.booktrope.com

CPSIA information can be obtained
at www.ICGtesting.com
Printed in the USA
FFOW03n1349240615
14577FF